HEARTWARMING

Her Cowboy Wedding Date

—

Cari Lynn Webb

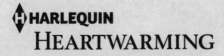

H HARLEQUIN
HEARTWARMING

HARLEQUIN®
HEARTWARMING™

ISBN-13: 978-1-335-42679-6

Her Cowboy Wedding Date

Copyright © 2022 by Cari Lynn Webb

For questions and comments about the quality of this book, please contact us at CustomerService@Harlequin.com.

Harlequin Enterprises ULC
22 Adelaide St. West, 41st Floor
Toronto, Ontario M5H 4E3, Canada
www.Harlequin.com

Printed in U.S.A.

Recycling programs for this product may not exist in your area.

Cari Lynn Webb lives in South Carolina with her husband, daughters and assorted four-legged family members. She's been blessed to see the power of true love in her grandparents' seventy-year marriage and her parents' marriage of over fifty years. She knows love isn't always sweet and perfect—it can be challenging, complicated and risky. But she believes happily-ever-afters are worth fighting for. She loves to connect with readers.

Books by Cari Lynn Webb

Harlequin Heartwarming

Three Springs, Texas

The Texas SEAL's Surprise
Trusting the Rancher with Christmas

City by the Bay Stories

The Charm Offensive
The Doctor's Recovery
Ava's Prize
Single Dad to the Rescue
In Love by Christmas
Her Surprise Engagement
Three Makes a Family

Return of the Blackwell Brothers

The Rancher's Rescue

The Blackwell Sisters

Montana Wedding

Visit the Author Profile page at Harlequin.com for more titles.

To the readers—your dedication to romance inspires me every day.

Special thanks to my editor, Kathryn, for continuing to believe in me and my stories. To my writing crew, whose support hasn't ever wavered—I'm forever grateful and blessed to have you in my life. And to my family—you are my backbone and my reason for everything. I love you more than you could ever know.

CHAPTER ONE

"GIVE HIM BACK, TESS." Carter Sloan filled the open doorway of the apartment behind the Feisty Owl Bar and Grill. His worn cowboy hat was pressed low on his forehead. Resolve framed his frown and shadowed his usual charm.

Tess preferred an irritated Carter. When he aimed his charm at her, it always set her back. And the last time she'd been flustered by a man, she'd ended up married to him. *Fool me once.* She frowned back at Carter. "I don't have *him*."

That was a lie. The *him* being Carter's grandfather, Sam Sloan, who happened to be one of Tess's favorite Three Springs residents. And the same person Tess had helped hide in the Feisty Owl apartment.

It was the same place where Tess spent her mornings. The kitchen in the unrented apartment was twice as big as the one in Tess's compact apartment over the Silver Penny General Store. She needed the modern appliances and open space to create. After all, dreams were on the line. *Her dreams. For her life.*

Fortunately, Tess's Grandma Opal had taught Tess the best way to soothe a riled cowboy like Carter was through his stomach. Tess lifted a chocolate truffle toward Carter, smiled wide to cover her secrets then added a cheerful command to her words. "Here. Try this."

Carter shoved the whole truffle into his mouth and spoke around the chocolate. "It's good."

But was it ten thousand dollars good? Tess walked back to the kitchen and sent a silent thank-you to her grandmother. Still, the candy and the cowboy could use a few tweaks to bring out their best. And when it came to the chocolate, she had to have the best.

Carter shut the front door and picked up another truffle from the tray on the granite island. "Is there whiskey in these?"

Carter's palate was refined as expected. He was the master distiller and creator of the Misty Grove Distillery. Tess nodded. "Your whiskey."

"These are really good." Carter finished the second one. "I could sell these in my tasting room. Clear a nice profit we could split."

She wasn't sharing her potential profit or her dreams this time around. All she needed was to win the Best Up and Coming Chocolatier competition at the Chocolate Corral Festival, and the subsequent cash prize for the final restoration to her grandparents' general store. Then she'd be on her way to having everything she wanted: her family around her and work that supported her in the one place her grandparents had called their true home. Life would be perfect, and she'd finally be truly happy. All on her own terms.

She eyed the always-business-first cowboy. "Why can't I have Sam? He's been a big help at the general store. He has more suggestions for candy flavors than a product development team for a national company." More importantly, she liked Sam. He didn't unsettle her like Carter always did.

Carter kept his perceptive gaze on her. "My grandfather needs to come home where he belongs. With his family."

Home. Belong. Family. Those words rattled easily from Carter as if it was all that simple and straightforward. Yet, Tess hadn't had a real home or people calling her back to the place she belonged in years. But she was building all that for herself now.

"I'm not going home." Sam's shout rolled down the staircase leading to the apartment's rooftop porch and gave away his presence. The older cowboy worked his way down the stairs and stopped in the middle of the family room. He crossed his arms over his plaid button-down shirt and scowled at his grandson. "I'm officially on a Sloan family strike."

"You don't have him." Carter frowned at Tess. Frustration rolled off the cowboy thicker than the Texas summer heat.

"Okay. You caught me. I lied." And she'd do it again. *Maybe.* Tess stuffed her hands inside a pair of oven gloves and held them up. Still, nothing blocked that flicker of awareness she always felt around Carter. "Sam offered to help with the candy making for the Baker sisters' upcoming family reunion and I happily accepted."

"Man needs to go where he's wanted." Sam lifted his chin.

Carter scrubbed his hands over his face. "You can't go on strike from the family, Grandpa."

"I just did." Sam smoothed his fingers over his stark-white beard. "Here are my terms. You have to tell my former brother, that traitor who you invited into my house, to leave and then we can talk."

"This isn't a negotiation." Carter braced his hands on his hips. "I'm here to take you home."

"I'm staying here now," Sam countered. "Wes and Abby told me I can stay as long as I like, and they own this place and let Tess use it. I get to stay free of charge too. Wes was raised to take good care of his elders."

Tess winced and watched Carter. He never flinched from his grandfather's jab and seemed to settle more firmly into the grandson-grandfather standoff. Carter's voice lowered. "You can't live here, Grandpa."

"Why not? It's not like I'm alone here." Sam motioned toward the kitchen. "Tess lives across the street, and she's been here almost every day to cook something. She lets me help and even asks my advice and opinion on things. She listens to me."

It was true. Tess checked the timer on the oven. Sam being there was a bonus. She always liked listening to his stories about growing up in Three Springs with her own grandfather. Sam offered her a connection to her grandparents, whom she still missed so much. But with five grandsons, Sam wasn't ever really alone at the Sloan farmhouse. "If you're worried about him, I could sleep in the guest bedroom here."

Sam's grin reached his eyes. "That's a splendid idea."

Carter's frown deepened. "Tess is not moving in here with you."

"She can if she wants," Sam challenged.

"It's no problem." Tess pulled a brownie pan from the oven and set it on the island near Carter. As if more chocolate might possibly relieve the strain tightening across Carter's face. "Then Sam won't be alone." And neither would Tess at her apartment.

It was almost a win-win. If not for Carter's obvious resistance.

"Our family looks after each other." Carter's gaze and tone were firm. "We always have."

Something in Carter's words hinted at a deep-rooted duty as if no one could look after them as well as he could. Tess looked after her own now, from her sister and cousin to her neighbors and friends in town. When everyone was happy around her, she was too. More importantly, she finally felt as if she belonged, and she didn't intend to lose that feeling.

Except Sam and Carter looked far from happy. And that negativity didn't belong in the kitchen where she needed to create chocolate that was decadent enough to win first place. Tess quickly sliced the still-warm brownies into squares.

Carter speared his arms to the sides and announced, "If anyone is moving in here with Sam, it's going to be me."

"You're not invited." Sam picked up a truffle and shook it at his grandson. "Not after what you did."

"I did nothing wrong." Irritation curved around Carter's words. "Uncle Roy is your only brother, Grandpa. Where else would he stay if not with us? The Sloans never turn their back on family. You taught me that."

"Roy Sloan *was* my brother." A stubborn resolve settled into Sam's eyes. "He's not family anymore."

Carter's mouth thinned.

Tension swelled around the sweet scent of chocolate and the two men. Tess slid the brownie pieces onto napkins. *Dessert is inspiration for your sweet tooth, Tessie. Time to be inspired.* Her grandfather had always ended that declaration with an eyebrow waggle and big grin. If her homemade fudge brownies gave these two cowboys a small reprieve and a moment to reset, she'd consider that a dessert success.

"What was it you used to tell me about my brothers?" Carter accepted the brownie from Tess. His grin lacked humor. "I remember now. *Son, you can't exchange 'em or trade 'em in so you better learn to live with 'em.*"

"I know full well what I told you. What's between me and Roy is best left well enough alone." Sam held his palm out for a brownie and faced Tess. "Now, Tess, if we're going to be roommates, we need to set some ground rules."

Carter coughed and placed his unfinished brownie down. Tess poured a glass of milk and pushed it across the counter toward him. Carter looked as if he wasn't ready to leave any of it alone. He opened his mouth. "Grandpa..."

The front door swung open, cutting off Carter's words. Tess's sister burst inside. Paige's worried glance bounced from one to the other. "Good, you're all here." Paige picked up the brownie knife and carved out a large center piece. "We've got a big problem."

"Then you've come to the right place." Sam patted Paige's shoulder. "I'm certain my new roommate and I can solve any problem you've got. We make a good team. Let's hear it."

"Tess is not your roommate, Grandpa." Carter opened the refrigerator, twisted the cap off a soda bottle and leaned against the counter.

"We'll talk about that later." Tess studied her sister. "What's wrong?"

Paige's boyfriend, Evan Bishop, grimaced from the front entryway. "Abby and Wes's wedding planner skipped town to elope in the Bahamas."

Tess flattened her palms on the granite counter and reminded herself that she could more than handle whatever came at her. "Eloped? In the Bahamas."

Paige finished off her brownie and cut out another piece. "Afraid so."

Tess and Paige's cousin, Abby, was set to marry Wes Tanner in two weeks. As the maid of honor, Tess had been beside her cousin for the venue choosing, the menu tasting and every wedding dress fitting. Everything but the wedding vows had been decided. Abby had planned every detail of her dream wedding day over the past six months. It was all set. Panic pushed Tess's pulse into a fast beat. "The wedding planner can't just be gone."

"Does it matter? Everything is already handled for the wedding." Carter looked and sounded calm as if an AWOL wedding planner was no more of a nuisance than a pesky horsefly. He added, "That's what Wes and Abby told me when I dropped them off at the airport for their flight to Florida yesterday."

Abby had told Tess and Paige the very same thing the night before last while she finished packing for her five-day conference. Wes had decided to join Abby to add a few vacation days to the end of Abby's work trip. It was a pre-honeymoon, but even more a celebration. The paperwork for Wes to officially adopt Abby's three-month-old daughter, Faith Rose, had been finalized. Now only the wedding vows needed to be recited and Abby would have the family she always dreamed about. Tess had seen Abby's wedding to-do spreadsheet with every task marked as complete. The wedding planner's impromptu departure shouldn't matter but the distress on Paige's face worried Tess.

"It was all handled." Evan polished off his brownie then finished Carter's untouched glass of milk.

"*Was* being the key word." Defeat dropped over Paige's words.

Tess pressed a hand to her suddenly queasy stomach.

"What does that mean exactly?" Carter rubbed the back of his neck. Uncertainty crossed his face.

"As of this morning, all the wedding vendors backed out." Paige looked grim.

Tess's stomach pitched sideways. "That's not possible."

"The vendors never received their deposits from the wedding planner." Evan considered the dish of brownies then studied the truffles. As if more chocolate would sweeten the bad news.

"Then we pay the vendors ourselves," Carter offered.

Sam reached into his back pocket and pulled out his wallet. "How much do you need?"

"It's not that simple." Paige smiled at Sam and set her hand on his arm. "The vendors have already booked Abby's wedding date with other clients who were willing to pay."

"How can we only be hearing about this now?" Anger vibrated through Tess. How could this happen to her cousin? Abby had been through so much. It wasn't until Abby had moved to Three Springs and fallen in love, that she found a place she belonged. A place that included Tess. Abby's wedding would be the start of the life Abby had always dreamed about. Now the wedding planner threatened to rob her cousin of that too.

"The vendors contacted the wedding planner about the missing deposits, but not Abby and Wes. As far as the couple knows, the vendors were paid." Evan rinsed the glass in the kitchen sink and frowned. "Now Wes and Abby's money seems to be funding the wedding planner's elopement instead of their own wedding."

"But Abby has to have her dream wedding," Tess insisted. Tess's own wedding had been far from perfect, and that bad luck had continued into her marriage. Tess refused to let that happen to her cousin. After all, a perfect wedding day was the start to a perfect life. And if her cousin's life was perfect in Three Springs, then Tess's family wouldn't leave her. Tess grabbed her sister's hand and held on.

"What are you saying?" Carter eyed Tess.

"We have less than two weeks to organize a wedding." Tess leveled her gaze on Carter. "And it has to be perfect."

CHAPTER TWO

No. Nope. No.

Carter had come to collect his grandfather. That was all. He was about to launch his whiskey after months and months of planning and had no time for drama—family or wedding.

Tess stared at him as if his refusal to help was out of the question.

Grandpa Sam wasn't of a mind to leave yet. Carter would change his grandfather's opinion soon. But he was not planning a wedding too.

Tess could turn her compelling gaze on the others. He was immune to her, even if her expressive green eyes reminded him of a meadow and endless possibilities. He had his future set and needed to concentrate on a business that required all his attention. Carter yanked his cowboy hat off his head and tapped it against his leg as if that would disrupt Tess's appeal.

"Okay, we need to talk next steps." Tess clapped her hands together.

Carter's next steps involved a distributor conference call, a video meeting with his marketing firm and running through the maintenance inspection list with his staff at the distillery.

"There's no time to waste," Tess added. "We need to make a complete wedding task list."

"That makes sense." Evan pointed from Tess to Carter. "Could you and Carter possibly handle that part?"

Now, that made very little sense. Wes, the groom, had promised Carter that Carter's best-man duties would be limited to the bachelor party and standing witness at the ceremony. Nothing more. Carter narrowed his gaze on his longtime friend. "Why can't you help?"

"Riley is at her first day of summer camp and I've got a schedule full of meetings today," Evan explained. "One of which is with Clyde Hill Food Group. The management team wants to sell more Crescent Canyon beef in more of their grocery stores."

Reasonable explanation. Difficult to refuse. Carter wanted his friend's cattle ranch to thrive. But Carter had a full day too. His whiskey launched nationally in two weeks. He had business priorities, not a wedding agenda. He should be heading toward the door. *Now.* His gaze landed on Tess and stuck as if she was his top priority.

"Consider me your all-around bridal DIYer." Paige smiled and pulled her cell phone from her pocket. "I was in a wedding once with a real bridezilla. We had to take a bouquet-making class and pass it."

"What if you failed?" Evan asked.

"Simple." Paige tapped on her phone screen. "You were out of the bridal party."

Carter could use an effective exit strategy right about now too.

"Well, good news. There are no tests for this wedding." Tess set a notepad on the counter beside the brownie pan and picked up a pen. "And no one needs to fear being kicked off either. It's all hands on deck for this one."

But a pair of those *hands* looked to be defecting. Carter narrowed his gaze on Tess's sister.

Paige stepped back toward the front entrance, one step and then another.

"Paige, you aren't leaving now, are you?" Carter called out, stopping her retreat. "There's your cousin's wedding to fix."

"And I promise these hands will be on deck later, but right now the Picketts need me." Paige flashed her phone screen toward Carter. Excitement and urgency spilled through the veterinarian's voice. "Their poor mare hasn't had the easiest of pregnancies and her labor just started. I really have to go."

"I do too." Evan tapped the watch on his wrist. "Or I'm not going to make it to the city on time.

And the beef and Clyde Hill Food Group wait for no one."

In the kitchen Tess filled a travel mug with coffee and seemed completely unmoved by everyone's hasty departures.

Panic rimmed the edges of Carter's voice. "What about the wedding?" The one that needed to be perfect.

"I will help." Even more excitement curved around the anticipation in Paige's words. "But this will be my very first equine delivery. I don't want to miss anything."

"I remember my first delivery like it was yesterday. My dad woke me up in the middle of the night." Sam wrapped a brownie inside two napkins. "Then the foal was breech, but Doc Wilson got it turned around straightaway. That mare went on to have six more foals, every one breech too. Their offspring are still on the farm today thanks to Doc Wilson and then Doc Conrad. Real good, reliable horses too."

Doc Conrad was currently Paige's mentor and partner in their veterinarian practice. And the pair was setting up a small animal clinic in downtown Three Springs to the delight of the locals. An animal in need trumped wedding prep. And the Pickett family's farm supplied Carter with their organic barley for Carter's whiskey. Carter wouldn't stop Paige.

"Go. Hurry. Send pictures of the foal." Tess pressed the to-go coffee mug into her sister's hand then hugged her sister quickly. "I'll answer the clinic phone calls so you can concentrate on your patients. I've worked out a new greeting. Three Springs Pet Clinic, how can we make your pet's day?"

"That's brilliant. You're a lifesaver." Paige smiled at Carter. "My big sister really is the best person I know. She's always so positive and reliable. You're going to love working with her."

Except Carter loved to work alone.

"I'll do whatever I can for the wedding. I promise." Paige reached for the front door handle. "Just text me and tell me what you need."

Carter needed Tess's sister to do the emergency wedding planning with Tess. Not him.

The last wedding Carter had attended had been several years ago. He'd skipped the ceremony, dropped a check in the gift box at the reception and departed after he'd greeted the blissful couple. Weddings always made him prickly. Two people pledged a commitment and declared their love in front of an audience as if more witnesses proved the bond was strong enough to endure real life. That blissful couple had hit a rough patch two years in and divorced last May.

Carter didn't understand all the fuss involved

in a wedding. He glanced at the kitchen counter and the carefully crafted truffles and artfully designed candies. Tess would want the fuss and more. In fact, she'd expect it. He was definitely not the right partner for her.

"Count me in too. I'll be better with the heavy lifting than the bouquet making." Evan laughed and followed Paige out the front door.

Carter's grandfather accepted two to-go mugs from Tess. The woman was like everyone's personal barista. His grandpa walked toward the entryway. Now his grandfather was defecting too.

"I'm off to meet Boone at the Owl." Sam toasted Carter with the twin mugs. "We had to move our historical committee meeting to this morning. Dylan is taking us with him to look at a new barbecue pit he wants to purchase this afternoon."

Boone and Sam had known each other since childhood. The two cowboys were best friends, coconspirators and always up to something. Not all of it good. Carter crossed his arms over his chest. "What about Wes and Abby's wedding?"

"I am doing my part." Sam smiled. "Keeping Boone distracted while you get this wedding back on track. This news would upset him and that's no good for his heart."

Boone had suffered a heart attack last year.

And he'd been given a clean bill of health at his most recent checkup. Carter had been at the celebration at the Owl, toasting to Boone's continued good health. Carter eyed his grandfather; suspicion skimmed the back of his neck.

"Boone thinks of Wes like a son," Sam added. "Abby and Wes are his family now."

"So are we." Carter and Wes were best friends. And Boone was like a second dad to Carter and his brothers. Carter wouldn't knowingly hurt Boone ever. Or want to cause him any stress. News of the AWOL wedding planner could do just that.

"Exactly." Sam eyed Carter. "And family always looks after family."

Carter accepted he was going to be the last one remaining in the wedding planning emergency. But he wasn't going to miss an opportunity to turn the tables on his grandfather. "What about Uncle Roy?"

"Roy wants something, or he wouldn't be here." Sam's voice deepened into dire. "Mark my words."

"What if Uncle Roy wants to make amends?" Carter pressed.

"If he'd wanted to do that, he wouldn't have waited so long." A melancholy clouded his grandpa's face. "You know what takes a decade to plan? Revenge."

"You can't mean that, Sam." Tess's eyebrows buckled together in alarm. "Roy is your only brother."

Yet, shared bloodlines weren't always enough to guarantee trust or loyalty. Carter's parents had proven that much.

"Roy disowned me and our family years ago." Sam's mouth thinned inside his thick white beard, and he eyed Carter. "I haven't forgotten that, and neither should you."

Carter hadn't forgotten. He could recall the look of hurt on his grandfather's face after the fateful phone call with Uncle Roy. But his grandfather had never shared any specific details. He'd simply looked at Carter and said: *I did right by my family. I know it even if my brother refuses to see it. And I'd do it again too. He'll come around.*

What if he doesn't? Carter had asked.

That's the thing about doing what's right. Sometimes you lose too. Yet, you gotta do it anyway.

Uncle Roy had never come around. And the divide between the two brothers had only widened over the past ten years. Until two nights ago.

When Uncle Roy had called Carter and announced his plans to return to Three Springs the following day. Then Uncle Roy had declared his intentions to set things right. Carter had assumed it was with Grandpa Sam. Unease pinched his conscience.

Sam walked to the front door and tipped his head at Tess. "See you tonight, roomie."

The door clicked shut behind his grandfather.

"Roomie?" Carter tossed his hat on the bar stool and squeezed his forehead.

"I know it's not ideal, but I think it's for the best." Tess covered the brownies with tinfoil. "Sam won't be alone if I stay here."

"He won't be alone if he comes home." Even Carter heard the lack of conviction in his voice. He had to figure out what his uncle really wanted. And he doubted he could do that with his grandfather around.

"Look." Tess touched Carter's arm. "I can talk to Sam, and you can talk to your uncle. Then maybe we can find a way to bring them back together."

Her sister hadn't been wrong. Optimism oozed from Tess. But he wasn't soft; he was practical and private. Yet, the warmth of her hand on his arm pressed against those cold places inside him as if testing his resilience. "This is a Sloan family thing. I'll handle it."

"Sure. Whatever." Her words were too casual, unable to fully conceal her dismay.

His slight had upset her. He shouldn't worry.

She wasn't his family. Not his responsibility. Not someone he cared for like he did his grandfather and brothers. Carter cleared his throat. "I do appreciate the offer, though."

Her smile was there and gone. Her fingers flexed on his arm before dropping away. "Well, we need to put together that task list."

"Fine." Carter set his hat back on his head and settled into his priorities. Number one was getting on with his workday. "But we have to walk and talk. Whiskey Wind is outside waiting."

"Who is Whiskey Wind?" she asked.

"My horse." Carter opened the front door. "He has to be ridden every day or he becomes seriously cranky and then he's hard to handle."

Tess gaped at him as if Carter was the hard to handle one. She said, "You seriously left your horse outside like a parked car."

"He's fine," Carter said. "It's not like he could've come inside anyway."

Tess chased after him, flipping off the lights as she went.

Outside, Carter walked over to the muscular dark bay thoroughbred he'd left loosely tethered to the sidewalk bike rack. "Sorry about the delay, Whiskey."

"You always talk to your horse?" Tess smiled yet kept her distance.

Carter untied the reins and nodded.

"Well, since we're walking and talking, I need to get the dogs from Boone's house." Tess stepped off the curb and crossed the street toward the historic houses on the other side of the railroad tracks. "It's my day to walk them. I'll be right back."

Tess rushed off before Carter could stop her. This wasn't a morning stroll. He had places to be. The walking was only outside to get his horse. The talking was meant to be a quick sidewalk conversation about next steps.

Carter led Whiskey Wind over to Boone's Craftsman-style house. Within minutes Tess appeared on the porch between two excited dogs. Ginger, the chocolate Lab, lunged toward the stairs. Tyne, the cream-colored Lab, rushed after her sister. Tess scrambled after the pair. Her sandaled feet slipped on the stone walkway.

Carter sighed and stepped forward to intervene.

But Tess righted herself, tugged on the leashes and ordered the enthusiastic dogs to sit. "Sit. Down. Now."

Even Carter stilled. *Impressive.*

"Everyone is going to behave today. Got it?" Tess kept her attention on the dogs.

Carter kept his focus on her. She was entirely too intriguing. And a distraction he couldn't afford.

The dogs' tails brushed eagerly against the grass like windshield wipers set on high. Their pink tongues flopped out of their mouths sideways. And Tess's stern face dissolved into a grin. "You're both lucky you're so cute."

And Carter was lucky it took more than appealing shop owners to sidetrack him. Still, he decided the walk would need to be a short one.

Tess and the dogs joined him and Whiskey Wind. They followed the railroad tracks away from downtown, then turned on Sunray Pass, once a livestock loading area for the railway stock cars and now nothing more than dirt and tumbleweed.

Tess transferred the leashes to one hand and clutched her phone in the other. "Okay. Let's start making that to-do list."

He had no time for all that. Carter switched Whiskey's reins to his other hand. "We need to stick to the basics—a location and food."

She stiffened beside him. "There is nothing basic about a wedding, especially not my cousin's wedding."

Carter slipped on a pair of sunglasses, better to block the sun's glare and Tess's all-too-expressive green eyes. "How about the essentials, then?"

"Well, the wedding essentials include a venue, a caterer, flowers for the bridal party, and the reception. A minister to officiate. A photographer. A DJ." She continued rattling off even more essentials. "We need to arrange music for the ceremony. Not to mention rent tables, chairs and place settings as well as a sound system. Announcements about the venue change need to be sent and posted on the couple's website. We should consider an email blast too. Also, we need to settle on a new menu and complete the seating chart."

Now they both needed to breathe. He said, "You forgot to mention the less than two-week deadline."

She looked grim.

But she was supposed to be the positive one.

Still, Carter excelled at time management. He ran through her essentials, but he doubted Tess would let him cross any off. They were definitely in over their heads. He hadn't felt such a distinct kernel of panic since he'd climbed into the shoot at his first rodeo in high school. "We should call Wes and Abby. It's their wedding day. The bride and groom should make the decisions."

"They already made the decisions." Tess stopped again. The dogs kept their noses to the ground and moved around Tess, forcing her to turn to keep from getting tangled up. "And now we're going to make sure those decisions come to life."

"But do they want us to do this?" Carter pressed.

"We have to do this," Tess stressed. "Or they won't have their dream day."

Carter clenched his jaw, grinding his teeth together—the ones the orthodontist had claimed would be perfectly aligned after three long years of braces in high school. Yet, his bottom teeth had moved back into crooked. Carter considered the braces a waste of time and money. And he'd vowed to make the best use of both throughout his life. It was going to take time and money to reinvent the couple's dream day. But would it be worth it? "We should tell them what happened. They might make different choices now."

"Like what?" The dogs wandered in opposite directions, then circled back, twisting their leashes around Tess's legs once more.

"Delaying the wedding." Carter shrugged. "They could decide to elope and skip all the fuss."

"A wedding is not a fuss." Tess untangled herself and the dogs, then started walking again. "And it can't be skipped over like TV channels during commercials."

"You're one of those, aren't you?" Carter slanted his gaze at her.

The dogs veered off again, earning a sharp

heel command from Tess. She eyed Carter. "One of those what?"

"Romantic types." He liked the spark crackling across her round green gaze. It was the kind of spark even a pessimistic cowboy like him could get used to. "You planned every detail of your wedding when you were a little girl, didn't you? Had pretend weddings in your backyard and all that stuff."

"Is it romance or weddings you don't like?" That irritation was quickly apparent.

"Does it matter?" he countered. He didn't trust any of it, especially the love and honor part. And that was the core of it all. Without that, what was left? Nothing more than an empty heart and nothing he wanted for himself.

The dogs circled Tess again, noses to the ground, tails wagging.

Carter stopped Whiskey Wind, dropped the reins and shook his head. "This is getting us nowhere."

Tess fumbled with her phone and Tyne's leash. "What are you doing?"

Carter unhooked Ginger's leash, then Tyne's and released the dogs with a command to run. "I'm freeing you and the dogs. Now the dogs can have fun and you can too."

"What if they run away?" Tess gathered the two leashes.

"They won't." Carter picked up the reins again and rubbed Whiskey along the bridge of his nose. "And besides, Whiskey Wind can chase them down."

Tess considered the horse. "He's quite stunning for a horse, isn't he?"

"I like to think so." Carter guided her over to the horse's side. "Ready?"

"For what?" The reserve in Tess's voice was obvious.

"For a ride," Carter said.

"I don't have time for fun." Tess shook her head as if a horse ride wasn't her idea of fun. "There's way too much to do."

"If you ride, you can take notes." Walking and typing were definitely not cutting it. The pace was too slow, and the conversation kept constantly veering off track. It was past time to focus. Carter added, "And then we'll all be having fun."

"I don't have very much experience riding a horse." Tess twisted the dog leashes around her wrist. But there was interest in her gaze.

"I'll be right behind you." Carter hoped he sounded encouraging. "And Whiskey Wind is better at this than we are."

"There's no saddle." Tess frowned.

"Adds too much weight." Carter ran his hand

along the horse's neck. "We both prefer to ride bareback."

Tess chewed on the corner of her bottom lip, but her curiosity never wavered. "I won't hurt him, right?"

"No, and we won't be taking a very long ride." Only long enough to get Tess back to her store quickly so Carter could get to the important things like securing the Sloan family legacy for the next few decades. And slow walks and wedding chats were not included anywhere on his business strategy for now or the future. He linked his fingers together. "Put your foot here. I'll give you a boost and you can use his mane to help yourself swing up."

Tess impressed him. She was up, albeit with his assist, and seated on Whiskey Wind after only four tries. He swung up behind her and adjusted his weight as best he could for the horse. He wrapped his arms around Tess and felt her shift toward him. He frowned. To get her back to her store quickly, he'd brought her even closer to him. He hadn't accounted for that. He nudged Whiskey Wind into a faster pace and then whistled for the dogs like he'd heard Boone do often.

"So back to the wedding," Tess said.

"I'm not going to ruin Abby and Wes's big day or anything like that if that's what you're thinking," Carter admitted.

"But it's hard to get excited about something you don't like." Tess relaxed against him.

He could like riding with Tess. But that was as far as he'd go. "Look, it's not my wedding day."

"You don't have to sound so relieved," Tess teased.

Carter's smile twitched into place. He added, "And you should know, I think weddings are fine for other people."

Not someone like him who believed business deals had better odds of being honored than wedding vows. Carter slowed Whiskey Wind in front of Boone's house, dismounted and helped Tess off the horse.

Tess faced him and grinned. Satisfaction wove through her words. "Then it looks like we're on the same page."

"What page is that?" Because it certainly wasn't the same love and marriage page. Tess had been married before. Carter hadn't ever come close to considering marriage. Not even as an afterthought.

"Not calling the happy couple because it would ruin their big day." Tess's grin never faltered as if she believed she'd won him over.

"I'll give you five days, Tess." To prove he wasn't that easy to win over. Carter held up his left hand and spread his fingers wide. "If we can't arrange their wedding before this Sunday, then we call Abby and Wes and confess."

"Fine." Tess stretched her arm toward him. "But if we succeed then you have to dance with me at the reception."

Carter set his hand in Tess's. One small tug and he'd have her in his arms. Right now. The woman was complicated, fascinating and a combination he really should avoid. She deserved more than a cynical cowboy like him. "And?"

Tess tightened her fingers around his. "And admit not all weddings are bad."

Weddings were bad. As for her hand in his, *bad* wasn't the first thing that came to mind. "Deal."

CHAPTER THREE

WATER BOWLS REFILLED and treats given, Tess checked on the dogs one last time. They were curled up together on the couch and looking as if they intended to stay that way for a while. Tess shut Boone's front door and turned around, surprised to find Carter standing beside Whiskey Wind on the side of the street. Surprised, but not disappointed.

Tess slowed her steps, which did nothing to slow the sudden uptick in her pulse.

There was something appealing about the cowboy. And that could be hazardous to much more than Tess's wedding vision. Still, he wasn't permanent. She was with him only until the I-dos and then they went their own separate ways. She could handle him and any thread of attraction until then.

Tess joined Carter on the empty street. "I thought you two would've left already."

"Answering a few texts and emails." Carter tucked his cell phone into his back pocket, gripped the reins and walked beside Tess.

She slanted her gaze at him. "I thought you might've been researching possible wedding venues. What with our tight timeline and all."

He looked at her as if he'd forgotten all about the AWOL wedding planner. "You won't approve of my venue suggestion."

They crossed over the railroad tracks. "What is your suggestion?"

"The courthouse."

"You're right. I don't approve," she said.

"Hear me out." Carter held up his hand and glanced at her. "A civil ceremony can be a sound, very prudent, financial decision for a couple."

Her pulse pounded. She knew the argument for a civil ceremony all too well. Her dead husband had used it on her for their wedding and won. Carter even had the same persuasive tone and endearing half grin Eric had always relied on to get his way. Tess would not back down this time.

A perfect wedding for Abby and Wes meant a solid foundation for their marriage. Tess's marriage had started off on the wrong foot and never recovered. And, selfishly, if Abby was happy and settled in town, Tess would be less likely to end up alone. "You're right. I need to handle the wedding venue."

"Fine," he said. "I'll handle the flowers."

Tess frowned. "I don't think so."

"You can't take the entire to-do list," he said. "That's hardly efficient."

"We're planning a wedding, not a productivity seminar," Tess argued. "Some things like finding the perfect venue or picking out flowers can't be rushed." And other things like *rushing* to the altar should be avoided all together.

"You can hear that ticking clock, can't you?" He arched an eyebrow at her.

Tess waved her hand. "You'll go into the florist shop and pick the first flowers you see."

"Definitely." He chuckled. "And if they have enough in stock, then I'll place the order."

"But sometimes you need to take a little extra time to look, really look, for the right thing. To make sure you don't miss anything." Tess stopped at the corner beside the general store and faced Carter. "It could mean the difference between finding the predictable thing or the perfect one. And you can't be rushed."

Carter swung up onto Whiskey Wind's bare back and glanced down at her. He'd removed his sunglasses and his gaze, sharp and inviting, searched her face as if she was the puzzle he needed to figure out. The spread of his smile across his face was anything but rushed. "We'll try it your way, Tess. But come Sunday, if there's no venue and nothing checked off, it's my way."

She was really going to enjoy proving the

stubborn cowboy wrong. Tess crossed her arms over her chest, blocking that quick beat of her heart, and kept her gaze fixed on him. "Bye, Carter."

"See you later, Tess." One corner of his mouth tipped up into a crooked grin as if he'd answered his own unspoken questions about her. Then horse and cowboy were gone, galloping away from her.

Tess spun around on the sidewalk and paused, taking in her audience. Breezy and Gayle Baker stood outside the Silver Penny General Store, wore too-wide smiles and waved eagerly at Tess.

The Baker sisters rivaled Boone and Sam in their matchmaking maneuvers. But Tess was a widow. When it came to love, she'd bought the ticket and taken that ride and like those spinning teacups at the amusement park, she'd walked away queasy and disoriented. And definitely not interested in a second go-around. Tess lifted her chin and headed toward the storefront and the women. "Good morning, ladies."

"Taking a morning stroll together, we see." Breezy Baker's thin eyebrows boomeranged toward her forehead. "Such a lovely couple you two make."

"Such a wonderful way for couples to start their morning." Gayle Baker curved her fingers around the straps of her daisy-painted jean overalls and sighed. "Walk. Horseback ride. Doesn't matter as long as you do it together."

"Moments like those are sure to make you and Carter stronger as a couple. You want that, don't you, dear?" Speculation dripped through Breezy's voice like slow-brewed coffee.

A couple implied Carter and Tess were something more than two people forced by unforeseen circumstances to work together. "Carter and I are definitely not a couple."

"Not yet, dear." Breezy touched her head, fluffing the short white strands even higher. "But you can't deny it's fun to imagine, isn't it?"

"After all, what you imagine, you make a reality." Gayle *tap-tapped* her eyeglasses back into place.

What Tess imagined was restoring the general store completely back to its former state. Just the way it was in the framed photographs of her grandparents hanging on the walls all around the place. And she envisioned winning the prize money from the chocolate competition to make that happen. Tess pulled her store key from her pocket.

But the women crowded in front of the general store doors as if intent on capturing Tess in their matchmaking web. And even more of that speculation settled around the spry women deeper than their collective laugh lines.

"Everyone always thinks a date needs to be at night. It's just not true." The moon-round lenses only amplified the mischievous gleam in Gayle's gaze. "You can steal a kiss just as easy during the sunrise as you can under a full moon."

"Isn't that the truth." Breezy hummed.

Tess stubbed her toe on the step leading to the store's landing and grabbed the handrail to steady herself. There would be no imagining. And absolutely no stolen kisses with Carter. Her pulse kicked up again.

"You could really use a pair of sensible boots, dear." Breezy's eyebrows notched higher.

Gayle's knowing grin sparked in her clever eyes. "Easier to catch a cowboy in boots than sandals."

If Tess was interested in catching a cowboy. Her cheeks warmed.

It was only eight in the morning. A few hours past sunrise and already the sun had turned the heat meter to full blast. She had to get inside into the air-conditioning.

"Do let us know if you need any dating advice, dear." Gayle spread her arms out then linked one with her sister's. "We've always adored a good love story."

The petite but formidable pair beamed at Tess.

Tess held her smile in place. There were more than enough love stories around town already.

Tess had no intention of supplying them with another one. Still, it was one thing not to want her own love story and quite another to admit it out loud and risk becoming the Baker sisters' next matchmaking priority.

Tess worked her way around the pair and unlocked the doors to the Silver Penny. "What brings you to the store so early today?"

"We've a family reunion update." Gayle followed Tess inside and tucked her hands into the front pockets of her overalls.

"More like a family reunion fiasco," Breezy added. "And today when we're supposed to be putting out the donation bins for Three Springs's summer pet supply drive. We can still leave a bin inside the store, can't we?"

"Definitely." Tess turned the closed sign to open, flipped on the lights and worked her way to the back of the store.

"We had to call a special meeting of the donation drive committee this morning in the book nook." Gayle frowned. "It's not reserved, is it, Tess?"

Tess had created the book nook in the front alcove of the store. Every committee and club in town from Boone and Sam's historical committee to Abby's town event committee met in the alcove. Last month the Bookmarked Book Club and the board members of The Roots and Shoots

Garden Club had arrived on the same day to use the alcove. A rather animated argument had ensued. Now a clipboard hung on the wall for the locals to reserve the space in advance.

Tess moved behind the checkout counter and turned on her laptop. She had special orders to fulfill for several customers and a wedding venue to locate. Then it was back to her chocolate sampler. She had one more chocolate to create, if only she could figure out the secret ingredient in her grandmother's recipe. It was that ingredient that had transformed Grandma Opal's spiced ganache truffle from good to amazing. And Tess had to have amazing. "Sorry, but I haven't looked at the sign-up since Monday."

"I'll go check." Breezy drifted down an aisle. "Gayle, fill Tess in on the reunion."

Gayle eased onto one of the empty stools where Boone and Sam usually sat. "Have any of your fudge hiding back there, Tess?"

Tess walked into the back room and took her sampler glass dish out of the refrigerator. She returned, set it on the counter and lifted the glass-domed lid. "Help yourself."

Gayle eyed the fudge samples on the glass dish. "It seems Aunt Frances was talking to some of her cousins about the reunion. And then those cousins started talking to more family. And well, now the RSVPs for the reunion seemed to double overnight."

Tess paused on her way to her computer and turned back to the older woman.

"Gayle and I weren't even aware we had so many relatives out there. It's quite startling." Breezy slid onto the stool beside Gayle, plucked two pieces of fudge from the dish, then grinned at her sister. "The book nook is open."

That was welcome news for the sisters. The news about the increasing family reunion guest list was not so welcome news for Tess.

"Of course, we can't wait to meet everyone." Gayle's eyebrows pulled together. "But it means we need more of everything, including the desserts you're creating specially for us."

"We need to double our order." Breezy bit into a piece of honey-and-brown-sugar fudge. Her eyes closed and she sighed. "Brings me back to our great-nana's fudge. Haven't tasted anything as good until now. You could win awards with this, Tess."

That was what Tess intended to do. But first, she had a wedding to rescue. And now the Baker sisters wanted to double what was already a sizable candy order for their reunion the Sunday after Abby and Wes's nuptials. Tess rolled her shoulders, but still, the worry wove through her.

Breezy's eyes flicked open and settled on

Tess. "We'll help you, of course. Pay for the extra ingredients. Whatever you need, dear."

"Unless you don't think it's possible." Gayle peered at Tess. Disappointment hovered around her thin, slightly stooped shoulders. "It's just your grandmother's fudge with our homegrown pecans would be like sending our family home with some of the best parts of Three Springs. It would be so special."

Tess wanted everyone satisfied when they left her store. Satisfied customers came back. Not that she'd ever charge for her sample candy creations. After all, her grandmother had never charged. Even more, Tess wanted cheerful neighbors. Because happy neighbors welcomed her into their homes as if she belonged. Tess wiped a fingerprint from the glass dome on the sampler dish and tried to clear away her worry. "It's not going to be a problem. Your family will have their candy favor bags."

"Tess, you are a true gem like your grandparents," Gayle announced. "How can we thank you?"

She was the grateful one. The Baker sisters had made her feel welcome from her first day in Three Springs. "You wouldn't know of any large venues in town?"

"What kind of large venue are you looking

for exactly?" Breezy picked up a piece of butterscotch fudge inside a cupcake holder.

"There's the rodeo arena," Gayle offered.

"Something a bit nicer than that," Tess hedged.

"Do you want someplace fancy like for a wedding, dear?" Breezy angled her head at Tess.

"Something like that." Tess polished the glass dome even more and kept her expression neutral.

Breezy inhaled, the sound just shy of a gasp, and touched several of the rings on her left hand.

But this was bigger than the Baker sisters' couple goals for Tess and any potential gossip. Tess was playing for keeps when it came to her family.

But she needed a venue to make Abby's dream come true. Tess pushed back her shoulders and looked at the pair. "Do you have any ideas for such a venue?"

"There was that lovely greenhouse out on Doyle's old farm, but the roof collapsed last winter." Gayle pulled out her cell phone and tapped on the screen.

"I recall going to a wedding at the gymnasium in the high school," Breezy offered. "For Ethel and Vernon Gaines. They both taught at the high school for years."

"Other ideal wedding locations include a library, museum or railroad station." Gayle read from her phone. "The nearest library is in Belle-ridge."

"And a library would be better suited for our Tess anyway." Breezy touched her clip-on earring and nodded at Tess. "On account of you once being a librarian and all."

"Good point." Gayle squinted at her phone screen. "For a proper museum, you'd need to head to the city. We've got the former train station, but it's hardly fit for the birds nesting there. Perhaps you could have the ceremony outside and use the train depot as a backdrop."

"If you want outdoors, why not the Starfall Campground?" Breezy suggested.

"So we've got the gymnasium, the campground and the former railroad station." Gayle set down her phone and finished her fudge. "That's a rather good start."

It was a good start to building Carter's case for calling the bride and groom. Without a venue, Abby's wedding would be ruined. And if Abby gave up on her dream, what else would she have to give up later? Tess pushed her words around the pinch of panic in her throat. "You've given me places to look into."

"Glad we could help, dear." Breezy smiled. "Although you should really check in with Carter about a venue. Some things should be decided together, even if you are only in that imagining phase."

Tess pressed her lips together. Protesting her couple status would only encourage the matchmaking pair.

The shop bell chimed. Celia-Ann Guthrie, Three Springs's longest-serving former mayor, hurried toward the counter and eyed Tess. "Did you mention Carter Sloan? Is he here by chance?"

No. Hanging out in her store wasn't Carter's pastime. Nor was he hers to keep tabs on. "I'm afraid he's not here."

Celia-Ann's shoulders slumped as if she deflated.

Breezy eyed Celia-Ann. "What do you need with Carter anyway?"

"A driver." Celia-Ann stuck her straw hat on the counter and lifted the lid on the fudge dish. "For the tractor parked outside."

And Celia-Ann assumed Carter could drive one. Tess supposed he probably could. He'd grown up on a wheat farm after all. Still, she'd rather watch Carter riding his horse than driving a tractor. As for riding along, she'd join him on Whiskey Wind. Tess reached for a pair of scissors and cut a long strip of wrapping paper and her train of thought. She was too busy for rides with Carter, on horseback, tractor or truck.

"Who parked a tractor out front?" Gayle frowned.

"I did." Celia-Ann's dry chuckle crinkled through her words the same way her fingers crinkled the cupcake wrapper holding the fudge.

"Celia-Ann," Breezy admonished. "You're not supposed to be driving anything. Not a scooter and especially not a tractor."

"Don't I know it. Seems my eyes are failing me faster than a falcon chasing its dinner." Celia-Ann shook her head at Tess. "I was good on Old Copper Mill Road into downtown. Nothing to hit but tumbleweed out there. I fear it's not the same in town."

Tess set the piece of plain brown wrapping paper on the counter. Several of her special orders had arrived last night, and she'd included free gift wrapping for her customers. "Where are you headed?"

"Whitney Carson at Cider Mill needs to use it. Her fencing collapsed on one side of the farmers' market." Celia-Ann shook her head. "And wouldn't you know they delivered the new wood posts clear on the other side."

"We dropped off our flatbed this morning," Gayle explained. "Now with Celia-Ann's tractor, it'll be less work for Whitney."

"Why don't we leave the tractor parked outside?" Satisfied she had found a workable solution and hadn't disappointed anyone in the process, Tess smiled wide. "Someone can drive it tomorrow."

"Whitney told me she intends to fix the fence herself." Gayle pursed her lips. "Tonight."

"She can't work on it any other time in the day," Breezy added. "What with running the farmers' market alone and taking care of her boys too. I think her only free time is when she sleeps."

Tess was well acquainted with little sleep. But she knew it would all be worth it soon. The store would be back like her grandparents had and showing a profit, and her family would be nearby.

"I'm exhausted for the poor dear." Celia-Ann rubbed her eyes.

"We try to help her out as much as we can. She's a hard worker. Same as you, Tess." Breezy smiled at Tess. "Could you take the tractor, Tess?"

Tess knew all about running things by herself. She knew the stress and exhaustion. And Whitney also had her sons to raise. Tess felt for the single mom. But recently, Abby and Paige had been encouraging Tess to embrace the words *no* or even *I'm sorry but I can't* more often. Tess plunked a box down in the center of the wrapping paper, worked her voice around her twinge of regret. Letting people down always soured her stomach. "I can't drive a tractor."

"There's nothing to it." Breezy shooed her argument away with a swish of her wrist. "I'd drive it myself but we've appointments at Bec's."

"Tonight is bowling league." Celia-Ann smoothed a dent out of her straw hat.

Gayle tucked her silver hair behind her ear. "We've been on a winning streak since we started having our hair done the same day we bowl. We can't change now, or we might not win the first-place trophy."

Tess wanted to win first place too. And to do that she needed to get back to her chocolate creations, courtesy of Grandma Opal's recipes. Not take tractor driving lessons. Tess rolled her refusal around her mouth.

"The tractor, the heat and the wind will ruin our hair," Breezy added. "And that would ruin our focus tonight."

Remember, Tessie, always look after your neighbors and they'll look after you too. That's how it works. Grandpa Harlan had watched over Tess, Paige and his neighbors all year round. And Tess wanted to be as successful in town as her grandparents had been. She knew what she had to do. Tess added the last piece of tape to her wrapped box and said, "I'll drive the tractor to the farmers' market."

CHAPTER FOUR

"YOU HAVE GOT to be kidding me." Carter slowed Whiskey Wind from a gallop to a standstill on the private road connecting the farmhouse and the distillery. As if Whiskey Wind's speed had distorted the typically picturesque view and scattered his usual delight for his home and all he'd been building.

But at a full stop, his disbelief only doubled as irritation rolled through him.

Dozens upon dozens of holes, each deep enough to hold several whiskey barrels, extended from the farmhouse's back porch toward the wheat fields and the distillery in long rows. The land had been entirely pockmarked and wrecked. In a matter of hours. Whiskey Wind and Carter had exited the stables before sunrise, and everything had been as it should be.

Now nothing was like he'd left it. *Nothing.* That would teach him to linger with a woman, however appealing she was.

A tractor sat in the center of the disarray like a giant glaring X marks the spot.

His brother Ryan reclined inside the tractor, his hands stacked behind his head. Ryan's boots were crossed at the ankles and rested on the top step leading into the cab. To a passerby, his brother looked asleep. But there was nothing relaxed about the stiff set of Ryan's jaw or the impatient tap of the toe of his boot against the other. Uncle Roy stood inside the tractor's front loader that waited on the ground.

Carter nudged the horse and headed toward the standoff.

Uncle Roy flailed his arms wide, pointed at Ryan and shouted. Carter's brother was clearly the only thing standing in Uncle Roy's hole-digging demolition way. The wind swept his uncle's exact words out over the fields. The very same wheat fields Carter should be checking right now. Harvest day loomed. That irritation flared sharp and bright.

Carter reined in Whiskey Wind beside the open door of the tractor cab. "What is going on?"

"I'm starting to agree with Grandpa. Uncle Roy is pure, unfiltered trouble." Ryan's voice was drier than the dust the tractor tires kicked up. "He dug up all this land. Now he refuses to get off the front loader until I give him the keys. If I do that he'll keep going and plow straight into the distillery."

That wasn't going to happen. The Sloan wheat fields alone extended well over a thousand acres. The only untilled land was on the north side. Uncle Roy could've practiced his front-loader skills out there. But he'd chosen the back acres between the farmhouse and the distillery. It wasn't an accident.

Mark my words. My brother wants something and it's not a family reunion. Carter rolled his shoulders, but his grandpa's warning only clung to him like a mosquito swarm.

"I'm not getting off here until I have the keys to the tractor." Uncle Roy widened his stance inside the front loader's bucket. "I have real important work to do."

First his grandpa had declared a Sloan family strike. And now his uncle seemed intent on tearing up the family's land. Carter didn't have time for a family revolt. He had a business to run, wheat fields to plow and a national whiskey launch to oversee. That irritation knocked into frustration. Carter ground his teeth together.

"Can we trade Uncle Roy for Grandpa?" Ryan's tone was calm, his expression neutral. Ryan had always been the slowest of the Sloan boys to rile. A trait that had kept Carter from acting before thinking on more than one occasion growing up.

Ryan continued, "We can make Uncle Roy stay at the Owl apartment instead of Grandpa."

Tess was staying at the Owl apartment now too, but she wasn't family. And didn't belong in this dispute. She'd be smack dab in the middle because she couldn't keep out of other people's troubles. Still, he should admire her for all she was doing for her family.

"I'm staying put." Uncle Roy wiped the back of his hand across his forehead and smeared more dirt across his face. He pointed at the front loader under his mud-caked boots. "Right here."

"That's fine by me." Ryan took off his baseball hat, scratched his head and muttered, "Then he won't drink the last of the coffee and eat the last of Ilene Bishop's almost-famous apple cake like he did this morning."

Ryan might be slow to rile, but he was surly in the mornings, even more so without coffee. Carter took a deep breath, elbowed his frustration aside and reached for his diplomacy. The kind he'd been using on his brothers to gain their cooperation since they were little kids. "How about we all get down and talk in neutral territory?"

"If I get off, Ryan will drive away." Alarm flashed across Uncle Roy's face. He shouted, "I'm not going anywhere!"

"Fine." Carter dismounted and approached his uncle the same way he'd approach an agitated bull, alert and cautious. "Ryan and I will come to you."

Ryan climbed down and stretched his left leg.

Carter watched his brother. Ryan had been home from the rodeo circuit for the past ten days rehabbing a hamstring injury from his last bronc ride. His brother should be concentrating on getting better and back to rodeo where he wanted to be, not chasing down their uncle and a tractor. Carter aimed his irritated gaze at Uncle Roy.

Ryan joined Carter. "What's the plan?"

That one simple line had been traded between the two brothers more times than Carter could count. From corralling cattle in the pastures to strategizing reasonable excuses for missing curfew again to scheming how to get their younger brothers to do all the chores. "I'm working on it."

Ryan nodded, quick and concise, trusting there'd be a plan.

Carter considered his uncle. Dirt covered Uncle Roy from his cowboy hat to his jeans. "Uncle Roy, what are you doing exactly?"

"I'm digging on my own land." Uncle Roy climbed out of the front loader and wiped his hands together. "Nothing wrong with that."

"Except you're ruining the land." Ryan turned his baseball cap backward on his head.

"It's not your property anymore, Uncle Roy.

You sold your half to Grandpa." It'd been a decade since Grandpa Sam had purchased his brother's half of the farm. Grandpa Sam had finally accepted that his carefree brother really had no intention of ever returning to their family's farm.

"Your grandfather pilfered it out from under me." Roy threw his arms over his head, knocking his cowboy hat completely off his head and onto the ground.

Grandpa Sam had paid his brother more than market value. His grandpa had included Carter in the details from the drawing up of the purchase agreement to cutting the check. But it wasn't an argument Carter wanted to start. Too many emotions shadowed his uncle's face, and those emotions made reasoning hard to hear. Besides, it'd been a fair business deal for both parties.

"I want back what's rightfully mine," Uncle Roy stated.

"You want the farmland back." *Never happening.* Carter gathered his sudden unease close and tried for indifference. Grandpa Sam and Carter had bought the acreage to expand the wheat crop. Then they'd slowly converted the nonfarmable acres into the distillery. It was all to ensure the farm sustained not for a year, but for decades to come. Uncle Roy had never cared about the land or its longevity.

"The land?" Uncle Roy scratched his cheek and gaped at Carter. "I don't want the land. I never had the right touch for the wheat. I've been told more than once in a season that I lack patience."

Carter's patience was starting to run low too. He could use some of Tess's optimism. Instead, his words were blunt and bracketed by frustration. "What are you doing, then?"

"I want what I buried here years ago." Sweat dampened Uncle Roy's plaid shirt, and determination framed his deep frown. "It's mine."

"What did you bury? A treasure chest?" Ryan kicked a clump of dirt into one of the oversize holes.

"It's better than all that." Roy considered Carter. His bushy salt-and-pepper eyebrows rose into his forehead and held. "It's my original moonshine recipe."

"What?" Ryan coughed, but the surprise remained in his words. "Are you really thinking of getting into the distilling business too?"

Uncle Roy was the original wanderer. Never rooted in one place for more than a year, two at the most. When Carter was a kid, he'd wanted to follow in his uncle's footsteps and plant his boots across as many state lines as he could. Live carefree and only for himself. But then he'd grown up and understood what responsibility and duty really meant.

"I don't need to start distilling." Roy set his hands on his hips. "Carter is already doing it with my recipe."

Carter crossed his arms over his chest, better to hold back those churning emotions. Still, anger tweaked his words into curt and clipped. "Uncle Roy, what are you saying exactly?"

"You're using my original recipe in your fancy distillery over there." Uncle Roy flung his arm wide then jammed his thumb into his chest. "And I deserve my share of the profits. It's only fair."

Fair would've been his parents fulfilling their responsibility and raising their five sons. Or at least paying his grandparents instead of forcing them to scrimp by for all those years. *Fair* would've been his uncle coming home to offer his help when the boys had been kids and his grandparents overwhelmed. Instead, Carter had stepped in as a naive, untested seven-year-old farmhand, determined to help any way he could.

Carter reached up and squeezed the back of his neck. Old resentments and anger and pain pushed for release. Carter wrestled the past back where it belonged. Besides, emotions never had a place in the wheat fields, whiskey barrels or business deals. "So you're searching for a recipe you buried somewhere out here to prove you deserve a stake in Misty Grove."

Ryan tensed beside Carter.

"Can't make demands with nothing to stand on," Uncle Roy said. "That's not right."

Still, his uncle could spread his rumor and damage Carter's reputation in the industry. Even though Carter had created the bourbon whiskey blend himself. Every barrel from the very first one had originated from Carter's own mash bill of corn, wheat and malted barley.

But Grandpa Sam had been at Carter's side, offering input and advice on each step from the yeast to the mash bill. Was there truth to his uncle's claims? Doubt poked at him, and Carter shoved back. Family should always be loyal to family. "You can't keep digging up our property for obvious safety reasons."

"Don't you see? I have to." Uncle Roy wiped a hand over his mouth. A tremor twitched through his dirt-stained fingers and his gruff voice. "I got nothing else and nowhere left to go."

His uncle just disclosed his weakness and his desperation. It was a powerful combination to take advantage of. But Uncle Roy was family. Still, could Carter buy his uncle's silence? At least until he spoke to his grandfather. The back of his throat burned.

"Don't suppose you'll let me have a stake

in the distillery on my word," Uncle Roy suggested.

This will always be your home. You have my word. Grandpa Sam had sealed that declaration with a firm handshake. And a seven-year-old Carter had learned the real value of a promise. And Carter had given his own promise that day to always look after his family. And that included lost souls like his uncle. "Let's compare recipes. You tell me what's in your recipe and we'll see how close we are."

Ryan slanted a startled look at Carter.

"So you're admitting you used my recipe for your whiskey." Uncle Roy puffed out his chest.

Ryan nudged a clump of mud off a tractor tire. "How could Carter use it if it's buried out here?"

"Because my conniving brother, your grandfather, memorized it too." Roy frowned and cut his hand through the air. "Go ahead and ask him."

Carter was going to do just that. "I intend to."

"Well, I'm not reciting nothing. When I find the recipe, written in my own hand, it'll prove I came up with it. Not Sam." Roy stabbed his finger into his chest. "Then I'll get what's rightfully mine."

Carter crossed his arms over his chest again. Tess's wide green eyes and patient smile flashed in his mind. But he wasn't soft like her. Yet, the harsh edge in his voice dulled. "What is it you think you deserve?"

"It's what I want." Roy's hand shook again, giving away his distress and a hint of fear. "I'm a Sloan too."

"There are different ways to go about becoming a part of the family again." Ryan widened his stance and mimicked Carter. The Sloan brothers stood shoulder to shoulder and often eye to eye against their adversaries.

"A man needs to stake a claim. Prove he belongs to be accepted." Roy tugged on his earlobe as if clearing the uncertainty from his own words. "Never mind. I'm finding that recipe."

But who would Uncle Roy hurt in the process? No one if Carter could help it. "Where exactly did you bury it?"

"That's the thing. The land has changed. No thanks to your new buildings and all that." Uncle Roy's chin tipped toward his chest; his mouth dipped down. "What was wrong with leaving the land like it was? Open country and good fresh air feeds a person's mind."

And a profitable farm and distillery fed Carter's family and his employees' families. "There will be no more digging, Uncle Roy."

"You say that as if you're the one in charge now," Uncle Roy huffed.

"I am that person," Carter said.

Uncle Roy opened and closed his mouth, then ran his fingers through his salt-and-pepper curly hair as if that news rattled him.

There had been two purchase agreements drafted a decade ago. One to purchase Uncle Roy's land. And the second for Carter to purchase a majority stake in the Sloan family property. Carter picked up his uncle's cowboy hat, brushed the dirt off the rim and handed it to him. "While you chose to explore life beyond Three Springs, I chose differently. I've put everything I have into our home." And he would protect it with everything he had too.

"You're telling me you own the farm now." Roy smashed his hat over his short, curly hair and braced his hands on his hips.

"The documentation is at the farmhouse," Carter said. "In my office. We won't even have to dig for it."

"Or you could take our word for it." A stubborn defiance crossed Ryan's face.

"What about this tractor?" Uncle Roy asked. "Own it too?"

"I do," Carter said.

"It's pretty new." Roy hooked his thumbs in his belt loops and tugged his jeans higher on his waist. "Where'd you get all this money? That fancy distillery of yours, I bet."

Fancy had never been a consideration. The

old barns had been converted into rack houses to store whiskey barrels. Some of their whiskey was still produced in the original copper stills Carter and his brother Josh had built together years ago. The tasting room was no more than a nook notched out of the stillhouse's entryway. The distillery was a grassroots business, created straight from Carter's vision.

As for the money, that came from well-timed investments, diversified income streams and simple hard work. Day in and day out. No detours. And always putting family first. "I took care of the land, and it returned the favor."

"What about your brothers?" Uncle Roy asked. Both angst and pain crisscrossed his weathered face. "You cut them out too?"

Gotta know your lines, Carter. Know when they've been crossed. Right now, Grandpa. *And you really gotta know when to let 'em walk.* Carter never flinched and simply held on to his uncle's stare. Same as he used to with anyone antagonizing his younger brothers. Often times, silence sent a stronger message than words ever could.

Uncle Roy fidgeted with his belt buckle.

Like it or not, Uncle Roy was still family. And there was that layer of hurt deep in his uncle's gaze. Carter knew all about burying things deep. "Ryan, take the tractor back."

"Don't think that's going to deter me. I can still work a shovel. Just you watch." Resolve stiffened Uncle Roy's shoulders. He turned and stalked off.

Ryan climbed into the tractor cab. "That's the plan? Let him keep digging."

"He can't do much more damage with a shovel." Carter mounted his horse, adjusted the reins in his grip and watched his uncle pick up an old oilcan from a hole and tuck it under his arm. "As for the plan, we keep Grandpa away until we can fix this mess."

"There's no telling what Grandpa will do if he sees this." Ryan grimaced.

Looked like Carter needed to encourage his grandfather's family strike for a little while longer. And that meant extending his grandfather's time with his new roommate too. Carter supposed he'd need to clear that with Tess. And that would give him another reason to see Tess and her bewitching smile. The one that flared into her eyes and captured him completely. Not that he was hooked or anything like that. After all, the best things were best in moderation like a four-second pour of his single-cask straight bourbon whiskey. And some things were best if avoided all together.

But he couldn't deny he was looking forward to seeing her again, if only briefly. "I'm taking all the tractor keys before I leave for my meeting at the farmers' market."

"I'm headed to the horse sanctuary to help Tori with two new arrivals and then to physical therapy." Ryan stuck the tractor key into the ignition. "Caleb is at the fire station. Should Uncle Roy be left alone?"

Uncle Roy marched toward the farmhouse, looking more determined with every step, not defeated. Leaving his uncle unattended at home was clearly not an option. "Can't you take him with you?"

"Both the new arrivals have eye infections and colic. I can't watch over Uncle Roy and help Tori treat the horses." Ryan shut the tractor cab door. "You take him with you."

Carter was irritated with his uncle. That didn't mean he wanted the older cowboy to get hurt. *Family first.* That was Carter's long-standing motto. Thanks to his parents who only ever put themselves first. He sighed. "Fine. I've got him."

"How much more trouble can he cause?" Ryan laughed and started the tractor.

A lot more. Carter had once seen a cornered rabbit fend off a rattlesnake in an attack of claws and kicks. His uncle looked determined to fight too. Carter turned Whiskey Wind toward the stables and nudged him into a trot.

Carter had to be more efficient. He had to

stay ahead of any disaster his uncle might stir up. That meant getting things done quicker, including all those wedding tasks pretty Tess had put on her checklist. He was about to push the wedding planning into overdrive. He only hoped Tess could hold on for the ride.

CHAPTER FIVE

THE GENERAL STORE had been open for several hours, lunchtime was rapidly approaching and Tess had nothing checked off her to-do lists. She'd exhausted all the possible wedding venue options within an hour's drive of Three Springs. Every single location was booked, even the Belleridge roller skating rink. Not that it was in the running, but these were desperate times.

Instead of locating her customers' special orders, she'd shopped in her store with Delaney O'Neil, the local Realtor, to help stage a vintage farmhouse for its upcoming open house. Then she'd accepted temporary ownership of the Fowler family's hermit crabs, Sandy and Herman. She'd agreed to pet sit while the Fowlers vacationed in the Grand Canyon. The youngest Fowler child, six-year-old Oliver, had an endearing tutorial on proper hermit crab care, and Tess didn't have the heart to hurry him through his demonstration.

She glanced at her grandmother's well-used and worn recipe box next to her laptop. Not one of the index cards stuffed inside contained another copy of Grandma Opal's spiced ganache truffle. All Tess had was the original recipe card, the ingredient list fading by line and disappearing completely on the last line. And a stack of photographs of Grandma Opal and her making chocolate in her grandma's kitchen. She'd placed an express order for organic cocoa powder and specialty baking chocolate from a gourmet shop in San Francisco. But she knew she was missing that secret ingredient. The one Grandma Opal had always added, then whispered: *You only need a dash to set your taste buds singing.* Tess definitely needed those judges' taste buds to sing.

She had to make another batch tonight. Add an extra dash of cinnamon. Or ground allspice. She had to figure it out and soon. A large cash grand prize was on the line. The last of her savings was quickly disappearing. And she refused to become a burden to her family. There was no joy in that.

Her phone screen lit up with a new text alert. From Carter:

One trip to the farmers' market. Centerpieces are done.

But they hadn't discussed centerpieces. They hadn't even secured a venue.

A picture from Carter downloaded in their text thread. A picture of a flowering cactus.

Alarm gripped her. Tess stopped texting a reply, pressed the call button instead, then chanted, "Pick up. Pick up. Pick up."

Carter skipped over a greeting. "You didn't need to call to tell me thank you."

"I'm calling to say no." An urgency rushed Tess's words. "No. No. No."

"Does that mean you don't like the cactus centerpieces?" Carter's words sounded stretched as if the slower he spoke the higher chance he'd hear what he wanted to.

"Where are you?" Tess asked.

"Cider Mill." Carter's long sigh reached across the speaker. "Look, it's all arranged with Whitney. But I have to go. Whitney and I have to discuss honey for Misty Grove. Go ahead and check the centerpieces off that list of yours. This is good progress."

The line went dead. Dread filled her. Tess stared at her blank phone screen. It wasn't progress. And it was far from good. Her cowboy was already proving hard to handle.

Tess tossed her notebook into an oversize tote bag, grabbed her shop keys from the hook on the wall and headed out of the store. Doors locked and the be-back-soon sign in the window, Tess raced around Celia-Ann's giant tractor. The Baker sisters were no doubt still at Bec's Salon for their bowling league updos. She couldn't interrupt that important ritual and risk being responsible if the women lost tonight. Tess hurried toward the Feisty Owl Bar and Grill instead.

"Boone. Sam." Tess rushed inside the Owl. Boone and Sam were perched on their usual stools in their usual spots at the far end of the bar. Paperwork was scattered in every direction around the cowboy duo. "I know it's the historical committee meeting, and I really hate to interrupt, but I need tractor driving lessons. Right now."

"Where you going in such a hurry?" Boone swallowed the last of his coffee and pushed the empty mug to the side.

"I have to get to Carter," Tess said. And stop him.

"What's he done now?" Sam drummed his fingers on the worn bar top.

"Cactus." Tess opened the cactus picture on her phone and flashed her screen at the cowboy pair. She skimmed over the centerpiece bit not wanting to alert Boone to any problems. "He chose cactus at Cider Mill."

Boone rubbed his chin. "Can't say I ever had much of a problem with any cactus."

"Me either." Sam shrugged.

"It's all wrong. Wrong. Wrong." Tess tried to erase the curt edge from her words. "There's no romance in a cactus."

"Romance," Sam mused.

Boone's eyebrows lifted. Sparks flared in both their gazes.

Tess rubbed her arms as if she'd been pricked by cactus spines. Or a pair of Cupid's arrows from a duo of self-proclaimed cowboy match-makers.

"Say, if it's romance you want, Sam and I can coach Carter on all that." Boone stood and straightened his shoulders. "Don't need to be sprinting all over town on a tractor for that."

"I want to get to Carter." To set him straight on a few things like the importance of sticking to the list. The wedding theme. The plan. It was supposed to be venue first. No jumping ahead. No veering off on his own.

Before she knew it, he'd have a courtroom booked, a succulent pot for a bouquet and a sensible defense for his choices. But she'd promised herself she'd do everything she could to make sure her cousin was content in Three Springs.

"Where's your car?" Boone picked up his cowboy hat from an empty stool and plopped it on his head.

"My car is at Ramsey's. It overheated last

night on my way back from Belleridge and I dropped it off this morning." Tess had been bandaging the old compact car for months now and putting the little bit of extra funds she earned back into the general store. Fortunately, she lived and worked in town and could walk almost everywhere she needed to go. But not the farmers' market. "And I told Celia-Ann I'd take her tractor to Whitney at Cider Mill. She needs it tonight."

"You should try Whitney's vanilla whipped honey and homemade biscuits." Boone patted his stomach. "If it isn't already sold out."

Sam nodded. "Can't find better. I've tried."

"I can't try anything until I get there." Tess set her hand on Sam's arm and tugged him toward the exit. "And I can't get there without those tractor lessons."

Boone trailed after them. "You sure you're feeling okay, Tess?"

"I'm great." Tess held open the doors. "Really great." And she'd be even better once she and Carter were on the same wedding page.

Boone nudged his elbow into Sam's side. "You think she's okay to drive?"

Sam shrugged. "She's a bit riled, but my Claire always said the best place to let off steam was outside."

The doors to the Feisty Owl closed behind

her and Tess inhaled. The old-timers preferred a slow pace, their coffee sipped, not chugged and distrusted fast-talkers and commotions.

"Look, I'm sorry for barging in on you and messing up your search for the missing Herring gold treasure." She held up her hands. "I just really could use your help. I want to catch Carter before he leaves the farmers' market. And I promise to help look for the missing silver coin and the treasure map for the Herring gold before your next historical committee meeting."

The pair studied her.

Tess tried not to fidget. Over the past year Boone, Sam and their friends had searched the entire basement of the general store for the missing centuries-old silver coin and the treasure map they were convinced was with the coin. Tess was beginning to believe the silver coin was lost for good and would become another part of the fabled Herring Gang legend from centuries past. But she wanted to support her two friends, not stomp all over their unwavering hope.

Finally, Sam nodded and grinned. "If you're gonna get to Cider Mill, we can't keep standing here talking about it."

Tess exhaled.

"It's a straight shot through town," Boone explained. "The only hard left is the turn onto the frontage road. Then it's two long curves and one bridge past the Bakers' gate and then you'll be at Cider Mill."

Forget the long curves, whatever those were, and the bridge. Tess had finally stopped and really took in the massive bright green giant looming outside her general store where horses used to be hitched a century ago. She'd have preferred a Clydesdale right now. "That's like a real farm tractor."

"Of course it is." Sam chuckled and ran his fingers through his white beard. "What'd you expect?"

"Something smaller." The back tires were as tall as Tess. Still, she refused to let one tractor sideline her. She had cactus to conquer and a rogue best man to bring around to her way of thinking. "Do I need a license to drive things like this?"

Boone's laughter spilled free. "You only need the will and the opportunity."

"And you have both." Sam bumped his shoulder against Tess's, his voice getting more excited. "The front loader isn't attached. Even better, it's got those fancy reverse alarms."

"Not that you'll be needing to back up." Boone smiled. "You get a real good view from the tractor. You won't miss nothing seated up there."

"Unless you miss the left turn. It comes on

quick like. It's all fields and fence around there."
Sam squinted at Tess. "You sure you're up for
this? You seem more prickly today than those
cacti you don't like."

It wasn't the cactus. It was a certain cowboy
making her feel prickly. "I can handle it."

Boone opened the side door on the cab and
motioned inside as if he was ushering Tess into
her very own fairy-tale carriage.

This was all Carter's fault. And Tess was certainly going to let him have it when she saw him.
But she had to get there first. Tess narrowed her
gaze on the tractor like a boxer sizing up her
competition. She adjusted her tote bag on her
shoulder, climbed the ladder-style steps up to the
enclosed cab and dropped into the padded seat.

"Best keep the side windows vented." Sam
used the sleeve of his shirt to wipe the sweat
off his cheek. "Been more than a few harvests
since the AC worked proper."

That small fact had barely sunk in before the
wily pair launched into their crash course on
tractor driving 101. There were more *don't be
surprised ifs* than any solid dos and don'ts. Finally, Sam paused for a breath, clapped his hands
and declared Tess in the know. Tess turned the
key. The engine rumbled, and her seat vibrated.

Sam shut the door and backed away. "Nothing to it."

Boone offered two thumbs-up and a crisp nod. "Go get that romance you're wanting."

There was a mischievous glint in their gazes and too-broad smiles. Tess wanted to blame the sun beaming from a cloudless sky. But she'd known the cowboy pair for more than a year and spent almost every day with them at the general store. Meddling and matchmaking was more than a pastime for the duo. But she'd have to deal with them later. Right now she had her sights set on a different cowboy.

She pressed on the gas pedal and rolled down Fortune Street. She'd motored past the downtown square, the old church and Ramsey & Sons Auto Repair, casting a longing glance at her compact car on a lift in one of the service bays.

Her phone vibrated on her lap. No doubt Carter sending more cactus pictures. She could only imagine what he'd pick for the bouquets and boutonnieres. She ignored her phone, swiped at the sweat on her forehead and pushed the tractor faster.

Twenty minutes later, her ears buzzing from the rumble of the tractor, Tess turned onto the frontage road, took the two long curves and the bridge. She turned to pull into the Cider Mill parking lot and came head to head with an oversize silver truck. An all-too-familiar silver pickup.

Tess shoved the tractor into Park, opened the door and stood on the ledge.

The truck door popped open. An all-too-familiar cowboy jumped out, hands on his hips, hat pulled down low.

Tess grinned.

Carter frowned and shouted, "Tess! What are you doing?"

She was taking a stand. Finally. And it felt good. Really, really good.

CHAPTER SIX

"You NEED TO back up, Carter," Tess hollered and pointed toward the empty parking spaces.

His truck idling, Carter stalked toward the tractor instead. He offered Tess a tight smile. "Tess, what is going on?"

"I'm delivering a tractor to Whitney." Tess patted the top of the door frame. "Celia-Ann Guthrie needed my help."

"Who's watching your store?" he countered.

Her store wasn't the point. "Look, you have to back up and park. My tractor lessons didn't include reversing this beast."

Resignation was there in the backward tilt of his head and his quick glance skyward. Then he turned on his boot heels and climbed into his truck. He reversed into a parking space as if he'd been a big-city valet in a former life and drove a two-door sports car, not a 4x4 truck. Tess pulled the tractor to a stop on the other side of Carter's truck and climbed down.

A gentleman, his salt-and-pepper curls fluffed in every direction like a frayed cotton ball, stepped out of Carter's truck and grinned at Tess. "I'm Roy Sloan. I'll take the keys and pull this around back for Ms. Whitney. And give you and Carter some privacy. I warned him about those cactus but no one listens to me."

Carter swiped his hand over his face as if catching his retort. Finally, he looked at Tess. "He's qualified, Tess. You can give him the keys."

Tess dropped the keys into Roy's palm and joined Carter on the walkway. His attention was fixed on his uncle and the tractor. Roy settled inside the cab, turned the tractor on and rumbled down a dirt road around the side of an old barn. Tess asked, "How does he know where to go?"

"Our meeting with Whitney was a working one just now. We helped move crates in the back," Carter said. "He'll be fine."

"Good." Tess faced Carter and got straight to the point. "We are not putting cactus on the reception tables. And we are not checking centerpieces off the to-do list."

"Why not?" he asked.

"This is not a Texas-themed wedding," Tess said.

"There's a theme too?" His eyebrows drew together beneath the brim of his cowboy hat.

"Of course," Tess said. "Every good wedding has a theme."

"Theme aside, Abby seems a bit unconventional." He crossed his arms over his chest. "How do you know she won't like the cactus centerpiece?"

"Because I was with her when she picked her flowers the first time." Tess gripped Carter's arm, wanting him to understand. To get it. "She chose peonies for the centerpieces. They symbolize happiness. And more peonies, roses and dahlias for her bouquet. Each flower choice was intentional and meant to come together in an elegant, romantic and magical arrangement."

"But she wasn't presented with the cactus option." Carter shifted and took her hand, tugging her beneath the Cider Mill sign and into the farmers' market. He squeezed her fingers. "We could call Abby and ask her opinion."

"You just want to tell them what happened, so you can encourage them to elope." Tess squeezed his hand harder. "And get yourself out of all this."

"That's not a bad idea." Carter grinned at her. "Eloping can be very efficient."

Or it could be a huge mistake. Tess tugged her hand free before she curved her fingers around Carter's to test whether their palms fit into that *this-feels-really-right* space. And then what? Even if it felt really right she couldn't trust it would last. *You're my now, Tess, not my forever.*

Tess shoved her hands into her pockets. "We aren't calling the happy couple, remember? We agreed."

"You agreed to leave the option open," Carter reminded her.

"And we agreed on five days. We still have four more days to go."

"Fine." Carter leaned forward to peer at Tess. "Are you sure this isn't about you having something against cactus?"

"It's not that." Tess searched for an explanation for the wedding-averse cowboy.

"Really? Because it feels like you don't like cactus." Carter walked through the fruit section and stopped near the hand-painted succulent sign. He picked up a small terra-cotta pot, then turned toward her. His smile and words earnest. "Look at this. It's a cactus that looks like bunny ears. Everyone likes bunnies, including me."

"I like bunnies too." Tess smoothed out her smile, but not that butterfly flutter in her stomach his teasing grin encouraged.

"Then what's wrong with this cactus?" He held the pot up higher.

"It's not a traditional wedding flower." It was all wrong. The same as it was wrong for Tess to be so interested in him so quickly. He was the best man and not in the running to be her man. Still, that flutter lingered as if fanning her attraction. She simply had to clip her curiosity and concentrate. "We want flowers not succulents for the centerpieces."

"Why do the centerpieces have to be flowers?" He set the bunny cactus back on the table.

"Because it's tradition." She traced her finger over the pale pink flower petal on a spiny cactus. "And my wedding was far from traditional. And not something I want for Abby."

"You say that like it was a bad thing," he said.

"I just wonder sometimes if we had stuck to tradition, would our marriage have turned out differently." She pressed her fingertip against the pointy tip of a cactus spine. Would it have hurt less when she'd discovered the man she thought was the love of a lifetime had only loved her for a moment?

"I'm sorry." Carter's voice was quiet and low. And thick with sincerity, drawing her gaze to his. "For what?"

He turned toward her. "For you not getting everything you wanted from your marriage."

She'd expected a partner. A teammate in her husband. Nothing complicated. She'd wanted what her grandparents had shared together. She'd been convinced she'd had that when she'd recited her vows. Then came the tears and grief, the broken promises and deflated dreams. She rubbed the sting from the tip of her finger, but not from her chest. "Thanks. At least now I know exactly what I want."

"Besides the perfect wedding for your cousin, what do you want?" The wide brim of his faded black cowboy hat failed to conceal the curiosity in his gray gaze.

She'd always liked watching the storm clouds roll in over the fields. Liked the feel of the air being charged. And the anticipation of that first crack of thunder. Grandpa Harlan had always claimed a thunderstorm was good for the soul. Could Carter be good for her? Could she want...

Tess blinked. The sun was beating down on her. Not a cloud in sight. Not a raindrop on the radar. Yet, the air around her seemed to crackle. "Success. I want to be successful like my grandparents were."

"We all want that." His voice softened yet the swirling intensity in his eyes built. "Let's get specific. What do you want in a boyfriend?"

That was direct. Tess cleared her throat but not her connection to Carter. Why wasn't she walking away? Telling him to mind his own business. This was about wedding bouquets, not sharing truths. Not getting to know each other. They had a wedding to plan, not a life to build. "I don't want one."

"Hypothetically, if you did." One eyebrow

twitched, the faintest of an arch into his forehead. His words dropped like a dare between them.

"I'd want a man who keeps his word." *Do you always keep your word, Carter?* Would this cowboy love with the same steadfast dedication he gave to his distillery? And with the same loyalty he had for his family? Because that kind of love would last more than a moment. Maybe even a lifetime.

"That shouldn't be hard to find." He stepped into her space.

"I didn't think so." She moved in closer as if she wanted to test her own resolve. "Maybe I just wasn't looking in the right places."

"Maybe." His gaze remained fixed on hers. "By the way, I always keep my word."

There was a warning beneath his promise. Still, she didn't retreat. "But?"

"But I'm definitely the wrong place to look." He pulled back. The smallest of a shift in his shoulders.

Hardly noticeable. But Grandpa Harlan had taught her the art of tells at the card table and in life. Unfortunately, she'd missed all the tells with her former husband, now deceased. That was love's fault. If not for love, she would've seen the truth. But she'd been so ready to fall head over heels and risk everything for love back then. Back then she'd believed love was the answer. She knew better now. She could be happier without it. No, she corrected, she was happier without it.

Now that she was back in the game, she intended to pay full attention. "Why are you the wrong place to look?" Not that she was looking in his direction. She had her own goals. Played for her own team now and liked it.

"Because I vowed never to fall in love." The rim of his cowboy hat shadowed his gaze, but not the warm rasp in his voice. "And you, Tess Palmer, are built to love."

Tess stilled. Completely and fully from the breath that was stuck in her throat to the lock of her knees.

Carter shifted his gaze over her shoulder, then straightened and grinned. "Hello, Freida. I'm sorry. Are we in your way?"

"I didn't want to intrude." Freida Hall clutched the handle of her round bushel basket and set it swinging in front of her. "You two looked to be having a private moment."

Carter chuckled. "As a matter of fact, we were discussing cactus. If you can believe it."

Freida's mouth pulled sideways. The Three Springs's council member considered them as if they'd presented a town ordinance for hopscotch games on all the town sidewalks.

Tess had her own ordinances to enforce.

Farmers' markets were strictly for fruit and vegetable selection, not testing connections to cowboys and discussions about love. *Built to love.* Maybe once upon a time. Her cowboy was wrong. Tess broadened her smile for the council member. "What's your opinion, Freida? Would cactus make good centerpieces for say a wedding? Not ours of course."

"Cactus is certainly a unique choice, isn't it?" The oversize bow on Freida's sun hat wobbled in time to Freida's back and forth head shake. "Just remember when it is your turn to head down the aisle, there's an order to things. You can't just skip ahead. And you certainly don't get extra points for being the fastest to the altar."

Tess had sprinted to the altar for her first marriage and suffered more than a bout of breathlessness for her reckless decision. And walked away with more than one regret. She certainly wasn't looking to repeat that mistake anytime soon. She glanced at Carter. Hard to imagine the business-minded cowboy acting impulsive or rash ever. Then she grinned at the council member. "Well, thanks for that advice, Freida."

"But I should get points for outside the box, creative centerpiece thinking." Carter smiled and presented the cactus. "Right, Freida?"

"Not everything is a competition, Carter." Freida arched an eyebrow at him, then ruined her admonishment with a small laugh. She tipped her head at Tess. "You've got your work cut out with this one, Tess. My Martin was the same. Still, I haven't regretted one day in the forty-four years I've been married to him."

"Oh no." Tess waved her hand between her and Carter. Her words flipped out one after the other. "We're not a couple like that."

"Martin and I weren't either, dear." Freida's laughter was as bright and cheerful as the yellow ribbon on her sun hat. "Until one day, we were. And the rest as they say is history."

Tess had a history with love too. And she'd closed that chapter. Yet, the longer she lingered with Carter in the hot sun, the blurrier those lessons learned became. She had to get back on task. Wedding decisions and chocolate creations wouldn't happen on their own. "It's been good to see you, Freida. We'll just get out of your way and let you proceed with your shopping."

The same Tess intended to get out of her own way and get on with her day. Carter matched Tess's brisk pace into the fruit section.

Tess ignored him, to prove she could, and skimmed her fingers over the watermelons squatting between the clementine oranges and blood oranges. Oranges had always been in her grandmother's fruit basket on the counter. Was it a splash of orange she needed in the spiced ganache truffle? She picked up an empty basket from the endcap and grabbed several varieties of oranges.

Beside her, Carter picked up a red apple and dropped it into her basket. "It's good to have options in your fruit bowl."

But it wasn't good to get caught up in his compelling gray eyes. She blurted, "What does *built for love* mean anyway? I'm not a house."

Carter massaged his neck as if trying to pull back his smile. "It's not a bad thing. It's just that you're wired to love, Tess."

"I'll have you know I gave love its walking papers." She was eyes wide open now. Love would never dupe her again. She added a pint of strawberries and two pears to her basket and moved on. "I cut those wires so to speak."

Carter laughed beside her.

She paused to look at him. "I'm serious."

"That's not how it works. It's who you are. You can't cut it out like sugar from your diet." Carter added a jar of vanilla whipped honey and biscuits to her basket. "In case you haven't had Whitney's honey, you won't find better around."

"Well, I did cut love from my life." Tess pressed her lips together and spun away before she tried to convince herself that she'd found better in a cowboy like Carter.

Carter stayed beside her, silent and watchful, through the rest of the fruit section and the vegetable aisles. And Tess almost forgot he was there. *Almost*.

Outside the greenhouse, he leaned in. His shoulder bumped her. He whispered, "What you are doing right now is proving my point."

She held a bouquet of white, pink and yellow snapdragons. "I'm picking out flowers. What does that prove?"

"For who?" he pressed.

"Margot McKee. She's having a run of bad luck after her boyfriend cheated on her. Then he just stopped paying his portion of the rent." Tess ached for the woman's heartbreak and considered the cheerful flowers surrounding the snapdragon's straight tall stalk. "I'm hoping when Margot sees them, she feels hopeful, not sad."

"See. It's who you are." Carter tapped the rim of his cowboy hat up, revealing his steady gaze. "You're wired to care about people, Tess. To love."

She leveled her gaze and challenged him right back. "What are you wired for?" Besides aggravating her.

"Business and practicality." He lifted his cowboy hat and smoothed his hand over his hair. "I'd tell you that you're wasting your money buying a feeling. The flowers die eventually, and the hope fades too."

Tess's smile dipped into a frown. Of course, Mr. No-Romance-Weddings-Are-Bad wouldn't appreciate the value of flowers. "But Margot will have the memory to hold on to. When she sees snapdragons, she'll remember how they made her feel." Tess walked to the checkout and handed the bouquet to the cashier. "It's like an instant mood reset."

"What flower resets your mood?" Carter's tone was casual.

"Sunflowers," Tess admitted. "Every time. What turns your mood around from bad to good?"

"Butter pecan anything." Carter pulled his cell phone from his back pocket and glanced at the screen. His face clouded. "Gotta take this."

Tess paid for the flowers and followed Carter to the exit. "Everything okay?"

"No. I need to get to the distillery. The inspector is on his way there now." Carter smashed his hat low on his forehead. "I'll drop you off at your store."

From his curt reply, Tess doubted butter pecan anything would improve his mood. "I can make other arrangements."

"You need to be at your store, Tess." Carter

typed on his phone, then shoved his phone in his back pocket. "And it's on my way."

"It'll take too long to drop me off," Tess argued.

Carter took her bags from her and headed for his truck. "It's not right. Your store being closed again. In the middle of the day. That's not good. In fact, it's a bad business practice to make a habit of."

"It's okay." Tess slipped on a pair of sunglasses. What wasn't okay was her continued interest in Carter. She had no couple goals. Neither did he. "The locals won't be wanting to shop anyway. They are either going to the carnival at the high school or the drive-in at Belleridge Park for triple threat night. Three horror movies for the price of one. Talk about a good deal."

"Another good deal is all the things you do for people." Carter shifted the bags to one hand and pulled his truck keys from his front pocket. "When do you collect on all the favors people owe you?"

"I don't." Tess slanted her gaze toward Carter. Something they didn't have in common. That should deter her interest in him. "You're frowning. You don't like that answer. You think I should be charging for all the things I do for people."

"I didn't say that," Carter hedged.

But he wanted to. She could hear it in his tentative tone. He didn't understand her. That should thrill her, not make her feel somehow adrift. As if his truly knowing her mattered somehow. "It's not always about the bottom line and making money."

"What is it about if not that?"

"Some things you do because it's the right thing to do." Why was she trying to explain herself? He either got it or he didn't. She added, "Or maybe you do something just because it's the nice thing to do."

Carter stopped on the walkway to the parking lot. "I can be nice and still want to make money."

Tess lifted her gaze to his. "I never said you weren't nice."

"And I'm doing the right thing for my family. I'm looking after their future." His jaw clenched, then loosened. "I vowed to do that no matter what it took."

Or what it cost him. And it had cost him. Surprise filtered through her. Tess searched his face. Saw the truth in the depths of his steel-gray eyes. Even more, she connected to the loneliness he seemed to accept like the inevitable dust coating his boots. He made no move to brush either off.

But Tess wasn't seeking common ground with

Carter. Or a connection that could strengthen those unwanted purely hypothetical couple ties.

"Carter. Your brother called me!" Roy hollered from outside the truck. "Get a move on. I want to speak to that inspector at Misty Grove."

"You're not talking to him," Carter called back.

Roy shook his head. "We'll see about that."

Carter started across the parking lot toward his truck. "I want to be nice. I really do. But he's making it difficult."

"Tell me about it." Her cowboy was making it difficult not to like him. But Tess had conquered bigger obstacles before. And besides, she wouldn't allow one business-minded, overbearing cowboy to change her heart.

CHAPTER SEVEN

WEDDING PLANNING, FEUDING FAMILY and one intriguing shop owner. Carter was gathering distractions faster than a grasshopper escaping the combine. Carter climbed into his truck and waited for his passengers to get settled and buckled up.

Roy shut the passenger door and grinned from the back bench seat. "You two work out your cactus quarrel?"

"We've come to an understanding." Tess shifted on the leather captain's chair to face him.

Carter understood those intense sparks cracking through her green eyes were entirely too compelling. Drew him to her and invited him to fall in. "What understanding was that exactly?"

"That we should leave all things romance related to me."

Uncle Roy chuckled. "Can't disagree with that one bit."

Tess's teeth bit into her bottom lip as if she fought back her laughter. Her expressive gaze connected with his.

But Carter wasn't falling in. He was single by choice, and it suited him extremely well. As for romance, he preferred not to complicate his life with all that. And he was more than fine leaving it all to Tess. Except he didn't want her to have to take on something else, like planning an entire wedding, all on her own. But that was just part of his best-man duties. Nothing more than that. Carter pulled out of the Cider Mill parking lot and stepped on the gas pedal. Everything he cared about was at home, not seated beside him an arm's reach away.

"Don't mind Carter's brooding, Tess." Uncle Roy's gruff voice disrupted the silence. "He's put out with me, not you."

Carter wasn't brooding. He was attempting to realign his priorities. To concentrate on his work and not on reaching for Tess. Not on taking Tess's hand in his. But he wasn't built to hold on for the long haul like his grandfather or even his uncle. Carter always kept his grip loose and free from those sticky entanglements. He drummed his fingers on the steering wheel.

Tess set her cell phone in the drink holder and rested her arm on the console. As if testing his determination to remain detached.

"And truth be heard by the angels above, I'm something sore with Carter too." Uncle Roy's voice was matter-of-fact.

Carter shook his head and frowned. *Someone save me from stubborn cowboys.*

Tess reached for him and squeezed Carter's arm as if she planned to do just that.

Carter kept quiet.

"I'm sorry to hear that." Tess's voice was thoughtful.

"Carter has been dragging me all over town today for his meetings." Frustration vibrated through Uncle Roy's words. "But I got real important work to be gettin' to. And being his sidekick is keeping me from it. I never asked to be his sidekick. That's not why I'm here."

Carter shook his head. His uncle's rambling was slow to roll off Carter's back and his own comebacks even slower to fade. But inside the truck, in front of Tess, was no place to air their grievances against each other.

"What kind of work are you doing?" Tess asked.

He wasn't surprised Tess probed. She most likely wanted to help as was her way. But Carter took care of his own and he would handle things with Uncle Roy too. He needed a quick conversation spin, away from family matters.

"Carter, you trust Tess?" Roy asked with suspicion.

Not the spin he'd been considering. Carter glanced across the truck cab at Tess as if she was the center of every conversation he wanted to have. Not simply a maid of honor he was obligated to assist. "I do."

"Sorry, Tess. I can't tell you anything," Uncle Roy said. "On account of you siding with Carter. It's nothing personal."

"I can't side with anyone if I don't know what's going on," Tess reasoned.

"Carter can tell you." A defiant edge scratched through Uncle Roy's voice.

Carter pressed his lips together then finally said, "It's a family thing."

"Certainly is," Roy huffed. "And the Sloans don't discuss family matters with outsiders."

"The Sloans don't discuss things within their own family either," Tess retorted.

"Now, that's not nice," Roy grumbled. "Carter, make her take that back."

Carter opened his mouth.

Tess jumped right into the pause. A stern urgency to her words. "It's true or you'd be talking to your brother, Sam, right now."

She didn't give in easy. Or back down. Qualities he usually admired. But he had distillery business to get to and a wedding to-do list to scratch off. He wasn't building a *what to like about Tess* list. Still, Carter kept his grin in check. "She makes a good point, Uncle Roy."

"Used to be Sam and I talked every day," Roy mused.

Carter shifted his gaze to the rearview mirror and saw the hurt work across his uncle's face before Roy glanced out the window.

Uncle Roy added, "Sometimes we even talked more than once in the same day."

"Don't you miss that?" Tess's voice softened into tender as if she felt his uncle's pain too.

"I don't miss people prying into my business." Roy's voice was gruff again. "'Course I miss my brother. Why do you think I'm here?"

Carter caught Uncle Roy's gaze in the rearview mirror. "I thought you were here for that important find."

"I am." Roy's face tensed, and his chin lifted. "My feelings have nothing to do with the search. That's all about business."

And taking a piece of something he'd never wanted to be a part of. Grandpa Sam and Carter had offered Uncle Roy the opportunity to come home and work with them. Uncle Roy had declined every offer over the years, always claiming he was living the good life. Then they'd bought Uncle Roy's half of the farm, releasing him to continue his good life. Now he was back, not to help, but to threaten what Carter had built.

"What are you looking for?" Tess asked.

"A piece of Sloan family history," Uncle Roy said.

"I hope it's easier to find than the silver coin the general store was founded on." Tess's smile was weak. "We've been searching for over a year for that coin that once hung in a frame behind the checkout counter. We haven't found it yet."

Carter hoped the moonshine recipe wasn't as elusive as the missing silver coin and the Herring gold treasure map his grandfather and Boone had been steadfastly searching for. Carter wanted that moonshine recipe. Wanted to know his uncle was mistaken. And he knew his grandfather would require proof otherwise the rift between the two brothers would only expand.

"Do you mean the Silver Penny General Store?" Uncle Roy asked. "Harlan and Opal's place in town?"

"They were my grandparents." Pride was clear in her tone. "I run the store now."

"They were real good people and friends." Uncle Roy sounded less standoffish and more wistful. "Millie and I used to go with Harlan and Opal to the stock show and rodeo up in Colorado every summer. Had the best concerts too that weekend in the Rockies. We always came here first, then traveled together."

"When was that?" Carter asked. "You never stayed at the farm."

"We always stayed at Autumn's Bed and Breakfast," Uncle Roy explained. "Autumn and Millie went to school together. And the rooms were full at the farmhouse with you boys. Millie always claimed you boys needed a good night's sleep in your own bed and a full belly to grow up strong."

That sounded like something his aunt Millie would've said.

"We always invited Sam and Claire, but they never wanted to leave you boys," Uncle Roy added. "Even for a night."

"Were they afraid of what the boys might get into while they were out?" Tess asked, her voice light.

"Something like that, I suppose." Uncle Roy's tone was careful.

That wariness Carter heard pulled his attention back to the rearview mirror. His uncle's gaze connected with Carter's. And Carter knew the older man knew the full truth. Carter had been terrified to be alone as a kid. He'd been afraid his grandparents would leave them the same as his parents. Carter had never shared his fear. He hadn't needed to. His family had somehow known and protected him anyway. And his uncle continued to protect his secret.

His uncle looked out the window. Carter concentrated on the road and turned over his uncle's words in his mind. It was the most his uncle had talked since he'd arrived at the farmhouse. Carter slanted his gaze at Tess. It was all her influence. He'd tried to block her out, but she'd slipped in and given him a glimpse of the uncle he remembered. He should be grateful, not more confused.

Did his uncle want profits and money or something else entirely?

Carter adjusted his hold on the steering wheel, untwisted his thoughts and focused on the road. The southern fence line of Martha Claire Horse Haven came into view. A dozen rescue horses and two foals, both born at the rescue last month, called the place home now.

"Whose idea was the horse sanctuary?" Uncle Roy asked. "Your grandma and aunt always talked about doing something like that years ago."

"My friend Wes had the rescue horses and no land. We had the land. Seemed like the best thing to do for the horses." The name honored both Carter's grandmother and Wes's mother. A bay paced the fence line in time with the truck. Carter rolled down his window. "That's Catnip."

"Catnip?" Tess smiled.

"The barn cats like to have their litters in Catnip's stall." Carter shook his head. "She's docile, gentle and protective. Out here, she plays like she's eaten catnip."

"That buckskin with the dappled gray mare in the pasture looks a lot like my Acorn," Roy chimed in. "That mare sure was one of the fastest horses around, beat those geldings something good in the roping events. Left the box so quick like I almost fell off at our first finals."

Tess shifted in the truck seat again. "You and Sam were part of a roping team, weren't you?"

"Since we were boys." Roy grinned. "We got pretty good too. Always talked about going out on the circuit to see if we could compete on the big stage."

"Why didn't you?" Tess added.

"Some talk is just that." The animation in Roy's tone faded. "Bunch of words that don't really mean nothing."

Too bad Carter couldn't decide what meant nothing and what meant something to his uncle. Carter clenched the steering wheel. Still, the short trip down his uncle's memory lane couldn't erase the damage Uncle Roy had caused on the farm in one morning. Carter turned onto Fortune Street. The general store came into view.

"I always used to shop at the Silver Penny." Uncle Roy was now upbeat, almost chipper.

"There was always good conversation and good candy to be had."

His conversations with Tess had always been on the comfortable, effortless end. Maybe it was the store. Or perhaps there was just something about the owner. Carter said, "Tess makes her own chocolates."

"They aren't exactly my own." Tess fidgeted and reached down to gather her shopping bags from the farmers' market in one hand as if his praise made her uncomfortable. "I follow my grandmother's recipes. I don't see any reason to mess with an already good thing."

"I'll have to stop in for a sample." Roy waggled his eyebrows up and down. "I always liked that almond buttercrunch Opal made. Have any of that?"

Tess shook her head. "But I'm happy to make you some."

"Well, isn't that kind of you." Uncle Roy grinned and shook his finger at Tess. "I knew I liked you."

What Carter knew was that he wasn't exactly *in like* with Tess. Intrigued, sure. Interested, slightly. The same way he was intrigued by experimenting with different casks for his whiskey to finish in and interested in the newest tractor models. But the charred American oak casks he used produced the whiskey he wanted. And his current tractors got the job done. Everything worked just as it was. And that included his personal life. "What about butter pecan fudge?"

"How about a trade?" Tess aimed her wide smile at him, grabbed his hand and squeezed.

Her smile lit in her gaze, drawing Carter into her impossibly round eyes. Inviting him to fall in.

"I'll bring the butter pecan fudge in exchange for more wedding planning." She added, "See you tomorrow morning."

"Looking forward to it." And he was. And that was slightly troubling. Carter let her fingers slip from his grip, then watched her climb out of his truck.

The single life suited him extremely well. He was in fact exceedingly content as a bachelor. But there was something about Tess that made him reconsider. Fortunately, it was as fleeting as the delicate scent of her dusk-laced perfume in his truck cab.

Still, Carter had to be vigilant. Cautious. Or before he knew it, he'd have her hand back in his and holes in his heart.

CHAPTER EIGHT

"I REALLY APPRECIATE the ride." Tess buckled her seat belt in the back row of the Baker sisters' SUV and wiped the sweat off her forehead.

"It's a good thing Breezy and I had second cups of coffee, or we wouldn't have still been at the diner." Gayle laughed from the front passenger seat.

Breezy slipped on her fire engine–red framed sunglasses and pulled out of the Lemon Moon Diner parking lot. "We're definitely glad you caught us in time."

"So am I." Tess was even more glad she wasn't forced to catch Carter in a tractor this morning.

As it was, she'd sprinted from the general store to the diner to intercept the Baker sisters and request a ride. The petite pair always ate breakfast at the diner every Thursday. It'd been their ritual for as long as the locals could recall. And a boon for Tess today with her car still in the repair shop and Carter attempting to duck out of the wedding planning with a short text. Need a rain check this morning.

And worse, no explanation and no response to her follow-up texts. Now Tess wasn't certain if she should be irritated or concerned about her cowboy. So she was headed to his farmhouse to find out.

"I don't think I've been this full in years." Gayle's beaded eyeglass chain dangled against her papery, rosy cheeks. "We had to splurge after our bowling league win last night. It's quite the coup."

"No team has gone undefeated in the league in over ten seasons." Breezy high-fived Gayle.

"That's something to celebrate." Tess smiled. She would celebrate when Abby and Wes's wedding was back on track. Then she could focus again on her chocolate sampler and give herself a chance to win like the Baker sisters.

"Speaking of celebrations, you're rushing off to Carter's first thing in the morning." Gayle peeked around her seat and blinked at Tess behind her round lenses. Delight lifted the lively retiree's voice an octave. "That's two mornings in a row."

Breezy hummed from the driver's seat. "It's good to establish a routine of spending quality time together every day."

There was nothing routine about Carter and Tess's time together. It would be all about wedding details. Like he'd agreed to yesterday. Tess wasn't letting him off the hook either.

Her cousin's dream wedding was rain or shine. The planning could not be postponed.

And if she was the tiniest bit excited to barge in and fluster him like he'd done to her yesterday, well, that was her secret. As it was, he'd traipsed around her thoughts all night long as if he belonged there. Once the wedding plans were finalized, she could put her cowboy out of her mind for good. The sooner, the better for the sake of a decent night's sleep.

"Do you ladies still want only the triple chocolate pecan fudge for your family reunion?" Tess pivoted the conversation away from more couple chatter. "I found Grandma's recipe for her chocolate pecan toffee and her vanilla pecan logs."

Yet, Tess still hadn't found the one recipe she needed for the competition. Without it, she'd have to go it alone and trust her instincts. But she'd done that before with her ex and had the broken heart to show for it. That only made her fret and fidget in the backseat.

"Those candies would certainly highlight our pecan crop." Breezy grinned in the rearview mirror. "We would have quite the pecan dessert display."

"I remember Opal's nougat inside her pecan logs." Gayle sighed and patted her chest. "Such a delightful flavor. Unlike anything I've ever tasted and still one of my favorite treats. I'll be thrilled to have them in my house again."

And that was why Tess had to have her grandmother's exact recipe. Grandma Opal's chocolates and candies were still remembered decades later. Tess wanted to have that kind of staying power too. Re-creating her grandmother's creations would give her that. "Consider your family reunion display complete."

"That's good timing." Breezy's joyful laughter streamed around the SUV, swirling with the upbeat country song about white sand beaches, stolen kisses and summer love. "We're almost to Carter's place and your mind is sure to be on other things than our desserts."

Her mind was going to be on wedding checklists and not a certain intriguing cowboy.

Breezy drove past the rod-iron gates for the entrance to Martha Claire Horse Haven and turned on a nondescript dirt road. A small, crooked private-property sign leaned into a tree trunk.

Gayle swayed her shoulders in the front seat in time to the upbeat music. "I always found summer to be a good time to fall in love."

Breezy hummed. "It's the long days that ease into those endless nights from sunrise to starlight. There's so much time to spend together. What do you think, Tess?"

There was no good time. Love could fool a person in any season. Besides, Tess knew the only surefire way not to be fooled by love was *not* to fall in love to begin with. She hedged, "Abby and Wes met in the summer, and it seems to have worked out for them."

"It certainly has." Gayle's face softened as if warmed by that truth.

The curvy road finally straightened, and the golden wheat fields gave way to pastureland surrounding a large blue-and-white farmhouse.

Gayle gasped, set her hand on the dashboard, then pushed her eyeglasses up her nose. "That's quite an eyesore in their front and back yards, isn't it?"

"Nothing romantic about that view." Breezy frowned and slowed the SUV in the large circular driveway.

Tess leaned against the center console, stared out the windshield and agreed. Massive holes dotted the land surrounding the Sloans' historic farmhouse. "Maybe Carter is testing out some new irrigation technique."

Breezy snorted. "He's a better farmer than that. And besides, Carter respects the land. Always has since he was a boy playing hide-and-seek in the fields. This all looks too careless to be intentional."

"I'm sure there's a good explanation." Tess

spotted Carter, who appeared more than fine in his usual cowboy hat, plaid shirt, jeans and boots. Carter's uncle, who stood beside him in front of a silver compact rental car near the four-car garage, also looked fine. Her concern unwarranted, Tess leaned into her irritation. *Rain check denied.*

Carter turned and narrowed his gaze on the SUV. He didn't look happy. Well, neither was Tess. She wasn't going to be brushed off so easily. Besides, she could handle one surly cowboy. After all, she had wedding priorities. She opened the passenger door and smiled at the Baker sisters. "Thanks for the ride, ladies."

"Phone us if you need a ride home, dear," Breezy called out. "We're heading to the Owl later to sample Nolan's latest barbecue creations on his new barbecue pit."

"And we'd love to hear about your day with Carter," Gayle chimed in.

"Thanks again." Tess shut the door. Breezy honked the horn, waved, then drove away.

"Tess, what are you doing here?" Carter's bewildered voice came from right behind her.

Nothing to do now but face her cowboy. Tess turned, patted the oversize tote bag on her shoulder and dialed her smile into brilliant. "I'm bringing the wedding to you."

"Didn't you get my text about needing a rain

check?" Surprise and confusion flashed across Carter's face before he turned and headed toward his uncle and another gentleman. "This isn't a good time."

Tess suspected there would be no good time for the eloping-is-efficient-and-romance-is-bad cowboy. She shaded her eyes with her hand and walked beside him. "What kind of landscaping project do you have going on?"

"That's not landscaping, Tess. That's my search and rescue. My important work that I told you about yesterday in the truck." Roy smoothed his hands over his diamond snap shirt and tucked the denim ends into his waistband. "And now Harris here is making a movie about Carter and the family."

The barely thirty-something gentleman stepped forward. The polish on his loafers matched the sheen above his forehead, glistening across his already receding hairline. His smile was relaxed, his voice eager. "I'm Harris Newton from Spider Silk Creative Group. I just arrived too."

Tess introduced herself and shook Harris's hand. "You're a filmmaker. That's fascinating."

Twin red spots burst across Harris's pale cheeks, matching the splotches on his equally pale arms.

Tess continued, "What kind of film are you making?"

"It's not a movie and it was scheduled for next week." Carter typed on his phone, hard, sharp, quick taps of his thumbs.

"It's a behind-the-scenes look into the distillery and the family running it." Harris adjusted the collar of his polo shirt around his neck as if trying to block the sunlight. "It's all part of the promotion campaign for Misty Grove's launch."

"If you're wanting to know about the Sloan family and the distillery, come with me." Roy rocked back on his boot heels. Excitement widened his eyes. "I'm looking for a piece of Sloan family history right now, in fact."

Carter's fingers clenched around his cell phone, and the muscles along his jawline flexed. "Uncle Roy, you can't take Harris digging around the property with you."

"Why not?" Roy ran his hand through his hair and tugged, fluffing the salt-and-pepper curly strands even more. Then he tapped a finger against his temple. "If it's Sloan family history Harris wants, I got all that stored right up here. We can dig and chat. What's wrong with that?"

For one, Harris needed to worry about the sun. Five more minutes out in the heat and Harris would need to soak his balding head and arms in an aloe bath all night. And second, Tess could feel Carter's frustration rolling off him.

Tess stepped closer to him, yet just far enough away she couldn't grab his hand to offer additional support. "I'm sure Harris has work to do to prepare for his film."

"I actually came early to set up and get my bearings." Harris shifted in his loafers and checked the sky as if searching for a wisp of cloud cover. "And I'd really like to get a lay of the land so to speak before I shoot any actual footage."

Carter's phone rang. Loud and shrill.

Tess slanted her gaze at Carter. "Do you need to get that?"

"A transfer pump is down at the distillery. It's responsible for moving the whiskey from the tank to the barrels." Carter silenced his phone and scrubbed his hand over his face. "I need to be troubleshooting and repairing it right now."

"Then you best be getting to the distillery, Carter," Roy declared.

"If Carter is heading there, it seems I will have some free time on my hands. I'd only be in the way. Tools aren't really my specialty." Harris held out his hands and smiled. "I'm better behind the scenes. If you've got spare gloves and a shovel, I can manage that much."

"I can't let you dig around the property." Carter frowned and shoved his phone into his back pocket.

"I've got new boots in the rental, and I really don't mind. It might lend depth to the video too." Harris headed off toward the compact car, then added, "Besides, it'll be good to move around after sitting on the airplane and in the rental car for so long."

"What about sunscreen? Have that in your rental too?" Carter mumbled. His head dropped back as if he searched for answers in the cloudless sky.

"I'll get the shovels." Uncle Roy hurried toward the work shed behind the garage, his steps brisk and spry.

"I have to be at the distillery, but that means I can't watch over them too." Carter straightened and shifted his hooded gaze to her. "Now do you see why I needed that rain check?"

Carter needed help, not a rain check. And she was there. The sooner she helped him, the quicker she checked off that wedding list and got back to her own things like her chocolate goals. And moving on from her unwanted cowboy connection. "I can watch over them for you, especially if you're worried about Roy falling and hurting himself like I am. And I even have sunscreen in my bag for Harris."

Carter shook his head and walked to the fence lining the property. He propped his forearms on the thick, notched wood of the top post and stared out over the pasture. Tension rode along the line of his clenched jaw.

Tess joined him and tapped her shoulder into his. "I know I'm not family, but I'm here. I'm willing to help if you let me."

Carter placed his boot on the lower fence post and kept his gaze fixed on the horizon. "It's so much bigger than a lost family trinket, Tess. And digging in the dirt."

His voice was grim. A disquiet dusted across her skin. "You know you can trust me, right? What's this really about?"

He exhaled, long and deep until his shoulders lowered. Then he tipped his head and searched her face as if seeking a reason not to trust her. Finally, he said, "Uncle Roy believes he buried the original bourbon whiskey recipe for Misty Grove somewhere on the property."

Tess's mouth dropped open. That disquiet sank deeper.

"Uncle Roy claims he's owed a portion of the profits and a stake in Misty Grove. When he finds his original moonshine recipe, he'll have the proof." Carter flicked his wrist toward the fields and the rows upon rows of holes. "But I created the mash blend and the yeast profile from scratch. My great-granddad brewed his own moonshine same as his father and his grandfather before him. Nothing remains except empty bottles and best guesses about their exact recipe. At least that's what I was always led to believe."

Fear, just a hint, skimmed over his face. And the worry was there seated deep and sure in his gray eyes. She asked, "What does Sam say?"

"He doesn't know yet. I wanted to talk to Grandpa in person if he'll speak to me." Carter pushed away from the fence. "But there hasn't been a good time."

Now Roy had captured Harris's attention. "And a family feud could make for a compelling storyline in Harris's film."

"Even just a rumor could cause reputational damage to me and the distillery." That alarm sparked in his gaze. "We can't afford that. Not to mention the cost and time of a legal brawl if Uncle Roy takes it that far."

Tess couldn't imagine Roy, with his cotton-ball soft curly hair and belly-deep laugh, taking his own family to court. Then again, she'd been fooled by charisma and charm before. "And you think family disputes should be settled privately among family."

"Absolutely. That was my plan," Carter said. "Get Grandpa and Uncle Roy to sit down at the same table and talk. But Grandpa moved downtown, and Uncle Roy has gone rogue."

"Now Harris is here, and his focus should be

solely on Misty Grove," Tess said. "And not on Roy's ownership claims."

"I barely have the distillery established. I've spent the past ten years refining the whiskey and Misty Grove's flavor profile to make it instantly recognizable but unique. Now it's ready to launch nationally. It's all I've been working for." Carter paced away from her, then back. He flung his arm toward the fields. "The launch is how all this keeps enduring and surviving."

"It's your legacy," she said.

"It's the Sloan family legacy," he corrected. "I'm just here to make sure it sustains."

He sounded as if he was the default leader, not the trailblazer and driver behind the distillery. Yet, she wasn't there to debate whose legacy it truly was. "You can't have Roy spilling a family dispute to Harris and risk it going public."

"The distributors could see the distillery as unstable and an investment risk. Any ownership changes could trigger doubts about the continuity of Misty Grove's flavor profile. They could question the integrity of future releases." Carter wiped a hand under his chin and frowned. "Why stock it if you can't guarantee the quality will be the same year after year? That's how you build brand recognition that matters."

It all mattered. And it all weighed on Carter. She could see it in the creases around his eyes.

Hear it in his uneven exhales. He wasn't asking for her help. She was giving it anyway. Same as she would for all her neighbors. That she wanted to hold his hand while she did it wasn't significant. At least she wouldn't let it be. "Do you have an extra work shirt in your truck?"

He stilled and watched her. "Why?"

"Because I'm going digging too." Tess lifted her chin and summoned a little determination. She may not be his family, but he needed her.

Carter squeezed his forehead. "And if I say no, you're not going digging too, then what?"

"Don't bother." Tess set her hands on her hips. "I'm sure you think I'm interfering, but I know how to keep Roy quiet."

"How exactly do you plan to do that?" Uncertainty slowed Carter's words. "Find the fabled moonshine recipe first?"

"We can only hope I'm that lucky." Tess braced her hands on Carter's shoulders, leaned in and captured his full attention. Just as she wanted. That she wanted to close the gap and hold on to him as if they were some kind of team was only noteworthy if she failed to keep her distance. She locked her knees. "I'm going to give Harris another brilliant cover story. A centuries-old legend is already in play in Three Springs with a missing silver coin, treasure map and buried gold. What could be better?"

His gaze dipped to her mouth, then lifted. And a different sort of warmth swirled through his eyes, scattering that earlier worry. "A lot of things come to mind."

Her heart skipped. Tess tensed her fingers on his shoulders as if she was the one needing support. She arched an eyebrow. "You have to admit it's a good idea."

He shook his head, the barest of movements, and held her gaze for another beat. That heat flared in his eyes and trapped Tess. But one small step forward would be a risk too far. She'd come to ensure her cousin's love story continued, not listen to her own foolish heart.

She released him, breaking their connection, then retreated into that safety zone. And caught her breath. "Just trust me and give me that shirt, please."

Carter turned and walked toward his truck. He opened his passenger door, reached inside and pulled out a gray-and-blue plaid shirt. "I can't believe I'm going along with this."

"There will be no talk about a missing moonshine recipe, copyrights and stakeholder shake-ups." Tess accepted the soft, worn shirt and that her heart was racing because he'd agreed. And those butterflies flipping in her stomach were from excitement, not attraction. "Does that make you feel better?"

"No." Carter whipped off his cowboy hat and scrubbed his hand through his hair, tangling the dark brown strands that brushed against his collar. The worry and fear were there still, slightly duller, but ever present. "It feels like absolute chaos brewing and I'm not quite sure how to stop it. I just know I have to."

"You realize you don't have to handle all this by yourself." Tess tied the long ends of the shirt at her waist and buttoned several holes over her white tank top.

"My brothers have their own lives now. As it should be," Carter said. "That means the farm, distillery and all that goes with it are my responsibility."

His shoulders were straight, his stance sure. Still, she sensed a weariness inside him and yet despite that, she understood he'd willingly take on more if he had to. All in the name of family. She admired his loyalty and commitment. But even he could only handle so much on his own. "It's going to be okay."

"Always the optimist." His grin lingered in the corner of his mouth.

She rolled up the shirtsleeves and tipped her head, wanting to draw out his full smile. Wanting to know she made a difference. "You do know that you are going to owe me for this."

"What do you have in mind?" He moved into

her space and freed her hair from beneath the shirt collar.

His movements were brisk and impersonal, yet the brush of his fingers against her neck sent her stomach in a deep, rolling somersault. And a considerate Carter became difficult to discount. She blurted, "Wedding planning is up next. And don't say you don't have time. You have to eat lunch. So we'll make it a working session over lunch."

"Fine. You're going to want these." He handed her a pair of work gloves, then tucked her hair behind her ear and drew his thumb across her cheek. One slow, soft caress as if Tess was the only thing on his mind. "Don't forget the sunscreen. Your cheeks are already turning a pretty shade of pink."

He turned at Roy's shout and headed for the garages.

Tess exhaled through her dry throat. She was a widow. Carter was a handsome single cowboy. She wouldn't apologize for her attraction, but she wouldn't encourage it either. After all, Tess knew where she stood on her own. It was relationships that made her lose her balance. All she had to do was just tread softly around love and then she'd avoid its notice all together. Tess joined the others. "Got another shovel somewhere?"

"Tess, welcome to the search crew. It's good to have your support." Roy handed her his shovel, frowned at Carter, then turned toward the work shed. "I'll be right back."

Beside her, Carter stiffened. Tess shoved her hand inside a glove rather than reach for him as if picking her team. "Carter, we'll see you at lunch."

"Fine. Don't get too close to the road." He pulled out his truck keys and walked away.

Within seconds his truck tires were kicking up pebbles and dirt and Tess was on her own. Time to prove she was more than an interference in his life.

Roy returned with another shovel and started for the fence. Tess flanked him on one side and Harris the other. Tess reached into her tote bag and handed Harris a tube of sunscreen. "You're going to want this."

Harris smeared the sunscreen down his nose and across his cheeks. "What are we looking for? Those holes look big enough to hold a large treasure chest."

"Funny you should mention it." Tess rubbed sunscreen onto her face, pleased she had such an easy opening into her cover story. Maybe luck was on her side. If only Carter could see her now. "There's a legend in Three Springs about a band of outlaws who looted train depots and towns around here. Then one night the outlaws stole from a small community not far from here."

"That was their first mistake." Roy held his hand out for the sunscreen. "Folks around here don't take to stealing and cheating, even back then. And it was three sisters who decided to make things right and they took back the gold and silver from the Herring Gang late one night."

Harris shaded his eyes with his hand and glanced out at the horizon. "And you think that gold and silver is out there somewhere."

"Of course it's out there." Roy pulled a pair of gloves from his back pocket and tapped them against his leg. "Victoria McKenzie, who was the only one who survived that night after the outlaws chased her sisters down, ended up with the treasure. It's got to be somewhere, doesn't it?"

"I suppose." Harris nodded and his eyebrows pulled together. "But what do you think is here?"

"Best I can reckon, a treasure map." Roy opened the gate in the fence.

Tess gaped at the older man. Boone and Sam believed the treasure map was tucked inside the frame of the silver coin that used to hang on the wall inside the general store. The silver coin was said to be part of the original Herring Gang treasure. The silver coin had been found in the river by Tess's own ancestor, who had then been inspired to open the Silver Penny General Store. "Why would the map be here?"

"I heard folks talking about the legend this morning at the Lemon Moon Diner." Roy grinned at Harris. "It's white asparagus week at the diner. You should stop in. The whole town's been in there this week for their tarts and fancy quiches. Can't find better."

"I'll make a point to check it out later," Harris said.

"Anyway, while I was waiting on my quiche and talking to my old friends, I got to remembering stories my granddad told us as kids." Roy stepped over to a hole and studied it. "Figured it can't hurt to look again. Might be I missed something the first time."

"So there still might be a missing treasure out here." Harris's voice was animated.

"It's rumored to be hidden in Silent Rise Canyon." Tess shifted around the dirt inside a shallow hole. "Having lost both her sisters, Victoria declared the loot cursed and she and her new husband buried it, letting love be their legacy and not gold."

"Why not keep the gold?" Harris scratched his fingers under his nose.

"The couple didn't want to bring bad luck to their marriage and their kin." Tess wasn't so different from Victoria McKenzie. She certainly believed a couple couldn't have too much good luck on their wedding day. She doubted Carter would find her connection to the legend inspiring. Still, the thought broadened her smile.

"That's why it makes sense for the treasure map to have been buried here. The northern end of the Sloan property meets the edge of the canyon." Roy tapped his shovel into another hole and lifted out a dented old oilcan. "And the Sloans have been married on this land since Three Springs was founded."

She wondered if Carter intended to continue the tradition. But her wedding-opposed cowboy probably assumed his brothers would keep the tradition going. And for reasons she dismissed that idea didn't sit well.

"Every Sloan has been married here?" Doubt crossed over Harris's face.

"It's not so hard to believe. Folks didn't have many options like they do now." Roy patted his head, peppering his white hair with dirt. "We got lots of places to get hitched around here from the farmhouse to the stables and even the pond."

"Did you marry here?" Harris worked his shovel through the dirt in an awkward scrape.

"Millie and I married at the farmhouse." Roy touched his fingers as if reaching for his wedding ring. "Sam and Claire recited their vows out at the pond."

Tess unearthed another oilcan and set it beside the one Roy found. "That was quite an impressive tradition."

"It was until Carter's mom broke it. Lillian flat out refused to marry here. Had to have her wedding in the city." Roy shook his head. Regret covered his words. "Broke Sam's heart something good too. It's no wonder she ended up divorced. Things that important need to start out on solid ground like the kind you find right here."

Tess agreed and shifted more dirt around inside a hole. Carter never mentioned his parents. Not even in passing. All she knew was that the Sloan boys had grown up on the farm and were by all indications Sam's pride and joy. And by all indications, Carter more than understood the value of the Sloan land.

Harris's foot slipped into a hole. He righted himself and wiped the mud from his new boot. "I'm confused. What does the Sloan wedding tradition have to do with a missing treasure map?"

"Don't you see? The Sloans chose love over the gold too." Roy scooped another oilcan from his hole and tossed it toward the others. "If the Sloans had the map, I believe they hid it on this land and got married the same as Victoria McKenzie and her husband did."

"And they put down roots and built their future home on something solid, rather than with cursed, stolen gold." Tess leaned on her shovel handle and smiled. "You have to admit there is something charming and entirely satisfying about the whole idea."

"I knew you'd see it like me." Roy beamed at her.

"Then shouldn't we leave the treasure map alone?" Harris used his shovel for balance. "Given its link to cursed gold, bad luck and all that."

Tess nodded, delighted for Harris's unintended assistance. Her luck was holding. "It's probably for the best. We could head inside and get an early start on lunch."

"I'm sure there's an expiration date on curses." Roy was sounding more and more confident. "And we aren't using the gold to build a legacy anyhow."

But Roy's missing moonshine recipe could alter the legacy Carter had been building himself. Tess squeezed the shovel handle.

"What are we doing with it if we find it, then?" Interest and anticipation curved across Harris's face.

"Well, I reckon we have to find it first and then decide." Roy laughed.

Tess shrugged. "What now?"

"We keep digging." Roy shuffled off to another hole.

That meant Tess too. Tess scrambled after the older cowboy. She couldn't leave Roy alone with Harris. Carter was counting on her.

And that mattered entirely too much to her. Even more, she didn't want to let Carter down.

Perhaps if she dug deep enough, she'd tunnel out of her growing fascination with Carter—a business-minded, romance-averse cowboy and the last person she should be starting to care about.

CHAPTER NINE

THE LUNCH HOUR was almost over when Carter walked into the farmhouse through the back door. He was late, but the transfer pump was operational. And the holes in his land hadn't multiplied. Small miracle there. And he knew who to thank.

His gaze skipped over the sandwich fixings scattered all over the kitchen island. That was nothing unusual in the Sloan house. In a family of five boys, it seemed someone was always eating. It was the family room that had him stopping in his grandma's drop zone next to the kitchen. Or what was supposed to be his family room. The space had been transformed into a bridal boutique, with only wedding gowns missing. And that gave Carter the slightest twinge of indigestion.

As for the woman at the center of the man cave makeover, she gave Carter complete pause.

He leaned against the kitchen counter and watched Tess. She still wore his plaid work shirt, tied at the waist, sleeves rolled up, and fluttered around the coffee table. She tore a page from a magazine and waved it at Uncle Roy.

Uncle Roy rubbed his stomach and shook his head. "Never had an appetite for fancy food like that. It's too small and too hard to pick up."

And Carter had never been quite so intrigued with a woman until now. That unsettled his work-first mindset and he refused to let this one wisp of a woman unnerve him any further. "Where is Harris?"

"Scouting the property for the money shots." Satisfaction stretched from Uncle Roy's wide grin, lifting his eyebrows into a waggle. "I gave him a list of suggestions."

"Someone should probably be with him." And by someone, he meant himself. But his gaze remained on Tess as if beside her was where he really wanted to be.

"Harris is fine." Ryan added slices of ham to his sandwich. "He promised to stay on the path and behind the fence line."

"And I gave him a cowboy hat from the work shed to block the sun." Tess smiled.

Carter checked the clock on the wall. He'd give Harris ten, fifteen minutes most, then go and find him. His marketing rep getting injured on his property would hardly be considered good client-vendor relations. As for the woman invading his world, she was hardly good for his peace of mind. "Tess, have you eaten?"

"No." Ryan piled a handful of shredded lettuce onto his stack of cheese and meat. "I offered to make her a club sandwich, but she was too busy with her vision."

Tess hugged the magazine to her chest and swayed. "I've been trying to explain to your uncle and brother the importance of a wedding theme."

"I explained I like to see things." Roy tapped his finger against the side of his head. "Not imagine them."

"Then she started all this." Ryan waved one hand around his head, pressed his other palm down on the bread and flattened his sandwich. "She took over the pool table, the couch and now the dartboard like some sort of bridal ninja. It's frightening, really. One minute it's our perfect hangout spot and then it's a bridal showcase."

"She hasn't stopped moving." Uncle Roy's eyes widened as Tess tore another picture from her magazine. "I blame you and the cactus, Carter. It all started with that cactus."

"What cactus?" Ryan lifted a sandwich half and took a large bite.

"No. No. Not happening." Tess shook her head and pointed to what used to be their tournament-size dartboard.

Magazine clippings, paint swatches and fabric scraps covered every inch of the mahogany wood cabinet, including the two chalkboard scoreboards and the entire dartboard.

"Does anyone see a single cactus on this vision board?" Tess continued, her words brisk and clipped. "I think not."

Carter saw the single smudge of dirt on Tess's cheek. Entirely too distracting. He grabbed two slices of bread and a paper plate. "I chose cactus from Cider Mill Orchard for the centerpieces yesterday."

"And I un-chose them." Tess lifted her chin and stared Carter down.

Was that another smudge of dirt under her chin too?

"Nothing wrong with a cactus." Ryan opened a bag of potato chips. "Did you know cactus drink from the fog?"

Carter nodded, not that he was interested in cactus facts. He was, however, increasingly fascinated with Tess and the dirt smears on her face he wanted to remove. Instead, he smeared mayonnaise across the bread and said, "I already explained the practicality of cacti."

There was nothing practical about the way he was drawn to Tess. But he'd only stopped in for that working lunch Tess suggested. It was all he had time for. He had to ensure the combine was ready, the mills cleaned and prepped for the up-coming harvest and that the maintenance stayed on schedule at the distillery. Satisfying his curiosity about one shop owner wasn't included on any checklist.

"We don't want to be practical." Tess held her hands out toward the dartboard cabinet as if it was some priceless artwork. Any plea in her words was muted by the firm determination in her tone. "Let's concentrate on the vision board, please. It's our guide."

"Well, my stomach is guiding me to the kitchen." Uncle Roy washed his hands in the kitchen sink and smiled at Ryan. "I'll take one of what you're having."

Ryan grabbed the loaf of bread. "It's my specialty."

Carter finished the sandwich, added a handful of chips to the plate and carried it over to Tess. "Lunch is served."

"I'm not that hungry," Tess said.

"We can share it." *Share it.* Carter didn't share things. Unless there was something to gain from it. Still, he held the plate out toward Tess.

Satisfied when she picked up a half, he placed the plate on the corner of the pool table and looked at a bridal magazine declaring six hundred and sixty-seven dazzling details to inspire every bride. His stomach twisted. He was inspired to gather up all the wedding clutter and Tess and remove every bit of the romance from his house. But that, he feared, would not be enough to erase the imprint Tess had made on him already.

He left the magazine on the pool table with the dozen others and grabbed a chip. "Do you always walk around with an entire shelf of bridal magazines at the ready?"

"I bought them last night at The Book Brook in Belleridge." Tess grinned around her bite of the BLT sandwich. "I may have lingered too long at the bookstore, but I miss being surrounded by books."

"You drove to Belleridge last night," Carter said. "For magazines."

"I borrowed Paige's car. I had to pick up the books for the book club meeting scheduled for next week. Then Freida asked me if I would mind grabbing her organic eucalyptus oil from Health Dash Depot. And Old Town Pet Market finally had the special koi fish food that Lynette Kinney has been waiting for." Tess picked up another magazine claiming to know the most brilliant dresses of the season and grinned. "I found these other ones when I went to the kids' secondhand boutique for Corine Bauer. Corine's twins are getting so big, they've already grown out of most of their clothes."

Carter dissected her errands. One was an indulgence. And all the others were favors. Favors did nothing to boost her bottom line for the general store. Surely, she understood that. "Who was working at the store?"

"I closed early." Tess finished her sandwich and wiped her palms on her shorts.

"You can't be closed more than you're open." Carter grabbed more chips. "That's a bad business practice." And something of a habit.

Spending time with Tess could become something of a habit for him. Good thing he had work and his family to keep that from happening.

"I like my business practices. And besides, I can't be in two places at once." Tess set her palms on the stack of magazines and inhaled. "None of that matters. It isn't relevant."

Business was always relevant. Especially when that business supported a family, even if it was only a family of one.

Tess leaned in, grabbed a chip and whispered, "By the way, I'm so good Harris wants to do a documentary on the Herring Gang legend and the treasure hunt. The missing moonshine recipe never came up."

"Harris works for a marketing firm, not Three Springs." Although a documentary might help bring traffic to Tess's general store. He wanted that for Tess, but not at the expense of his distillery. Carter chomped down on a chip. A documentary about a lost treasure would take time to put together. He needed his whiskey promoted now, during the national launch, and that required Harris's complete focus.

"It'll be in his spare time. Filmmaking is Harris's hobby." Tess straightened and set her hand on Carter's chest as if he was the one needing to reset his priorities. Her voice lifted. "Now we need to concentrate."

And not on the warmth of her palm against his shirt. Too bad, really. But she needed to concentrate on her general store. Profits didn't just happen. He could help her. Help her identify her potential income streams and grow her business. He was good at that. Carter's gaze shifted to that smudge on her cheek. Suddenly, it wasn't balance sheets and profit margins he wanted to discuss.

But getting closer to Tess Palmer was bad for his own equilibrium. The distillery, farm and his family rounded out his life; adding another person would set him completely off-kilter. He sighed and wondered if he should ignore his interest. "You want to concentrate on the vision board, I suppose."

"Exactly." Tess's smile pushed into her cheeks. "We really need to focus."

"I don't need to focus." Carter eased away

from her, proving he could disconnect his interest. He considered the wall and his unrecognizable dartboard cabinet. "I can hit the bull's-eye blindfolded."

Tess's eyebrows drew together, and irritation curved across her mouth. Even that he found attractive too.

"I'll take that bet," Ryan announced.

Carter turned and looked at his brother.

Ryan set Uncle Roy's finished sandwich on a paper plate and pulled out his wallet. "Twenty says you miss."

"What's going on?" Caleb, the youngest but tallest Sloan brother and an identical twin, walked inside. He checked for mud on his boots in the drop zone, hung his cowboy hat on the hook near the back door and ran his hand over his volunteer firefighter T-shirt.

"It's BLTs for lunch. Tess has launched a bridal takeover. Harris, you'll meet him soon, is making a film about the family." Ryan stuck the butter knife in the mayonnaise jar and wiped his hands on a towel. "And Carter is getting ready to prove his imaginary dart skills. Bets are now being placed."

"Count me in." Caleb grabbed the other half of his brother's sandwich before Ryan could hide it and took a big bite. A quick shoving match ensued, then Caleb added, "Another twenty says his dart doesn't even stick in the board."

Uncle Roy reached into his back pocket, pulled out his wallet and revealed a large selection of bills tucked inside the leather folds.

"I'll double it." Uncle Roy slapped a twenty on the kitchen island. "My money says Carter won't land in the outer ring, let alone the bull's-eye."

Carter rubbed his hands together and considered his dartboard turned bridal vision. He stepped closer and frowned. "Is that a picture of a swan ice sculpture?"

"Yes." Tess lifted her chin. "There's one with twin hearts and the couple's initials too."

"It won't last an hour in this heat." Talk about a waste of money. Carter rubbed his chin, but his confusion still colored his words. "Why would you want an ice sculpture?"

"It's not about the ice sculpture." Ryan waved the butter knife over his head like an awkward magic wand. "It's about the feeling it evokes. Right, Tess?"

Tess aimed her delighted smile at Carter's brother and nodded. "You were listening after all."

Ryan grinned and assembled another sandwich.

Carter crossed his arms over his chest. "And what feeling is that exactly, Ryan?"

His brother shrugged, tossed his head back and laughed. "I have no idea."

"Don't look at me." Caleb cradled the bag of potato chips. "Weddings are good for a champagne toast and cake. Gotta have the cake, or it isn't a proper reception."

"Ice sculpture could be useful if the animals are invited. Keep the water cold and all." Uncle Roy sat on a stool at the kitchen island and looked at Tess. "Are the animals invited too?"

"We're organizing a wedding, not a petting zoo." Tess touched her forehead and swiped her fingers across her eyebrows.

His grandmother used to do the same. Then she'd claim the boys were giving her a headache and shoo them all outside to spend their pent-up energy. Gran Claire would tell them not to come home until they heard the dinner bell. Carter supposed he could grab Tess's hand and take her outside for a reprieve. But he figured she'd keep talking wedding out there or in here. Carter located his darts on the end table, resting on yet another bridal magazine.

"Abby and Wes's wedding needs to be filled with as much charm and romance as we can fit into the day." Determination reinforced Tess's words.

"There's nothing charming or right about that swan ice sculpture." Carter narrowed his eyes and shifted his stance, aiming his dart for the cabinet.

"Or the champagne with the fruit floating in it. That's on the board too." Ryan rubbed his stomach. "Never liked the taste."

"I always hated mint chocolate." Caleb brushed his hands through his hair, tousling the wavy strands in every direction. "Gran Claire always promised I'd get a taste for it. Never did."

Tess moved to stand in front of her visionary creation and waved her arms as if drawing everyone's attention back to her and away from culinary dislikes. "What's on this board is inspiration for us. Not exactly what we're going to do."

"Then why did you go to all that work covering up a perfectly fine dartboard?" Ryan frowned.

"So you had something to see, and we had a road map." Tess pointed at Carter and set her hands on her hips. "Carter, you will not throw darts at my vision board."

"I kind of need to." Carter rolled the darts between his hands and ignored the alluring spark in her eyes. After all, he wasn't interested. "Bets have been wagered."

"Save it for later," Tess said. "We have too much to do."

Carter shook his head. "I'm afraid that's not how it works in the Sloan house."

"Grandpa taught us not to walk away from challenges," Caleb declared. "They only make you stronger in life."

Tess touched her eyebrow again.

Carter swallowed his laughter.

"Our own granddaddy raised Sam and me with the same values," Roy announced. Pride curved from his face to his shoulders. "Grand-dad believed in hard work and never backing down."

Tess eyed Carter. He shrugged one shoulder at her and worked to keep his expression neutral.

"Would you like to get in on this, Tess?" Ryan asked.

Carter studied her. Would she bet on him or against him?

Tess steepled her hands together, set them in front of her face and inhaled as if searching for patience. "If this bet gets satisfied, can we please concentrate on all things wedding?"

"If we have to." Carter stretched a disgruntled thread through his concession. In truth, he was slightly more disgruntled about not getting to spend the rest of the day with Tess. But he had work to do and work always came first. He couldn't afford to veer from his goals now.

"One dart only." Tess's eyebrows arched. She

considered Carter for a beat then said, "My money is on Carter."

Something close to pure joy ignited in him. Only Carter bet on himself. Not too many other people had. It was one dart. Foolish, really. Yet, her words had his confidence soaring.

Carter aimed and threw the dart. It landed squarely in the center of some kind of infinity image and stuck. "Bull's-eye."

Ryan and Caleb walked toward the dartboard. Ryan scratched his fingers through his dark beard. "We can't even tell."

"Don't touch that board," Tess ordered.

Ryan pulled up short and spun around to consider Tess.

"It's a heart and infinity symbol intertwined." Caleb examined the board closer. "He hit the image dead center like Cupid's arrow."

"I win," Carter declared.

Yet, it was Tess who celebrated like she'd won.

And suddenly, Carter wondered if there was more at stake than a dart game.

CHAPTER TEN

THE NEXT AFTERNOON Tess finished resolving a countertop issue with the contractor at the soon-to-be-opened Three Springs Pet Clinic for her sister. Paige and Doc Conrad were on the other side of town at Haystack Hills Farm, treating an outbreak of pneumonia in the farm's sheep herd. Outside the clinic Tess pulled out her cell phone. A delivery notification flashed across her screen. Her special-order organic chocolate and cocoa powder had arrived. *Finally.*

Now Tess had to get to her chocolate before the heat ruined it. She sprinted down the sidewalk past the Double Rainbow Arts Center toward the Rivers Family Hardware. Then she pulled up.

Carter stood in front of the Silver Penny, her delivery box cradled under one arm.

She downshifted into a fast walk and kept her eye on the chocolate box, not the cowboy.

"Hey, Carter." Her voice sounded breathless, not cool and composed. That wasn't right. She'd seen him yesterday. There should be nothing particularly heart racing about him standing there now. She inhaled deep yet her pulse kept pumping. "What are you doing here?"

"Pecan delivery, courtesy of the Baker sisters." He tapped the vacuum-sealed bag balanced on top of her chocolate box, then frowned at her feet. "You should really consider a good, practical pair of work boots. They are always worth the investment."

No. She didn't need boots or homegrown cowboys who made her reconsider things like second chances. "I work in a retail store and live in an apartment above it. My sandals are more than practical."

"Not when you spend the day running around town for everyone." Carter handed her the pecan bag.

"Librarians, even former ones, don't run," Tess stated.

"They do here in Texas." Carter coughed as if catching his laughter. "And if you're not going to look after yourself, I suppose I'll have to do it. What size shoe do you wear?"

"I'm not telling." She'd missed him. And that was definitely not something she wanted to stand around and consider too long. Or at all. She reached for the delivery box.

He backed away. "You didn't answer my question."

And she didn't have time to linger and risk a cowboy distraction. That would only lead to heartbreak. Then she'd have more than melted chocolate on her hands. Tess checked the street for cars before stepping off the wooden sidewalk. If she crossed the road, maybe she'd find a cowboy repellent on the other side.

"Hey, wait up." Carter easily matched her pace. "Your store is behind us, by the way."

"But I need the pecans and that box at the Owl apartment." And she needed to realign her interest in Carter. She had award-winning chocolate to create, prize money to win and a future to build. And Carter wasn't her future. "Let me guess. Breezy asked you to bring me these pecans."

Carter switched the box to his other side. "How did you know?"

"Breezy called me earlier to tell me that she was sending the pecans by special courier." Tess should've known the crafty matchmaker would've sent Carter. She pulled the Owl apartment keys from her tote bag.

"Breezy and Gayle stopped at the farmhouse to meet Harris this morning," Carter said. "Seems word has already traveled around town about the documentary. You really sold the Herring Gang legend to Harris yesterday. It's all Roy and Harris can talk about."

Tess covered her face with her hands but failed to stop her laughter.

"It's not funny." Carter's grin was small and quick.

"It kind of is." Tess bumped into him and tempered her amusement into a chuckle. "How did the Baker sisters hear about the documentary anyway?"

"My guess is straight from Harris when he stopped in at the Lemon Moon Diner that morning. Haven't you heard about white asparagus week?" Carter's voice was resigned. "Now Harris is staying at the farmhouse too."

Tess opened the door to the Owl apartment and turned back to look at Carter. "You're kidding?"

"Not even a little." Carter followed Tess inside the apartment. "Grant's room is empty with him in Dallas for his fellowship, so Uncle Roy offered it to Harris this morning. Then Uncle Roy asked to be an executive producer on the documentary."

"At least you'll know what Roy is telling Harris now." Tess set the pecan bag on the counter and glanced at Carter. "Where are Harris and Roy, by the way?"

"Ryan nominated Caleb to watch Uncle Roy today," Carter said. "And then Ryan offered to take Harris out to the sanctuary to meet the horses."

"And now you have a break." Tess smoothed out her grin. That wasn't an invitation for him to take a break with her. She wanted him to leave and get back to his work. Then she'd get back to hers.

"You remember that kid's game hot potato?" He leaned against the granite island as if he intended to stick around.

She nodded, her attention stuck to him as if she wanted him to stay. Tess took the chocolate box and wondered how to shake a cowboy.

"Well, I feel like we're playing hot potato only with Uncle Roy. Just passing him around. It has to stop." Carter slipped off his cowboy hat, brushed at it and settled it back on his head. "I came into town to find my grandfather."

She should tell him where Sam was. Wish him luck with his family matters. She had her own matters to see to. Tess put the unopened box in the refrigerator. "What are you going to tell him?"

"That's the problem." Carter paused and stared out the window as if it suddenly held all the right answers. "When Grandpa finds out about the documentary and Roy's involvement, he's going to be upset. When he finds out about the moonshine recipe, that's going to make him angry. And then he's going to look me in the eye and tell me this is what happens when I don't listen to him."

"But your heart was in the right place." As for Tess's heart it never seemed to be in the right place. That unattached and unconnected place. That safe, unbreakable place. She found herself walking around the counter and reaching for Carter as if they both needed the connection. "That counts for something."

Carter dropped his gaze as if considering her hand on his arm and his next words. Finally, he raised his gaze back to hers. "Only you would tell me that."

"It's true." The Sloans often declared: family first. Tess always assumed Carter added an addendum: family first, but not before business. But seeing his property yesterday and that he had allowed his uncle to dig it up and the mix of worry and stress on his face now, she was beginning to wonder. "Even if you don't want to admit it. Or that you even have a heart."

"Maybe I don't have to tell Grandpa Sam anything yet." Carter attempted a smile and stuffed his hands into his pockets.

That was for the best. Tess needed to reach for her dreams not a cowboy. "The Baker sisters were at your farmhouse today and yesterday. You can expect the entire town all the way out to the state line knows about the holes and the documentary by now."

Carter scrubbed his palms over his face. "When did it all become so complicated?"

Tess wanted to know the very same thing. One AWOL wedding planner had tangled her up too. But it was only ever supposed to be about her cousin's dream wedding. Nothing more. Nothing heart tempting. Tess held out her hand to Carter. "Come on."

He kept his arms locked against his sides. "Where are we going now?"

"I know where Sam and Boone are." Tess adjusted her tote on her shoulder and headed for the door. "Let's go. It's time to talk to your grandfather."

"You don't have to come with me." Carter followed her outside.

Tess lifted one shoulder. "It's no problem."

"But it's not your family's feud."

"Doesn't mean I don't care about Sam and Roy." *Or you.* Tess picked up her pace on the wooden sidewalk. Perhaps if she started running, she'd outpace her growing feelings for her cowboy.

"Still, you should be back at the Silver Penny." Carter matched her quick tempo.

"I can handle everything." And by everything

she meant her attraction to him too. It didn't have to be anything if she didn't allow it to be.

"But while you're handling everything for everyone else, who's taking care of your store?" Carter frowned at her. "The store is your livelihood."

"I'm not looking to expand nationally and triple my profit." She was looking for roots. To belong. "I just want to be surrounded by my family." Then she'd finally be happy.

"But you still have to make a profit," Carter argued.

"It's not always about the money." Tess swiped at the sweat beading on her forehead. Carter and she were too different to be compatible. He wanted profits. She wanted satisfied friends. Even more basic: he wore boots; she wore sandals.

"But sometimes it has to be," Carter pressed. "Like when bills are due. Loan payments. Electricity. Grocery bills."

"The general store building is paid for," Tess argued. "I'm covering my other expenses." Barely, but she was making it most months.

"But you can't fund improvements to the building," Carter said. "What about an emergency fund for unexpected repairs?"

"I have a plan." It hinged on chocolate and a quick influx of cash. Even she recognized it wasn't a sound business strategy. Yet, right now it was all she had. "I've been restoring the space back to what it was when my grandparents ran it."

"What about your vision? Your dreams for the space? Dreams are important, not because you follow your passions, but because you want to change something in your life for the better." Carter stopped in the center of the square and faced her. "That's why I started the distillery. It's okay to want more than what your grandparents had."

"My grandparents did well for themselves. What they built was successful here." And it was reliable and comfortable. And proven to work. No risks involved. Tess added, "If I can have that, I'll have enough."

"Why not take a risk anyway?" Carter asked.

"It's not in my nature." That she'd concluded after she'd risked everything for love and lost in her first marriage.

"But what if you're missing out on something even better by not taking that risk?" he asked.

Her dead husband had drawn her out of her comfort zone. And she'd willingly gone, embracing the spontaneity and freedom. But love, it turned out, wasn't any kind of safety net. And her life hadn't been better. "Let me ask you.

Why hasn't the process of whiskey distilling changed much over the past hundred years?"

He chuckled. "Because it works."

"Exactly," she said. "Sometimes it's okay, good even, to follow the blueprint of the past because it works. And even more, it's okay to be content with what you end up with."

"Are you content?" His gaze searched hers.

"I'm working on it." She was tired deep into her bones most nights. But that helped her fall asleep faster. And if that lonely crept in, she'd outrun it during the day and let exhaustion squash it at night. "What about you? Are you content?"

A hint of a smile played around his mouth. "I plan to be."

Her hand brushed against his. She started walking again before she linked her fingers around his and held on. "When is that exactly? Do you have a specific date marked on your calendar?"

"Not a date," he said. "Just a goal."

"Your goal is tied to money, isn't it?" They walked across the square toward City Hall.

"If I say yes, it'll prove you were right about me." His voice was dry. "That I'm only interested in profits and money. That it's all that matters to me."

Could I matter to you more? She wasn't willing to take any kind of risk to find that out. She glanced at him. "I hope you reach your goal and find that contentment."

"Back at you." He reached up to capture the strand of hair the wind blew across her cheek. "When will you know you're finally content?"

Right now. All she felt was content and all she wanted was to know how to hold on to it. "When my family is permanently settled here in Three Springs and happy."

She reached for the door of City Hall, not Carter's hand and that kind of contentment. Because the last time she'd lingered outside the city hall in Chicago, she'd reached for love and ended up a widow, in debt and brokenhearted. And she'd vowed never to trust her heart again.

CHAPTER ELEVEN

CARTER'S BOOTS TAPPED against the gleaming hardwood floors of Three Springs's City Hall. He'd expected Tess to walk with him over to the Feisty Owl to find his grandfather. Grandpa Sam and his longtime friend Boone split their days between the general store and the bar and grill. The pair were staples at both locations and usually at the center of anything going on in town.

Tess led him down a small hallway in the back of the building. She touched the door handle and glanced at Carter. "You ready for this?"

He was ready for his interest in Tess to pass. Good thing he was a patient man. As for the feud, that he had to end and soon. "Is it that bad?"

"Depends on your viewpoint." Tess opened the door to a tiny, water closet–size room wide enough to hold a card table and three metal folding chairs.

Boone sat in one chair. His grandfather in the other. Papers of every size covered the folding table. More rolls of blueprints sat stacked on the empty chair.

"Grandpa. Boone." Carter stepped into the small space but kept his back inside the open doorway. Apprehension pricked the back of his neck. "What are you two doing?"

"Figuring things out for ourselves." Boone set what looked to be an old-school protractor on the table.

"It's our only choice as it seems my own family intends to leave me in the dark." Sam squinted at Carter the same way he squinted at a spider to determine if it was the poisonous kind or not. "As if I'm the one causing all the trouble."

His grandfather's shoulders sank as if defeated. Or worse, disappointed. In Carter. Carter always hated disappointing his grandfather, ever since he was a kid. It sat heavy and awkward on his chest like a bronc kicked him in the ribs. "I'm here now to talk."

"You're only here because Breezy and Gayle stopped at the farm," Sam charged.

That was partially true. Carter crossed his arms tightly over his chest. "And to bring you home."

"We'll see about that." Sam's frown softened into a warm smile he aimed at Tess. "Tess, did you get those pecans from the Baker sisters?"

"Sure did." Tess smiled in return and leaned

against the wall as if making more room for Carter and his frustration.

Sam's smile widened. "That's good to hear."

Pleasantries would get them nowhere. "Look, Grandpa, I'm sorry if you felt left out. I wanted to fix things before you saw what happened."

"What were you planning to do with the Herring gold when you found that?" Sam's eyebrows burrowed together over his nose. "Hide the treasure too?"

"There's no treasure." That declaration dropped out, abrupt and brisk, before Carter could stop himself.

His grandfather winced. His fingers sank into his thick white beard as if he'd lost his breath. Boone narrowed his eyes on Carter; disapproval hardened his expression.

And regret burned the back of Carter's throat. Hurting his grandfather was worse than disappointing him. But there were things that needed to be said, however unwelcome.

But the Three Springs legend about the Herring Gang was just that: a legend. A story best told around a fireside. It wasn't meant for business hours and workdays. The two old-timers were both searching for the impossible. There was nothing productive about that. The treasure maps and the gold had been lost long ago if they'd ever even existed at all.

It had to stop. Carter stepped forward, ready to launch that truth so they could get back to what mattered: ending the feud and securing the Sloan family home and its future for decades to come.

Tess reached for a falling paper. Her gaze connected with his. She gave him a small, clipped head shake. Carter pulled back, cleared his throat and checked his words. "There can't be a centuries-old treasure on our property. Or you two would've discovered it already."

"That's not what the chatter is around town." Boone tapped a finger against his ear.

Carter gave his grandpa and Boone points for their tenacity and continued conviction that the gold was theirs to find. The only thing Carter knew for certain was success came from hard work, not windfalls. And every minute he wasn't focused on work put that success even further out of reach.

"Word is Roy found money from the Herring Gang loot in one of his holes." Sam tipped his head and regarded Carter.

"And he's spending it around town too." Boone's mouth thinned inside his beard.

"Maybe Uncle Roy went to the bank," Carter said. "It's not lost gold he's using to buy mushroom and asparagus tarts from Lemon Moon."

Neither Sam nor Boone appeared the least bit swayed by that argument.

"Roy and I found old oilcans in some of the holes," Tess offered. "About a half dozen yesterday."

"You were up there digging too, Tess?" Sam shook his head, slow and drawn out. Discontent thickened his voice. "Even my own roommate is keeping things from me."

Carter stepped closer to Tess and said, "Look, Tess was helping me out. But you'd know that if you came home."

"And you know why I can't come home." His grandpa's attention snapped onto Carter like a bull sighting its target. "Now, if you'll excuse us, we have our own dig to plan."

Carter lifted his gaze to the ceiling then dropped his attention to the table and documents. He moved closer and read the land surveyor imprint and date on the top document. It was the plot and land survey plans for the entire Sloan property and farmland. Carter's patience evaporated. "This stops. Right now," he ordered. "No one is digging up any more of our land."

"We aren't asking your permission." Sam tightened the silver slide on his bolo tie and straightened his shoulders as if preparing to end the discussion. "Hear me now. We will be searching for that treasure."

Carter glanced at Tess as if he'd always looked to her for an assist in family matters. As if she was always in his corner. But Carter had been handling things alone just fine. He never required backup before; he wouldn't lean on Tess now.

Tess offered him a small smile.

You can trust me. That was what she'd told him yesterday. And he had. Spilled the family secret right there in the driveway. Then she'd stuck by him and insisted on helping him. But she couldn't help now. Carter was scared. And not even Tess's optimism could stop the whisper of fear brushing the back of his neck. What if Roy was right? And his grandpa had lied. And everything Carter had built wasn't really his idea after all.

In this house, we face every setback as an opportunity. And scared or not, we tackle it head-on. Gran Claire's words echoed in his head. Carter stepped to the table. "Uncle Roy is searching for the family moonshine recipe. He claims he buried it somewhere on the property to keep it safe. That's what he's been digging up the land for."

Sam tugged on his ear as if he hadn't heard Carter correctly. There was caution, not denial, stretching out words. "Roy was always burying things, even after he went and grew up. Got that from our Gran Esther, on our daddy's side."

"What's Roy want with his moonshine recipe now?" Confusion burrowed across Boone's forehead.

"To prove Grandpa and I copied his recipe for Misty Grove bourbon whiskey. He wants a stake in the distillery." Carter gave it straight the same way his grandfather liked his whiskey. Then stepped over his own fear and asked, "Grandpa, is it true?"

Sam bristled and smacked his palm flat on the table. "I have as much right to that recipe as Roy." Another smack. "Even more." *Smack.* "I stayed and put all I had into the farm." *Smack.* "While my own brother up and left me high and dry."

"You did a fine job growing the farm." Boone's voice was gruff. "And all on your own too."

Carter had thought he'd been building something all on his own too. For his family. But what he'd built could very well tear the two brothers further apart, not bring them together. A chill settled inside him. He'd only ever wanted to add value to what they had. To his family. "So there is an original recipe?"

"Of course." Sam tossed his arms over his head. "Same as Tess has the missing silver coin.

Same as there's a missing treasure map and sto-len loot."

Tess's arm brushed against Carter's. She steadied him, just by being beside him. Her hand in his would steady his heart. But for how long? Carter tucked his hand into his jeans pocket. "Grandpa, why didn't you tell me?"

"What does it matter now?" Sam gathered several pieces of paper and avoided looking at Carter. "It's done."

"It matters to me." Carter rubbed his throat, but his words still sounded tight. "It matters to Uncle Roy."

"My brother sold out long before I bought him out." Sam settled his cowboy hat low on his head, setting his face in shadows. But his words were uncompromising and bleak. "And he can't come back now wanting a piece of the family he abandoned."

How did Carter cut through so many decades of hurt and resentment? He glanced at Tess as if she was his anchor. His solution.

"I'm sorry for your pain, Sam." Tess rested her hand on Sam's shoulder. "But maybe if you talked to your brother. Really talked. You two could work things out."

"Tess is right," Carter said. Grateful she was there. "Grandpa, you have to come home."

"I'm coming home all right." Sam rolled up the land surveys. "But not to talk."

Carter set his hands on his hips and eyed his grandfather. Suspicion overtook him. "What are you going to do?"

"I'm going to find that moonshine recipe myself." Sam tugged on his bronze belt buckle and tilted his chin up. "Roy can't make any claims if he's not the one holding it, can he?"

Finders, keepers. This wasn't a kid's game. Carter gaped at his grandfather.

Boone stood, stretched his arms over his head, calm and casual as if they'd just decided where to eat dinner. He gathered more of the rolled paper. "I'm going too. I gotta help Sam."

Carter had walked in with a clear objective. But he'd only created more chaos. How was that even possible?

The old-timers collected the paperwork in a matter of seconds and set the small room to rights in less than a minute. Then they regarded Carter as if surprised to find him still standing there.

Carter squeezed the bridge of his nose and searched deep for a reserve of patience. The conversation wasn't closed. The discussion wasn't over. Nothing had been resolved. "We aren't finished here."

"Is there more you haven't told us?" Sam eyed him. "Did you let Roy move into my room?"

"What?" Exasperation quickened Carter's words. "No. That's ridiculous."

"Then it's time to go." Sam motioned to the doorway, shooing Carter aside.

Carter remained where he was. He just needed time to think of something that would fix all of this. All he knew was letting his grandfather dig, too, was a bad idea. He should've known the two stubborn cowboys wouldn't sit and talk it out.

Sam scratched his cheek. "You can't keep us here. You've work that requires your attention."

Carter's phone rang as if to prove his grandfather correct. He checked his phone, silenced the call and sent a quick text to his distillery manager. That was all it took for his grandfather and Boone to shake off their earlier tension as if they sensed Carter was already shifting gears too.

"Carter, you need to help Tess with her chocolate for me." Excitement and fondness softened across Sam's weathered face. "She's got a big chocolate competition that she's fixin' to win coming up real soon."

Chocolate. Chocolate wasn't part of any conversation that Carter needed to have. He glanced at Tess. Why had she told his grandfather and not him? He liked her chocolate. More than any he'd ever tasted. He'd even offered to sell it in his tasting room more than once.

"Sam." An uneasiness pinched across her face. "You weren't supposed to tell anyone."

"I didn't tell anyone." Sam released a small grin. "I told family."

Boone peered at them. "You two aren't going to get far as a couple if you don't learn to share with each other."

"That means sharing the good and the uncomfortable," Sam added. "It's the only way to make a relationship last."

"I'm not sure what you heard about Carter and me." Tess looked flustered. The breeze from the slow turn of the ceiling fan was stronger than her voice.

Tess's bewildered gaze collided with Carter's. *Adorable.* She looked adorable and endearing. Someone he could have wanted if…if only he was someone different. Carter skipped his gaze away from her.

"You two need a proper date." Sam stroked his fingers through his beard and studied Tess and Carter as if he'd found another more fascinating topic than his brotherly feud and a missing moonshine recipe.

"A date." Tess's hand fluttered around her throat as if the word got stuck there.

Carter's gaze slid to Tess and caught again.

Adorable. Hardly enough for a relationship. And he wasn't interested in dating. All dating and relationships offered was second-guessing and confusion. Besides, he couldn't afford that kind of detour, what with his family in disarray.

"There's the food truck rally with dancing in Belleridge tomorrow night." Boone's voice was entirely too encouraging. "Violet Myers says it's quite fun dancing under the stars. She's been pushing Wes to put in an outdoor dance floor over at the Owl for months now."

"I already told Harris about the food trucks when we were sharing a table at Lemon Moon this morning." Sam offered that tidbit with a heavy dose of zeal.

Carter wasn't the least bit surprised the wily pair had already met Harris. There wasn't a mouse that crossed the county line that his grandfather and Boone didn't know about.

"Nice fella that Harris." Sam grinned.

"Maybe tomorrow night Harris can find someone to dance with and get a little country swing into his two-step." Boone smiled and executed a quick step as if warming up for the dance floor himself.

The cowboy duo continued their matchmaking maneuvers, despite everything else going on. Impressive, really. Still, the two old-timers couldn't be encouraged. Carter said, "I have to…"

"Start listening to your grandfather," Sam finished for Carter. "You're taking Tess for a date and bringing Harris along with you."

"We already mentioned it to Paige." Joy curved around Boone's words.

The pair was efficient and productive for two old-timers who shared a running commentary about the creaks in their bones and less get-up in their get-up as the days passed on.

"Tess, your sister deserves a night off too." Sam's delight reached into his eyes. "There's been a constant line of patients for her since she got into town."

"Good to have Paige here," Boone said.

"You, too, Tess," Sam said. "And I forgive you for not telling me about all this. I rather like rooming with you."

"I like your company too, Sam." Tess's voice was genuine and sincere.

That compliment earned a broad smile from his grandfather.

Carter liked Tess's company too. But he didn't feel like smiling about it. Carter rubbed his forehead. "Sounds like it's all arranged, then."

"Leave things to us and they get done right." Sam chuckled and stroked his beard.

"What about Uncle Roy?" Carter couldn't keep the wince from his voice or his face.

"I'll gather your brothers and we'll organize our own search party at the farm." Sam sighed. "And we'll include Roy."

It was the start Carter needed. The two brothers in the same location at the same time. Now Carter just had to start a long-overdue conversation.

"You can't be digging at night." Concern creased around Tess's eyes. "It's not safe for anyone. What if someone falls and gets hurt?"

"Don't go worrying about us." Boone smoothly brushed away her concern.

"Someone has to look out for you both," Carter said. His voice firm.

"I told you my brother liked to bury things." Sam pointed at Carter and lifted his eyebrows. "But not all of it was in the ground."

"Where else do you bury things?" Carter asked.

"Inside attics. Walls. Under the ashes in the old fireplace." Sam scratched his cheek. "I'm sure Roy can think of even more places. Just need to get him to confess."

Carter nodded. He'd get with his brothers and set down some guidelines. No punching through walls. No climbing ladders for Boone, Sam or Roy. And definitely no digging outside in the dark. And first, before anything else, was that conversation.

Sam checked his watch. "Now, let us go. We have to be at the Owl for Nolan's barbecue samples before he runs out."

"Breezy and Gayle got themselves invites again." Boone shook his head. "We'll have to share."

Boone looked decidedly put out by that idea. Satisfied his grandpa and Boone would be occupied tonight, Carter stepped into the hallway.

Sam shoved several rubber-banded plot plans at Carter. "Here, take these. We might need them too."

The rest of the small group piled out of the workroom, walked outside and paused on the sidewalk in front of City Hall.

"Well, you've got a date with chocolate and with Carter, Tess." Sam chuckled. "For a chocolatier like yourself, what could be better than that?"

"I hear chocolate is the way to a person's heart." Boone laughed.

Tess shifted and fidgeted with the strap of her tote bag.

If Carter wasn't mistaken, a blush tinted her

cheeks a pretty pink. It was a color he was becoming more and more fond of.

And once again, Carter found himself hooked on the adorable shop owner.

mean a pretty place. It was a place to work, a coming in and eating food at the

And as always, Carter liked Nolan's cooking

Tin Sloan family bright gra

CHAPTER TWELVE

WITH THE SLOAN FAMILY land surveys stored in Wes's office at the Feisty Owl for safekeeping, Tess and Carter left Sam and Boone seated on their usual bar stools. The Owl's head chef, Nolan, wanted the duo to sample his latest barbecue pulled pork and chicken nacho creation and a potential new addition to the bar's menu.

Tess walked around the side of the Feisty Owl toward the apartment and glanced at Carter. It was time to shake her interest and her cowboy. "If your schedule is full tomorrow, we can reschedule the food truck rally for another night."

"I can fit it in," Carter said. The rim of his cowboy hat shaded his gaze, but not the challenge in his words. "What about you?"

"I can fit it in too." Tess lifted her chin, but it wouldn't be a date. Because dating her cowboy could be bad for her heart. And she'd given up on things that caused heartache. "I'll catch a ride with Paige and Evan and meet you there, if that works."

Carter nodded. "Harris and I are spending the

day together running through promotional ads and the script he's drafted for the promo video."

"A script sounds very official." Not like their date to the food truck rally. There would be nothing official about that. Tess pulled out the apartment key and opened the door. "By the way, I really don't need any help with chocolate."

One corner of his mouth tipped up. "I'm fairly certain you don't want my kind of help in the kitchen. But I consider myself a solid bet on taste testing."

"Is that right?" She dropped her tote bag on the hallway table.

"Yeah." He shut the door and moved into the small foyer.

"You aren't going to leave, are you?" She held her ground, proving she was charm-resistant.

"And risk my grandfather finding out?" He shook his head and his grin spread into a smile. "Sorry. You're stuck with me for a bit."

And that was the problem. The more time she spent with Carter, the more she wanted to be stuck with him. "Fine. But the kitchen is off-limits." *The same as my heart.*

"I can work with that." He pulled out his cell phone. "Mind if I make a few business calls? If you require quiet, I can head out to the porch."

"It's really hot out there." Tess opened the bag

of the Baker sisters' pecans and spread them out on a cookie sheet. Then she started prepping the island, keeping her tools within easy reach. "You won't bother me or the chocolate."

Carter tapped on the phone screen, set it to his ear and walked into the family room. His voice shifted into professional yet sociable. He never looked at Tess, yet she struggled to stop peering at him. And from one call to the next he remained efficient and friendly. And she was impressed by his knowledge and his ability to seamlessly transition from cask char levels to troubleshooting a weld on the production line to answering federal filing questions from his accountant. Carter had layers and those only drew her to him more.

His call ended and he caught Tess watching him. "Are you sure I'm not bothering you?"

"You're fine." She was bothered by herself and not entirely fine. It wasn't like she hadn't been around other men. Wes and Evan were staples in her life. But there was something about Carter. Something that made her all too aware of him, leaving her both happy and unsettled he was there. She cut open the delivery box and froze.

Carter was at her side in an instant. "What's wrong?"

Everything. "The cocoa powder exploded inside the box." The chocolate dusted the plastic Bubble Wrap and every corner of the box. She lifted the bag and stuck her finger in the hole of the bottom seam. It was empty and deflated, the same as Tess.

"I'm guessing you can't find this at Five Star Grocery Depot." Carter winced.

"It's organic cocoa powder and I had to special order it from a gourmet marketplace in San Francisco." Tess tossed the bag into the box and blinked back her tears. "There isn't time to get another shipment in before the chocolate sampler deadline for the contest."

"Can you call the competition coordinator?" Carter asked.

"The chocolate sampler has to be shipped on Saturday so it can only arrive on Monday." Tess tossed the box into the trash and stared out the window. "Monday is the only day they'll accept entries."

She wouldn't cry. It'd been a long shot anyway. Her ex would've called it a blue-sky reach. *It's fine to want to reach for rainbows and blue skies, Tess. But it's better for us not to stretch right now.* And she hadn't. Not for a home. A family. Or her dreams. But it was supposed to be her time now to have what she wanted. And she wasn't reaching all that far. Just enough to have what her grandparents had.

Tess washed her hands in the sink and rearranged her thoughts away from her past mistakes. "If my entry is one day early, they won't accept it. One day late, they won't accept it. There's a ten-thousand-dollar cash prize and rules for a reason."

"Right." Carter leaned against the counter. "That's not a bad payout."

"Tell me about it." It was supposed to have been her renovation fund for the general store.

"What now?" Carter asked. "There has to be a solution."

Tess shook her head. *Just be patient, Tess. When this investment pays out, we'll have everything we ever wanted and more. Trust me.* Tess had been patient. Worse, she'd believed her ex's promises. Then he'd died and the debt collectors had started calling. After paying everything off, her only solution had been Three Springs and the store.

"We can drive to the city. If we leave now, we'll get there before the stores close." Carter walked over to her and set his hands on her shoulders. "I know it's not a big west coast city like San Francisco, but maybe they have something."

Tess searched his face. "You'd drive almost two hours for cocoa powder."

"I'd drive you for cocoa powder," he corrected.

"I can't ask you to do that." *But can you hold on to me? Just until I remember I can stand on my own now.* Tess blew out a long breath. "Maybe it's not meant to be my year. We've got the wedding. I still have the Bakers' dessert bar to finish. Not to mention a list of customers' special orders. This is probably a sign."

"Or it's just a setback." Carter squeezed her shoulders, his voice encouraging. "You should enter that contest."

"I have to concentrate on my store like you've been telling me." And know when to concede. She drew her hands to her face and nudged his arms away. "Grandma Opal never had to sell her chocolate to pay her bills. She gave it away. Always said it was the giving and the joy on people's faces that was her reward. I need to follow her lead."

"Do you know when I got serious about whiskey making?" He picked up a brownie slice from the pan she'd made the other morning.

Tess held out her hand.

"My grandma entered my bourbon whiskey at the regional fair without telling me. My grandparents came home with a blue ribbon around the bottle." Carter broke his brownie in two and set a half on her palm. Then he continued,

"Grandpa Sam told me it wasn't a belt buckle from an eight-second bull ride, but it was still first place. And wheat might not be my ticket out of town, but it could be my ticket to success." Carter lifted the brownie piece as if to toast her. "What if your chocolate is like my whiskey? And it's the key to your success?"

All it takes is for one of these investments to hit it big, Tess. Then you can have anything you want. All she wanted now was to be happy. And she was happy, wasn't she? "I took a few cooking classes during college for fun. I'm not classically trained. I'm self-taught."

"That's how I learned the art of distilling and whiskey making." Carter chewed on his bite of brownie. "Why are you looking at me like you just tasted peanut butter in your brownie?"

"Because you're surprising me."

"I hope that's a good thing." He grinned and finished his brownie.

"I thought you would tell me to get back to my store and leave the chocolate to the culinary chocolatiers of the world." *We need to be strategic, Tess. We need to think about our plan for the future.* Too late, she'd discovered there had never really been an *our* or *a plan*. Only a *now*.

Carter cut another brownie piece and drew her out of the past. He said, "First of all, never leave the chocolate tasting to someone else. Always leave it to me."

Tess laughed; the lightness pulled her fully into the moment.

"And second, you're really good." Carter's tone was firm, almost insistent. "And you don't seem to want to take my word for it. I can sell whatever chocolate you create in my gift shop, and I don't make that offer to just anyone."

"But making candy brings me joy. The same as it did for Grandma Opal." Tess picked up a raw pecan from the cookie tray. "Grandma's kitchen was my favorite place growing up. She taught me everything about candy making and what it means to be a good person. It feels wrong to profit on what should be a simple kindness."

"But it's hard to offer that chocolate kindness if you can't afford the ingredients," Carter said.

"You think I sound silly." And maybe she did. "It's just that my former husband chased the money and that big payout that would set us up for life. Once we had that, we could do all the little things we'd put off."

"What happened?" His voice was quiet.

"It was always about the next big thing for Eric. He was always so confident. So sure the next idea would be the one. He made me believe it too." Tess wiped her hands on a towel. "But that payout never came. He died in a motorcycle accident. Took a corner too fast after a rainstorm, the same way he'd approached life."

"I'm sorry." His sincerity washed over Tess like a warm embrace.

"He was everything I wasn't." Tess wrapped her arms around her stomach as if she could hold on to that warmth. "Bold and daring and carefree. I was so sure our love united us. And when we got to that place he chased, it would be enough." She would be enough.

"I'm not sure he would've ever found it." There was an apology in Carter's voice. In his gaze.

Tess nodded. "After the shock and the anger and the tears, I realized all those little things we set aside and put off, those are what mattered." She spread her hands out over the candy-making supplies. "Everything my grandma Opal had taught me in her kitchen growing up is what matters."

Carter approached her and took her hand in his. "I think we need to enter the contest so you can keep doing what matters."

"You sound like we're doing this together." *Together*. There was such power in that one word. It was all she'd wanted at one time. Tess stared at their joined hands and warned herself to let go.

"We are." He linked their fingers together.

"My grandparents entered my whiskey. Now I'm going to pay it forward and make sure you enter your chocolate."

"I'm out of cocoa powder." And she was good on her own now. Making a place for herself that would last. Still, she kept her hand in his and added, "A key ingredient for Grandma Opal's spiced ganache truffles. It rounds out the sampler."

"You're out of that cocoa powder," Carter corrected. "There has to be something else we can use. Don't you have a hidden stash at your apartment? An in-case-of-emergency cabinet?"

He could be her in-case-of-emergency. The one that she leaned on. But would she be enough to love for more than a moment? Tess shook her head. She was playing it safe these days and it was working. A slow grin spread across her face. "I don't have an emergency cabinet, but Abby does. And lucky for us, my cousin has a bit of a hot chocolate addiction."

"Well, this is an emergency." Carter squeezed her hand, then released her. "Let's go raid Abby's cabinet."

"Let's do it." Tess headed for the front door, Carter right behind her.

This could work. Hope swirled through Tess once again. Abby wouldn't have the exact cocoa powder Tess had ordered. However, Abby had a collection of assorted cocoa powders she used to create what she declared was one of the finest cups of hot chocolate in the Lone Star State. Then Abby would always talk Tess into making her homemade marshmallows, which according to her cousin elevated her hot chocolate to divine.

Ten minutes later Tess had the cocoa powder arranged across Abby's kitchen island and the idea to blend the powders the same as her cousin did. Outside, Carter had Tyne and Ginger chasing after softballs he launched into the air.

"I have what I need." Tess walked out to join Carter and the dogs.

"Couple more throws, if that's okay," Carter said.

Tess nodded, reached down and scratched Ginger behind the ears. "I always wanted a big backyard like this. One with a real kitchen and working fireplace too."

"What did you have up north?" Carter threw another ball. Tyne barked and sprinted across the grass.

"A townhouse." Tess worked the ball loose from Ginger's mouth. "It was supposed to be the starter home. The temporary one until we found the perfect one with the white picket fence and front porch swing." Just like her grandparents had. Just like she'd always wanted for her own family.

Carter took the ball from Tess, launched it into the air and studied her. "A house doesn't seem like one of those small things you mentioned earlier. A house should be a priority for a family."

"It is for a lot of couples." Tess motioned to the screened-in back porch. "Look at Wes and Abby and what they've done to this place to make it their home."

"Were you in love?" Carter motioned for Tyne to sit and drop the ball. "Don't answer that. I don't know why I asked something so personal."

And Tess wasn't certain why she was telling Carter so much about her past. She should stop talking. Stop spilling truths that were meant to be her own. But there was something about being with him that reminded her of Grandma Opal's kitchen and made her feel protected. "I really wanted to be in love. Because when you're in love, your marriage is supposed to be perfect."

Carter frowned and raised his hand with the tennis ball. "Gran Claire always said marriage was a choice that had to be made every day."

"Eric chose to focus on that payout," Tess said.

He added, "At the expense of your marriage."

"He's not fully to blame," Tess countered. "I should've fought more. Spoken up." Maybe she would have if she'd been someone else. If her former husband had been different. Maybe if he'd loved her like he meant it. Not like she was just part of the chase.

His eyebrow furrowed. "And yet you still believe in love and marriage and all that goes along with it."

"I believe it for everyone else," Tess corrected.

"You could still have all that for yourself too." He kept his focus on her.

But could I have that with you? Tess touched her forehead as if reminding herself to think with her head, not her heart. "It's enough that my sister and cousin are on their way to having it."

Carter tossed both balls and lifted his eyebrows at Tess. "And it all starts with Abby's wedding."

"You have been paying attention." Tess smiled, pleased he was starting to understand. Even more, she was relieved to move on from that uncomfortable part of her past. Funny, she always considered herself foolish for the mistakes she'd made. But somehow Carter never made her feel like that.

Carter set his hands on his hips and watched Ginger and Tyne wrestle for the same ball. "If it all begins with the wedding as you claim, then why not have Abby and Wes recite their vows back here?"

"Here." Tess pointed at the grass. "Like right here in their backyard."

"Why not?" Carter rubbed his chin and turned in a slow circle as if surveying the entire backyard. Then he stopped and looked at Tess. "This is the place Abby and Wes are building their life together."

Tess's pulse picked up. Excitement stirred inside her. The idea gained traction. "Is there enough room?"

Carter scanned the backyard, then snapped his fingers and walked to the open gate in the middle of the fence line. The one that granted direct access to Boone's backyard. "If we include Boone's backyard, we'll have enough room."

Ginger and Tyne raced into Boone's yard as if testing out Carter's claim. Tess followed Carter and stood inside the open gate and searched for reasons it wouldn't work.

"You could have the ceremony in Abby and Wes's yard. Then move into Boone's yard for the reception and dancing." Carter moved beside Tess, shoulder to shoulder, and started pointing. "You could put one of those flowery arch things in that corner. Your fancy chairs with the ribbons and what was on your vision board thing? Birdseed for the runner."

"Did you just say *birdseed* and *runner*?" Tess didn't bother to hide her surprise.

"Yes. I did." But he didn't stop there. Carter continued the wedding layout into Boone's yard. "We hang those fairy light things you like over the dance floor and add in a fountain or two. Also on your vision board."

"You're serious?" Tess tried not to sputter.

"Two fountains are too much, aren't they?" Carter rubbed his chin. "Maybe it's a wishing well when you pass through the gate to the reception. Toss in a penny and make a wedding wish for the new couple."

Wedding wishing well. Fairy lights. "Are you okay?" Tess pressed her palm against Carter's forehead. "You're not having a heatstroke or something like that, are you?"

"I'm fine." Carter laughed and set his fingers under her chin, lifting her gaze to his. "Now you need to pay attention. I'm envisioning your perfect dream wedding day."

Her dream wedding. Tess could see it all and more. Much, much more. With Carter. Her breath caught in her throat. She tugged her gaze from his and fixed her focus over his shoulder.

It wasn't her wedding day. It was Abby's day. Abby's dream.

And that was all Tess wanted. Her family to be happy. That was enough, wasn't it?

Tess stepped around Carter, searched for her words and her voice. "How could we get an arch built in time?"

"Josh will be back next week from Colorado. He can build anything we want." Carter picked up the balls and whistled for the dogs, letting them onto Boone's back porch then into his house. "Paige can help with flowers and decorations for the arch."

"This could work." Not Carter and Tess—that wouldn't work. But everything else for everyone else that could work. Tess walked beside Carter back to Abby's house. Her hand brushed against his. Once. Twice. But she wasn't taking hold.

"Of course it'll work." Carter followed her into Abby's kitchen. "We just have to stay open to ideas. And we have to tell Boone what's going on with the wedding planner."

"Right." Tess picked up the cocoa powders from the counter and dropped them in a paper Silver Penny shopping bag. She linked her fingers around the rough handles. She wanted chocolate, not a cowboy. "I can talk to Sam tonight about our plans. I'm sure Boone will like our ideas."

Carter held the front door open, and they headed back to the Owl apartment. As if they were already headed in the same direction. *Together*.

Underneath the dim porch light, Tess turned to Carter. "You've come to the rescue twice today."

"Is that a problem?" He moved closer to her.

She didn't want it to be. She wanted it to be perfect. "Only that I'm supposed to be rescuing myself now."

"Consider us even." His warm gaze skimmed over her face. "You helped me with Uncle Roy."

She bit her bottom lip. "Do you think we can get Roy and Sam to talk?"

"Sounds like we're going to do that together." One corner of his mouth tipped up.

"Do you mind?" *Being together*.

He reached up, tucked her hair behind her ear and let his fingers linger, trailing across her neck as if testing whether he minded. Finally, he shook his head.

Tess set her hand on his chest, felt his heartbeat beneath her palm that matched her own. And she let herself fall. Into his storm-gray eyes. Into the moment. One small shift and her lips pressed against his. One soft kiss. One breath-stalling moment. One impossible wish.

Tess pulled back, pressed her fingertips against her lips as if to capture the feeling and her apology. "I shouldn't have done that."

"Why did you?" He stayed in her space. His voice quiet and contained.

"I don't know." Her words were breathless.

He reached up as if to touch her cheek, then pulled back. "You don't know or you're too scared to say?"

"You participated too." Her gaze collided with his. "Why did you kiss me?"

"Curiosity." His voice was still too reserved. Too quiet as if he'd lost it in that kiss.

Carter made her the dangerous kind of curious. The kind that tempted her to take chances. To risk more than she should.

He touched one finger to the brim of his hat. "'Night, Tess."

Her heart raced. She wanted to kiss him again. She wanted to push him away. "Careful, cowboy, or I'm going to think you're running scared now."

"Not scared." His gaze softened. "Call it self-preservation."

"What does that mean?" she asked.

"It means you make me consider breaking promises." Carter spoke so casually and so clearly. As if that truth was as indisputable as the change of seasons every year. "And that, Tess Palmer, makes you a wildcard. And wildcards are game changers."

With that, he tipped his hat and walked away. And Tess folded her hand. After all, she'd vowed never to let her heart go all in ever again.

CHAPTER THIRTEEN

"WHAT DO YOU wear to a date that's not really a date?" Tess slid a red sundress from a hanger, held it in front of her and glanced at her reflection in the floor-length mirror. The beading flashed in the light. "Way too much for food trucks."

And after the debacle of that kiss last night and without a do-over button, Tess wanted to feel pretty, confident and nonchalant when she saw Carter again. And if Carter saw her the same way, that wouldn't be so bad either.

She tossed the sundress on her bed with the half dozen others and checked her closet again. "This is why I don't date."

Only the ceiling fan squeaking on every half turn filled the silence.

She opened the bottom drawer in a thin, tall dresser and considered her collection of shorts.

A quick knock on her front door echoed down the hallway, followed by her sister's cheerful greeting. "Tess, we're here. Time to go."

"Shorts it is." Tess grabbed a pair of white

denim shorts and a tank top. Then yelled, "I'm almost ready."

"You're not even dressed." Paige stood in the doorway. A long summer dress floated around her wedge sandals, and her hair fell in waves around her shoulders.

Her sister looked like everything Tess wanted to be tonight. "I'm just running a bit behind. It won't take me long."

"Let me guess." Paige walked to Tess's closet and sorted through Tess's clothes. "You got tied up making cake pop bouquets for Corine Bauer's surprise birthday party."

The birthday bouquets had been finished several hours ago. Along with her work to-do list. Tess was running late because of a certain cowboy. But she wasn't admitting that out loud. "It was a busy afternoon." Mainly because she'd kept herself extra busy to keep from thinking about that kiss.

That kiss she wanted to be a mistake. But she couldn't quite find her regret. Worse, if she thought about it too long, she started to wonder about a second one. There shouldn't have been a first. There definitely couldn't be another. Tess walked toward the bathroom.

"Wait," Paige commanded.

Tess stopped, then turned around.

Paige tilted her head and studied Tess.

Tess tried not to fidget. Her sister would notice and then accuse her of hiding something from her. Like a kiss. A kiss with Carter.

Paige tapped her nose and grinned. "You can't wear that shirt. You need the lavender one. It makes your green eyes pop."

Tess didn't want her eyes to pop. She wanted her attraction to Carter to snap and fizzle away. She caught the billowy woven blouse Paige tossed to her. "Anything else?"

"Yes. Where are those silver starburst hair clips Abby gave you?" Paige opened the top drawer in the dresser. "We'll put in a loose French braid on the side and clip it with those."

"That's too much trouble." She wanted to look cool and effortless. Not like she'd spent the day mooning over Carter and that kiss. Tess walked into the bathroom.

"It's no trouble for you." Paige followed her into the compact space and pointed at the toilet. "Sit. I'm doing your hair."

Tess tugged the lavender-colored shirt over her head then slipped on the denim shorts. "It's just going to fall out."

"It is not. And it emphasizes your cheekbones and wide, round, gorgeous eyes." Paige pushed her onto the closed toilet lid. "Just wait and see. If you don't like it, you can take it out."

"Isn't Evan waiting in the truck?" Tess mumbled.

"He's fine." Paige laughed. "We picked up Jodie Hayes too. She's Riley's second grade teacher and she's the head counselor for Camp June Bug Jamboree this summer."

Tess knew Jodie Hayes. The elementary school teacher had tracked down Tess last week to ask her to run the cakewalk booth at the kids' carnival next month. Tess asked, "Why is Jodie with you now?"

"She's a Breezy and Gayle–approved match for Harris." Paige's laughter spilled around the bathroom. "Apparently, Harris and Jodie met at Lemon Moon the other morning. And Breezy and Gayle decided they needed a night out together."

"That's very efficient." So was her sister. Paige had finished Tess's hair, secured the hair clips and went right into applying makeup on Tess's face. "Is this necessary?"

"Absolutely." Paige lifted her eyebrows at Tess and aimed a soft blush brush at her. "We haven't gotten ready together for a date night in years."

"You're already ready." And it wasn't a date. At least not for Tess. She added, "And you look beautiful, by the way."

"Thank you." Paige dabbed the brush into the powder and swept it across Tess's cheek. "Evan's word was *stunning*. But then he's used to seeing me in my coveralls and rubber boots on the ranch. Anything I put on would've been an upgrade."

In fact, her sister glowed from the natural rosy tinge in her cheeks to the sparkle in her eyes that welled up from inside her. Joy filled Paige from her fingertips to her toes. And it was Evan who was responsible for her sister's continuous sparkle. It was everything Tess wanted for her sister. Tess glanced at Paige. "You're still glad you moved here, right?"

"Definitely." Paige added a touch of lip gloss to Tess's bottom lip. "I can't imagine being anywhere else."

Just what she'd wanted to hear. Tess's shoulders relaxed. She couldn't imagine not having her sister or cousin near her either. "I think we're done. I'm going to eat and chew off the lip gloss."

Paige handed the lip gloss tube to Tess. "Put it in your pocket and reapply later."

Tess took the lip gloss and glanced in the mirror.

"You look really pretty." Paige set her chin on Tess's shoulder and smiled into the mirror. "Promise you'll have fun tonight."

"Why do you sound like I don't know how to have fun?" Tess followed her sister out of the bathroom and took the sandals Paige handed her. "I know how to have fun."

Paige tossed her head back and laughed.

Tess lifted her voice over her sister's laughter. "My work is rewarding."

"So is mine. And Evan's and Carter's and everyone else's around town. But that's not the fun I'm talking about, and you know it." Paige sobered and wiped her eyes with her fingers. "When was the last time you did something because you wanted to do it? For the pure joy of it and no other reason."

She'd kissed Carter last night because she wanted to. But she hadn't been full of joy afterward. Tess buckled her sandal. "When did you?"

"Last night." One corner of Paige's mouth twitched.

"Really?" Tess arched an eyebrow.

"Last night, instead of chores, we took Riley for ice cream and went out onto the dock at the lake. Then Riley and I started a water fight with Evan, and we won." Paige held up a pair of earrings and checked her reflection in the mirror.

Of course Evan and Paige had fun. Riley was a kid and fun was a prerequisite for every childhood.

"I know what you're thinking." Paige turned around and eyed Tess. "But the ice cream at the dock was all my idea. With a little help from Grandpa Harlan."

Spontaneous ice cream outings had been something Paige and Tess had done with their grandparents. Grandpa Harlan would walk into the family room and declare: *Tessie and Paige, things have gotten too serious around here. What with chores and schoolwork and all this life stuff. There's only one cure. We need to inject a little fun. What's it gonna be today?*

Had Tess's life become stale and predictable? Not that there was anything wrong with that. She liked the routine. Preferred it after her short marriage to an impulsive, over-the-top man. But had she forgotten how to have fun? She grabbed her keys and walked out of the bedroom. "I promise to try and have fun tonight." To a point. She was drawing the line at spontaneous kisses with a certain cowboy.

"Thank you." Paige trailed behind Tess down the short hallway and outside onto the landing. "I'm just worried about you. And as your sister, I'm allowed to be worried about you."

"But you don't need to be." Tess locked the apartment door.

"Someone does," Paige argued. "You take care of everyone all the time. Who's taking care of you?"

"I am." Just like she wanted. Tess headed

down the exterior staircase. "And I'm doing quite well at it too."

"Maybe too well." Paige joined her on the sidewalk and frowned.

"What does that mean?" Tess asked.

"It just means that it's okay to let someone in again." Paige knocked her shoulder against Tess's.

Her sister was happily in love and wanted everyone around her to feel the same. Tess would settle for happy and leave love on the sidelines. "It's also okay to be happily single too."

"But are you happy?" Paige peered at her.

Tess lifted her chin and held her sister's gaze. "Yes."

"The really-happy-in-your-core kind of happy?" Paige pursed her lips and narrowed her eyes as if examining Tess like one of her four-legged patients.

Had Tess ever experienced that kind of happy? She'd imagined it at one time. With her former husband. But really felt it? She would remember, wouldn't she? Still, she managed a small nod. "I'm good. I promise."

"You'd tell me if you weren't, right?" Paige linked her arm with Tess's and the sisters headed for the street and Evan's truck. "I know I've been distracted by the renovations and my patient load and getting settled in Three Springs. But I'm always here for you."

"I know." Just as Tess would be there for her sister too. Whenever she needed her. Tess squeezed her sister's arm. "And I love that you're here now. Just within reach if I need a hug."

"I bet Carter gives one heck of a good hug," Paige said with an air of nonchalance that Tess wanted to steal.

Tess concentrated on keeping her voice even and easygoing. "Why are we talking about Carter's hugs?"

"Why not?" Paige nudged her elbow into Tess's side. "Tell me you haven't thought about it. He's good-looking, charming and going places."

That was how she would've described her former husband too. And that relationship had been all wrong. "Carter is also just a friend."

And hugging a friend like Carter wasn't a habit she wanted to get into. One small kiss had already tipped her off-kilter. But she would find her balance before she saw Carter and everything would be as it should.

"Friends turn into more all the time." Paige laughed. "Look at Evan and me."

"I'm good with friends." Friends was all she wanted. She added, "In fact, I'm happy being friends only with Carter."

"Fine." Paige waved to Evan in the truck and opened the back passenger door for Tess. "Just promise you'll keep the door open."

Tess had all but kicked the door open last night and kissed Carter. Then he'd walked away after calling her a wildcard. She'd never won big at any card table. And besides, all bets were off-limits when it came to her heart. "If I promise to keep a door cracked, can we talk about how cute Jodie and Harris will look together?"

"They will, won't they?" Paige said.

Inside the truck Jodie blushed and admitted she was nervous.

Paige climbed in and added, "That's sweet, but there's nothing to be nervous about, Jodie. You and Harris are two great people who deserve to have a fun night out."

Even sweeter, Tess never gave her sister that promise. And as far as she was concerned, all doors leading to Carter were closed.

CHAPTER FOURTEEN

"THAT WAS A productive day for sure." Harris set his camera on his lap and stretched his arms out toward the truck's dashboard. "I'm feeling pretty confident we shouldn't need any more film from the distillery."

"I should hope not," Carter said. As it was, it had felt like a full-scale Hollywood production, not a simple promotional video. Carter turned his truck onto the private driveway leading to the Sloan farmhouse. Harris had followed Carter around Misty Grove from the rack houses to the backside of the distillery and everywhere in between since breakfast.

"But I would like to get a shot of this drive onto the property for an opening sequence." Harris made a frame with his fingers, leaned toward the windshield, then picked up his camera. "Like it is now with the sun starting to set over the property. The golden wheat absorbing the orange sky."

One of Carter's favorite times. He slowed around a curve, loosened his grip on the steering wheel and relaxed into the leather seat. He was where he belonged. The fading sunlight streamed across the fields, setting the wheat crops to gleam like an invitation to pause and unwind.

Those setting sunrays had streamed across the front porch of Tess's apartment last night, sweeping an enchanting air around Tess and capturing Carter completely. He'd moved closer to her as if she was where he belonged.

He flexed his fingers, straightened away from that impractical idea and concentrated on picturing Harris's opening sequence. But all that came to mind was that blink-and-you'll-miss-it kiss Tess and he had shared on the porch. The kiss might've been brief, but there was nothing fleeting about its impact.

Still, Carter had never been rattled by a kiss before. He wasn't about to start now.

The hole-pocked land came into view, pulling Carter away from kisses under porch lights and dangerous diversions. He knew his priorities: his family, the farm and the distillery.

Now he had a feud to end to prove he could be counted on to take care of his family.

And kissing Tess, however tempting and however enjoyable, wasn't sustainable. Not like the distillery and the farm that would guarantee his family always had a home for decades to come.

After all, what he was building was worth sticking around for, not his feelings.

Harris leaned back as if changing his mind about that opening sequence and lowered his camera. "When did you say this part will be fixed? Now that we know there isn't a centuries-old treasure in the ground."

Not soon enough. Carter scanned the land and frowned. There looked to be more holes, not fewer. And Carter wasn't quite certain how that was even possible. He'd made Caleb and Ryan promise no digging and no ladder climbing on their searches with Roy and Sam that afternoon. With luck, they found the moonshine recipe today.

And hadn't called Carter because they'd wanted to surprise him with the news. *Unlikely.*

Carter would have better odds betting on a lawn mower in a tractor-pull rally.

"Wouldn't it be something if they found the treasure map and a part of the Herring Gang loot on your land?" Earnestness and hope laced Harris's voice. "They'd just need a coin like the one missing from Tess's general store."

"It would be something all right." Something like a complication. And Carter didn't want one more complication. He wanted to rewind. Back to when he was clear on his goals. Clear on exactly how to get there. When he wasn't looking at a certain general store owner and reconsidering what home meant.

His grandfather's vintage power wagon truck was pulling out as Carter drove in. Carter slowed beside his grandpa's dark blue truck in the driveway and rolled down his window. "Where are you two going?"

"Back to Boone's place." Sam hooked his thumb at Boone in the passenger seat of the single cab truck. "We need to check our paperwork on the legend to refine our search."

It wasn't supposed to still be about the missing treasure. At least Carter had gotten everyone to agree not to mention the moonshine recipe to anyone outside the family, until it was located. Small victory there. Carter tried for a neutral expression. "Find anything else interesting?"

"We need to cross-check some new information Boone and I came upon today up in the attic." Sam tapped his steering wheel.

Carter noted how his grandpa stressed the words *Boone and I* and excluded Uncle Roy's name. It was clearly going to be up to Carter to start the conversation between the brothers.

"Could be we got a map and treasure hiding someplace on our land." Sam's eyebrows wobbled up and down as he leaned out the window and shouted, "Did you hear that, Harris?"

Harris gave a thumbs-up sign. "Ready to hear all about it, Sam."

Carter was ready for it all to be over. No more wasting precious time. "What did you discover today?"

"Found these journals in the attic." Boone lifted the pair of worn notebooks from his lap.

"Written by my gran Esther." Sam smiled. "One is from before she was married to my granddaddy. She even talks about planning their wedding here on the farm."

Carter didn't need any more wedding conversations. "Uncle Roy might have information too."

"Wouldn't know about that." Sam smoothed his fingers through his beard and shook his head. "Ryan and Roy spent the afternoon searching the southern barn. Caleb was with us in the attic until he left for the fire station."

And Sam and Roy had never crossed paths all day just as Grandpa Sam had intended. Carter sighed and eyed the cunning older cowboy. It was past time to turn the tables on his grandfather.

"Well, good luck, Grandpa." Carter checked the watch on his wrist. "Harris and I are running behind and we still need to pick up the barbecue sauce from Nolan. We promised to deliver it to the Owl booth at the food truck rally tonight."

Sam's eyebrows creased. "When are you picking up your date?"

It wasn't a date. But Carter let that misconception slide and waved his hand as if he had all the time in the world. And that being punctual wasn't something he prided himself on. "Tess and Jodie are riding with Paige and Evan. They'll be fine until we get there."

Boone leaned toward the open driver's-side window and shouted, "You two can't be late for your dates."

Technically, if it wasn't a real date, Carter wouldn't actually be late.

"It's bad manners," Sam insisted. His fingers drummed an irritated beat on the door frame.

"Nolan needs help." Carter lifted one shoulder and set his amusement aside. Outmaneuvering the two old-timers didn't happen often enough. "What else can we do?"

Sam turned to his friend in the truck cab, exchanged a few words, then smiled at Carter. "Boone and I can get the sauce from Nolan and bring it up to Belleridge."

"You guys have other things to do." Carter shook his head. "I don't want to keep you from your important research."

Sam narrowed his gaze on Carter, then grinned beneath his beard. "Plans change."

Yes. Plans changed. And Carter was putting

the two brothers together. Tonight. Whatever it took. "If you're sure you don't mind, then we'll see you at the food truck rally."

"Hurry and get cleaned up," Sam hollered. "And don't be late for your dates."

Carter rolled up his window as Grandpa Sam's truck rumbled away.

Harris quickly stuffed his camera into its bag and zipped the cover. "I have to admit this is my first date in quite a while."

Carter parked the truck and glanced at Harris. Time to correct everyone. "It's just a night out with friends and good food. Nothing more than that." Because Carter wasn't letting it be more than that.

"You're right." Harris nodded and opened his truck door. "There's no need to be nervous."

Ryan and Roy appeared from the side of the garage. Both dust- and dirt-covered from their cowboy hats to their boots. Uncle Roy's hands were stuffed in his pants pockets. Ryan still had the slightest of limps. Carter should've never agreed to the search today without him being there. Ryan needed to concentrate on his rehab, not climb around decades-old barns.

"Change of plans," Carter announced and jumped out of his truck. "We're all having dinner at the food truck rally."

"What about your dates?" Ryan wiped a

hand across his forehead and studied Carter as if searching for some kind of a catch.

The only catch was Ryan's misuse of the word *date*. "Tess and Jodie will be there," Carter said, then improvised again. Problems at the distillery had kept Carter occupied all day. But tonight he wasn't working. And it was past time to end a feud. "Tess thought Uncle Roy might enjoy some real Texas chili."

"Hmm, we do have to eat." Uncle Roy rubbed his stomach. "I sure could use a spot of chili and rumor is I can find some that's worth a second helping there."

"Then we should get cleaned up and head out." Carter grinned. "We can meet back at the truck in fifteen, maybe twenty minutes."

Harris followed Uncle Roy up the back porch stairs.

"Best polish your dancing shoes, Harris." Uncle Roy paused to look back at the marketing rep. "Don't want to be stepping on anyone's toes tonight."

Ryan crossed in front of Carter, almost stepping on Carter's boots, and blocked him from heading into the house. "Dates are usually between two people, not a collection of people. You can't just invite more people on your date with Tess."

"It's not a date." How many more times did

he need to repeat himself? Carter wasn't driving Tess. Dropping her off. And he definitely wasn't kissing her again. And those were the rules of a date. Besides, if he was taking Tess on a real first date, it wouldn't be to a food truck rally with half the town. "It's. Not. A. Date."

"You sure about that?" Ryan turned and walked beside Carter toward the farmhouse. "Maybe Tess thinks it is."

"I'm sure she doesn't." Carter's voice was firm. He'd walked away last night and left her standing on the porch. He wasn't someone a woman like Tess should even want to date. "You don't need to come along."

Carter only needed his uncle and his grandfather there. Same place. Same time.

"Well, like Uncle Roy said, we do have to eat." Ryan opened the back door.

"You could eat here." Carter slipped off his work boots in Gran Claire's drop zone. *If it's muddy, dusty or dirty, drop it here. And just to be clear, if you've been out there, it gets dropped here.* Too bad there wasn't a zone to drop his tangled feelings about Tess into.

"I suppose I could eat here." Ryan hung his hat on one of the wall hooks and grinned at Carter. "But then I wouldn't get a front-row seat to your date with Tess."

"We need to seriously stop calling it that." Carter shoved his brother out of his way.

"But that's what it is." Ryan trailed after him toward the stairs.

"Look, I'm trying to get Uncle Roy and Grandpa to talk tonight," Carter confessed.

Ryan folded his arms over his chest. "Shouldn't your attention be on Tess?"

"Tess will understand." Carter gripped the rod-iron railing. "Uncle Roy and Grandpa have to sit down and talk things through."

"You think that's going to happen tonight?" Doubt shifted across Ryan's face.

"It has to happen," Carter said. "Why not tonight?"

"Because they both spent the entire day avoiding each other like it was a competition. One that they both intended to win." Ryan ran both hands through his hair and yawned. "Caleb and I were the go-betweens all day."

But tonight Carter would be there and he intended to be the difference. How, exactly, he wasn't sure yet, but he'd figure it out. It was what he did. "Sorry about that. Had to work on the forklift before we could move the barrels. Took longer than we anticipated, then Harris kept wanting to shoot more film."

"I'm capable of helping more around here,

Carter." Ryan frowned at him. "You just have to ask."

"You need to recover." And his brother needed to get back to his life—back out on the rodeo circuit where Ryan truly wanted to be.

"You don't have to always do everything yourself." Ryan followed him up the stairs.

"I won't be doing anything by myself tonight." Carter tapped his fist against his brother's shoulder. "You're coming on my date, remember?"

Ryan returned Carter's soft jab with one of his own and laughed. "You're going to owe Tess a serious do-over after tonight."

There would be no do-over. No second date. Because dates led to a relationship. And a relationship required things like commitment and sharing and teamwork. Carter was committed to his family and his business. And he couldn't risk splitting his attention. How could he be fully invested if he always had his mind somewhere else? And someone as good and compassionate as Tess deserved to be put first. Every time.

Fifteen minutes later and his hair still damp from the shower, Carter cruised down the bypass and turned up the country song on the truck radio. Ryan sat beside him, playing air guitar. And Harris and Roy hummed in the backseat.

The song ended and Roy leaned on the console between the front seats. His gray curls fluffed and clean. "Why aren't there any flowers in here?"

"Why would there be flowers in my truck?" Carter frowned. Grandpa Sam liked to call Carter's truck the Sunday-driving car because of the fancy leather and power windows. Then Grandpa would pat his vintage power wagon and declare it was made back when trucks were still trucks.

"What's Harris going to give his date?" Uncle Roy drummed his fingers on the console. "A handshake isn't gonna cut it."

A handshake wasn't exactly what Carter wanted to share with Tess either. Not that it was relevant to anything. Since he wasn't looking for *anything* between him and Tess. Carter glanced in the rearview mirror. "Harris, you should decide. It's your date."

"Is this a date?" Harris freed the top button on his polo shirt.

"Of course it is." Uncle Roy slid back onto the bench seat. "You're meeting a lady friend at the food truck rally, aren't you?"

"Flowers feel like added pressure." Harris rubbed his throat as if he'd been singing too loud to the radio.

"If that's all it takes, then Carter is going on a date too." Ryan tapped his fingers to the beat of the next country song.

Not this again. Carter kept his gaze on the road.

"Carter needs flowers." Ryan grinned from across the truck cab. "But Harris needs to keep things casual. No flowers for Harris's first date. Harris is right about the added pressure that flowers would add to the mix."

Tess and Carter hadn't been on a first date. There would be no flowers for anyone. Flowers always came with an awkward explanation attached. *Tess, these are for you. I'm sorry for walking away the other night.* Or: *Tess, these are for you. I was thinking about you all day.* Or: *Tess, these are for you. They remind me of your smile.* The one he wanted to see again. In the morning when he woke up. At night before he fell asleep. Of course, only if he was going on a true date with Tess tonight would he want all that.

But it wasn't a date. And he only wanted that conversation between his uncle and his grandfather to finally happen. "No one needs flowers tonight."

"Back in my day, we always brought a lady friend flowers." Roy's grin creased his face and twinkled in his gaze. "That's what a gentleman did. I'm quite certain your grandmother raised you to be a gentleman, Carter."

"I've given flowers to women before, if that's what you're asking." Carter couldn't recall the last time he'd bought flowers for anyone. Or even his last real date. None of that factored into the wheat field harvest or the distillery operations and was clearly inconsequential.

"My mom raised me to be a gentleman." Harris cleared his throat. "I should probably buy some flowers."

Clearly, Carter had to teach Harris how to take a stand. A stand against dates. And against older cowboys with outdated notions.

"I used to pick my flowers from the meadow beyond the back field." Roy grinned. "Drove all around to find Millie her favorites. She liked those purple wildflowers, daisies and violets. Took time and effort, but the smile on her face was always worth it."

Carter knew something about smiles too. And Tess's smiles were definitely worth it. Carter's voice sounded gravelly even to himself. "We are not picking flowers."

"There's no need to." Ryan's voice was entirely too chipper like he always walked through fields of roses for the sheer joy of it. "Now you can get all those flowers in one convenient place at Five Star Grocery Depot. I see their sign up ahead."

"Certainly takes the fun out of the search," Uncle Roy grumbled.

"How is scouring fields for flowers fun?" Even their current conversation wasn't fun.

"You've got a lot to learn." Deep affection wound around Roy's voice and bolstered the lingering sadness for the loss of his wife. "From the first time I held Millie's soft, pretty hand, I knew anything we did together was gonna be a fun adventure, even picking flowers."

Carter liked spending time with Tess. But his adventures were contained to the distillery and the farm as it should be. He didn't have time for picking flowers or things that took him away from his work. But Tess's smile. Her hand in his… Carter stepped on the gas pedal. "Lucky for me, I prefer my adventures solo."

"Until you don't." Roy laughed.

Carter took a hard right at the last minute and pulled into the Five Star parking lot. He slowed in an open parking space and shoved his truck into Park. His door open, he glanced at his passengers. Then arched an eyebrow at his brother as if daring Ryan to say something. Carter mumbled, "I'll be right back."

Ryan's smile grew in increments, but he managed to keep his thoughts to himself. Small wonder that.

"I'll go with you." Harris hopped out of the truck and swiped at his balding head as if brushing off those nerves. "Just to see if there's something that feels right for tonight."

Carter was starting to wonder if anything was going to feel quite right again. Surely, after the feud ended. And Abby and Wes exchanged vows. And Tess and Carter went back to their own lives. Surely, then all would be right in his world again and back to the way he wanted. He ignored the twinge of discontent and blamed it on unexpected interruptions.

"Jodie and I have been talking and texting." Harris touched the tip of a yellow rose in the floral section of the grocery store. "But I don't know her favorite flowers or even if she has allergies. She does like red licorice and keeps a secret stash in her classroom and in her nightstand."

"Then get the red licorice," Carter suggested. "It shows her that you were paying attention."

Something Carter had to stop doing with Tess. He knew enough about her already, from the way her green eyes flashed when she laughed to the way she always reached for him, as if she realized before he did that he needed the contact. The reassurance her touch gave. He definitely knew all he needed to about Tess. Yet, somehow it felt like it wasn't nearly enough.

"What flowers are you getting Tess?" Harris asked.

There really hadn't been an option. Carter had known the second he'd walked into the floral area. He reached for a bouquet in a white bucket. "Her favorite."

CHAPTER FIFTEEN

CARTER SKIRTED AROUND the dance floor, taking up a large chunk of the green space in downtown Belleridge. A lively country band performed on the stage anchoring one side of the dance floor, where Jodie and Harris were already several spins into a line dance alongside Paige and Evan. Uncle Roy had spotted the Four Fiddlers Tavern and persuaded Ryan to join him for a spot of whiskey first. More than a dozen food trucks waited on the streets around the park. The entire atmosphere was infused with energy and good cheer.

Carter headed toward the picnic tables, following the directions Tess had texted him.

He spotted Tess at a table off to the side. She toyed with a paper menu and her foot tapped to the beat of the fiddler's quick tune. And suddenly, Carter regretted leaving those flowers in his truck. He'd figured he'd give her the flowers later as if they were an afterthought. No big deal. Something he just happened to have lying around his truck.

But watching Tess now he realized there was nothing about Tess that could ever be described as an afterthought. And wasn't that a hazardous realization.

Those nerves Harris referenced earlier prickled through Carter. He ran his palms over his jeans. *Get it together already. It's not like it's a date.* Carter walked over to the table. "Looks like we've been designated as the table savers." *You look amazing, by the way.*

"Carter." She smiled.

Not the one that usually filled her green gaze as if her joy overflowed and had no place else to go. No, there was a reserve now. A caution that held her smile in check. She was guarded. And he worried he may have caused that.

"I can table save, and you can get food." She handed him a paper menu.

"It's fine." Carter dropped onto the bench across from her.

"You don't look fine." She tipped her head and eyed him.

"Sorry." *For not kissing you properly. For not being the man you deserve.* But Carter lived by his rules. And he hadn't lied last night; she was a wildcard and a game changer in a life he already had set. Carter linked his hands together and rested them on top of the menu. "I wanted to get Uncle Roy and my grandpa together to finally talk tonight."

"Here?" Tess pressed her finger on the metal table. One eyebrow arched.

"Ryan had the same reaction." Carter shifted back on the bench as if she poked him instead. "What's wrong with here?"

"It's crowded." Her eyebrow joined the other, both notching higher. "And far from private."

"Aren't you supposed to have uncomfortable conversations in public to avoid big scenes?" And temptations like kissing pretty general store owners again and upending a very well-balanced life. Relationships required attention he wasn't willing to give.

"I believe that's the recommendation for a breakup." A hesitancy surrounded her words. "Probably not for reconciliations."

"They're going to have to confront each other before they can reconcile." Carter skipped his gaze over the crowd. All he saw were couples. Entwined on the dance floor. Holding hands on the grass. Sharing ice cream and most likely finishing each other's sentences. Welcome to date night in Belleridge. But Carter was all too aware of his priorities. "Right now Uncle Roy and Grandpa are still successfully avoiding each other."

"Where are they?" Tess shifted and glanced toward the dance floor.

"Sam and Boone are working the Owl booth, selling barbecue sauce for Violet so that Violet can take a few turns on the dance floor." Carter settled his gaze back on Tess as if to prove to himself he could look at her and concentrate on more than wanting her to smile. Really, *really* smile. At him. Because of him. With him. He dropped his cowboy hat on the bench as if his hat was responsible for his fixation on all things Tess. "Ryan and Roy went to the Four Fiddlers. Apparently, Uncle Roy and Aunt Millie had their fourth date there and he wanted to toast their love story."

"That's sweet." Her gaze softened. She propped her elbow on the table and set her chin in her hand. "What now?"

I ask you on a real date. Just you. Just me. But that would be starting something he couldn't finish. And Tess deserved better. "I can't keep waiting on them. Have any ideas about how we can get them together?"

Surprise flared in her gaze. There and gone. Then one corner of her mouth tipped up into her cheek. "Grandma Opal always said if you want to bring people together, you just have to feed 'em and feed them well."

"Good thing for us, we're surrounded by

food." Carter picked up the menu and ran his finger over the offerings. "What's going to bring two stubborn cowboys to the table? Chili. Street tacos. Sliders. Chicken wings."

"I think we're going to need a little bit of everything." Tess waved to Harris and Jodie, who carried cherry-flavored soda bottles and wore matching big grins. The marketing rep looked flushed and far from nervous now. Apparently, date night agreed with Harris.

"Come on." Tess stood and motioned to Carter. "We have a family to bring back together."

And a feud to end. Not a relationship to start. Carter shoved his hands into his pockets and joined Tess.

Orders placed for beef sliders with the works, Texas red-hot chili bread bowls and spicy fried chicken wings, Carter sent a text message to Ryan about dinner being served. Tess went to find Sam and Boone. Paige and Evan joined Carter to help carry everything back to the tables.

Carter balanced the cardboard baskets in his hands and shook his head when he got closer to the tables. He hadn't realized he had needed to make seat assignments too. Roy was seated at one table across from Paige and Evan. Sam the other. At least the two brothers were still close enough to steal off each other's plates if they wanted to.

Jodie placed her cherry soda on the table, took Harris's hand and pulled him back out onto the dance floor for what she claimed was her favorite song. Paige grabbed Evan midbite and the couple followed Jodie and Harris. Ryan strolled over, set his beer beside Uncle Roy and sat. Carter dropped onto the bench across from his grandfather.

"Boone stayed at the booth. Told him we'd bring him a chili bread bowl." Tess sat beside Carter then whispered, "Sam and Roy aren't exactly at the same table."

"It's a start." Carter leaned toward her. She shifted, her knee tapped against his and suddenly Carter couldn't claim he was entirely disappointed in the seating arrangements. "It's the closest they've been since Uncle Roy returned home." And the closest Carter had been to Tess since that kiss.

"Now to get them talking." She reached over and swiped a loaded potato skin from the basket in front of Carter. "These are one of my favorite appetizers. I can never resist them."

Carter thought he knew what he could resist. But a pair of beguiling green eyes kept making him reconsider more than his favorite foods. He picked up a beef slider, listened to the light conversation around the tables and waited for an opening. Uncle Roy and his grandpa needed common ground. Carter was going to help them find it. A lull opened and Carter tested the water. "Uncle Roy, is that the best Texas chili you've tasted?"

"It's in the top five." Uncle Roy helped himself to a second chili bread bowl. "It's missing our mamma's secret ingredients. If it had those, I'd be a repeat customer."

"What's missing?" Tess picked up another potato skin. Her voice was playful. "Or can't you tell us because it's a family secret?"

"The secret is how it's all put together." Uncle Roy wagged his plastic chili spoon at Tess and grinned. "But I can give you the ingredients. It's missing coffee in the broth and vinegar at the finish."

"That's just plain wrong, Roy. Guess I shouldn't be surprised. You haven't gotten things right in decades." Carter's grandfather dropped his chicken wing on a napkin and pointed at his brother. "Mom always put dark beer in the broth and chocolate at the end."

"Maybe it was all those things," Tess offered. Her tone calm and encouraging. "True Texas chili has quite an expansive ingredient list."

And his uncle and grandfather had quite the stubborn streaks. Carter shoved the rest of the slider into his mouth. What had he been think-ing? This pair would probably find a way to dis-agree over what day of the week it was.

"It was always dark beer and chocolate." Sam flattened his palms on the table. "It's how we were taught and how I taught the boys."

"It was coffee and vinegar," Roy argued. "She always brewed extra the day before in that por-celain pot with them blue flowers on it. The one we chipped when we knocked it off the counter trying to get to the cookie jar first."

Sam dipped his chicken wing in the sauce, taking his time to coat it in the ranch dressing. Finally, he looked at his brother. "I remember getting to the cookie jar first that day. But you're wrong about the chili."

Uncle Roy shoved his spoon into his chili bowl and scooped out a large mouthful, then narrowed his gaze on his brother. "Shows what you don't know."

Carter's grandfather focused on his food. And a weighty, uncomfortable pause settled around the group. Ryan toasted Carter across the table as if to tell him *I told you this would happen.* Carter rolled his lips together and rolled back his shout of frustration.

"Carter, did your great-grandmother leave a recipe box in the farmhouse?" Tess's voice was casual as if she had all evening to hang out in the park and wait for the older Sloan brothers' anger to pass.

Carter scooted toward Tess until they touched from hips to knees and his exasperation at his family quieted. Shouting at his elders would hardly get the result he wanted. "I don't think I've ever seen a recipe box. Ryan, have you?"

Ryan shrugged. "I think she had a recipe book. Haven't seen it in a while."

"Your great-gran never measured anything or wrote her recipes down." Sam shook his head. "It was always a pinch of this or that, taste and repeat. Same as my Claire."

"Gran Claire always told me when you cook what you love, you don't need a recipe." Carter patted his chest and offered Tess a small smile. "Cook from your heart and your flavors will work every time."

"And does that work for you?" An amused grin twitched into place; even her eyebrows twitched. "Do you cook from your heart, Carter?"

"Carter doesn't cook." Sam chuckled. "Not from his heart or from a cookbook. Best know that up front, Tess. It's always good to know what you're getting into."

"Carter, you don't cook at all?" Tess gave him a perplexed look.

Sam shook his head back and forth slowly as if answering for Carter.

Carter glanced at his brother. Ryan lifted his beer to his mouth, barely covering his laughter in the red plastic cup, and offered no assistance. Carter clarified, "I know how to cook. I don't have the time."

"Or the want," Roy chimed in. "And things we want, we make time for."

This wasn't about Carter's culinary talents or lack of. Cooking a three-course meal wouldn't ensure his family always had a home to come back to. And that was all Carter had ever wanted.

Tess's arm brushed against his as if testing that claim.

He could want Tess's hand in his. But he didn't have the time. He crumbled a napkin in his fist.

"Still, I'm warning you, Carter." Sam's tone firmed in time to the shake of his finger. "When your brothers all move out, I'm not doing all the cooking alone."

His grandfather hardly cooked now. Caleb had inherited their grandmother's culinary skills and usually had something on the grill. Carter sighed. He supposed that wasn't an excuse not to pull his weight.

"You gotta cook sometimes, Carter." Uncle Roy tore a bite from his empty bread bowl and shook the piece of bread at Carter. "It's not right to always rely on everyone around you for a good meal."

"Sounds like Carter should have dinner duty tomorrow night." Ryan's big laugh finally burst free, rolling across the table and bouncing into Carter.

"I can handle dinner tomorrow night. Nothing to it." And if it got his family back at the table, even better.

"Fine, just don't make your chili with chocolate and beer." Roy picked at his bread bowl. "That's a bad combination."

Sam's hands fisted on the table.

"Grilled cheese and tomato soup. That's a good combination." And one his grandfather and uncle couldn't possibly argue about. Carter raised his hands. "And now on the menu tomorrow night."

"Grandpa Harlan made a wonderful tomato soup." Tess set her hand on Carter's arm and smiled at him. "I could give you the recipe. It's easy to follow and doesn't take much time to make."

What can I give you? Carter blinked. "That would be great."

"You know." Sam's voice smoothed out like the finish on Misty Grove's small-batch whiskey. "I always thought cooking was way more fun with a partner."

"Millie and I cooked together just about every night. It was always one of my favorite parts of the day," Uncle Roy mused. The creases around his eyes softened as melancholy spread through his words. "I still remember showing her how to make buttermilk biscuits with ham. She insisted on getting them perfect. We must've made five dozen batches that night. Each one harder and more burnt than the last. Laughed about that for years."

"Claire and I had never quite got the hang of those beef Wellingtons, but we sure had fun trying." Sam chuckled and shifted his gaze from Carter to Tess. "You know it might be best if you showed Carter how to make that soup, Tess."

Not again. His grandfather could tuck his matchmaking ways away. It was time to call his grandpa's bluff. Carter said, "Tess and I can make grilled cheese and tomato soup if you and Uncle Roy make the biscuits with ham for dinner. Tomorrow night."

Sam stroked his beard and considered Carter. "Roy, you still know how to use a rolling pin?"

Uncle Roy laughed. "Some things you never forget."

"Guess that only leaves dessert." Sam grinned. "Of course, that's if Tess is good with participating in Sunday family dinner night."

"Sure. Why not." Tess avoided looking at Carter. "I'm sure it'll be fun."

And Carter had to be sure to keep his distance from Tess. He knew his place. On the farm and in his family. He knew where he was meant to be. And tomorrow evening was about continuing the conversation between his uncle and grandfather. Repairing their rift. Not exploring what was between Tess and himself.

"Then it's settled." Sam stood and picked up a chili bread bowl. "I'm going to bring this to Boone and see if Violet wants another break to kick up her boots on the dance floor."

Roy wiped his hands on a napkin, gathered the empty containers and walked to the trash can.

Paige and Evan returned. Evan flopped onto the picnic bench. "I need to eat before we go another round out there."

"I think I could dance all night." Paige laughed and spun around. "The band is so good."

Evan rested his forehead in his hand and looked slightly ill. Carter pushed the plate of sliders toward his friend.

"If you don't mind going a beat slower, I'm happy to take a turn with you out there." Uncle Roy held out his hand to Paige.

"I'd be delighted." Paige took Uncle Roy's hand and the pair blended into the line dancers.

"Your uncle is my new hero." Evan went to work on the sliders and seasoned curly fries.

Carter laughed and stretched his legs out underneath the table.

"Tess, want to take a turn?" Ryan stood at the end of their table, gripping his cup in one hand and holding his other arm out.

Carter crossed his arms over his chest and narrowed his gaze at his brother. "Aren't you injured?"

"My physical therapist says I'm almost back to normal." Ryan grinned, revealing his teeth. "And besides, I'm not too injured to make sure Tess has fun too."

"I'd love to dance as long as you won't mind if I step on your toes," Tess said. "It's been a while since I've danced."

"As long as we're having fun, it doesn't matter," Ryan said.

Tess gathered the empty potato skin container and stood. "Let me just throw this out."

"You don't mind, do you?" Ryan set his cup on the table and leaned in close to Carter. "After all, it's not like Tess is your date, right?"

Carter lifted one shoulder and rammed as much indifference into his words as he could. "Go right ahead. Have fun."

Ryan's hand landed on Carter's shoulder and squeezed. "You're one stubborn cowboy, brother."

Tess returned and Ryan greeted her with a flourish of charm and glee. Then his brother twirled Tess out onto the dance floor, proving Gran Claire had worked her dance lesson magic with more than one grandson.

Carter tracked their progress across the dance floor. Watched Tess's cheeks get more flushed. His brother kept up what looked like a lively conversation without missing a step. And then Tess tossed her head back and laughed.

It was the smile Carter had been searching for all night. And it was aimed at the starlit sky and not him. For a moment Carter wanted to be the one to bring out her joy. To make her happy.

But Carter was built for income streams, revenue making and hard work. He was cynical and blunt. He wasn't made for green-eyed romantics. He knew nothing about romance and all the softer things women wanted. All the things someone like Tess should have.

Have to be mindful of a girl's toes and feelings, Carter. Don't want to be crushing either one. Gran Claire had always opened her dance lessons with that advice. Carter remained on the picnic bench.

No. It wasn't a date, but Carter still minded.

CHAPTER SIXTEEN

RYAN SPUN TESS one more time and guided her back into the two-step hold and circled them to the outside of the crowd of dancers. Tess smiled up at Carter's brother. "Thanks, Ryan. I forgot how much I like to dance. And I didn't even step on your toes one time."

"I'll be your partner anytime." Ryan's grin was mischievous. He gripped her hand and swirled her out of the dance hold, then spoke over her shoulder. Amusement floated through his words. "But I'm fairly certain my older brother wants to impress you with his dance moves first."

Tess's gaze landed on Carter and locked on. He stood at the edge of the dance floor, arms loose at his sides, his stance relaxed. But there was nothing casual about the way his gaze was fixed on her. As if she was the only one he saw. The only one who mattered.

And that awareness sparked inside her. Not quite so unsettling now. Almost welcoming. She moved toward him, Ryan beside her. Yet, her attention never strayed from Carter. She stopped only when she was close enough to see that same awareness in Carter's gray gaze.

"Have fun, you two." Ryan tipped his hat and disappeared into the crowd.

Tess swallowed, willing her voice into more than a breathless appeal. "Want to dance, Carter?"

"Thought you'd never ask." His closed-lip smile was slow, mysterious and more than rewarding.

Tess set her hand inside Carter's and set her heart on pause. The warmth in his gaze matched the warmth of his hand. But hearts weren't allowed to get involved. Or to get swept away. She'd keep her sandals fixed on the dance floor and quickstep until even love was too dizzy to snare her. It shouldn't be too hard. Once Abby and Wes exchanged their vows, Tess and Carter would go back to their usual routines. Routines that didn't include each other.

Carter spun her onto the dance floor for the cowboy cha-cha, kick-starting her pulse again. His arms came around her from behind as natural and effortless as her fingers entangling with his. And Tess lost herself in the dance and the moment.

Three more line dances and a two-step later, Tess fanned her face beside Carter and laughed. "Okay. I really need a drink."

"Me too." Carter offered her his arm and escorted her off the dance floor.

Tess slanted her gaze at him. "You've got some serious dance skills."

"You sound surprised." Carter grinned at her.

"I am. I didn't expect that." And she hadn't expected to want to grab Carter's hand now and head right back out onto the dance floor. Tess picked up a bottle of water from the table and watched Paige and Evan circle around the other dancers across the dance floor. Her sister looked graceful, free and inspiring. The same as Tess had felt dancing with Carter.

Carter leaned against the edge of the table. His voice was wry. "There's more to me than you know."

"I'm realizing that." Tess sipped her water and kept her gaze on her sister. Evan pulled Paige in close, and the pair blended together, completely content to be tangled up in each other. Confident the other one would catch them if they tripped up. But falling for Carter like that was a free fall into the unknown. And Tess couldn't trust love to catch her. It was safer never to take the fall in the first place.

"You held your own out there too." Carter tipped an open bag of candied pecans toward her. "Where did a librarian who dislikes running learn to dance like that?"

Tess bit into a pecan. The sweet cinnamon sugar glazed her words and the memory. "One of the good parts about my first marriage."

Carter shook a handful of pecans into his palm. "Gran Claire taught my brothers and me. She told us the time would come when we would want to dance with a girl. And she wanted to be sure we wouldn't step on any toes."

"She certainly accomplished her goal." Tess shifted her gaze to Carter, confident she had her heart and reaction to Carter under control again. "Do your other brothers dance as well as you and Ryan?"

"No idea." Carter shrugged. "I've never asked them to dance."

Tess laughed. "I forgot how much I enjoyed it."

"You didn't wear out your dancing shoes with your ex?" Carter asked.

"It was a short phase. Lasted about a month, which was something of a record for Eric." Tess brushed the cinnamon sugar from her hands and the sting from the memory. Although with Carter beside her, the memories stung less.

"Dancing wasn't his thing," Carter said.

"Long-term commitments weren't really his thing." Tess pressed her lips together.

Carter stilled beside her and shifted to look

at her. "But he married you. Isn't marriage one of those long-term commitments?"

There was a reserve to his voice. A distance in his words as if he didn't really want to know her answer. Just like she hadn't wanted to hear Eric on that fateful night. *You're my now, Tess. It was never meant to be forever.* Tess's voice dropped below a whisper. "I thought so."

Carter reached for her just as Paige and Evan walked up with Jodie and Harris close behind. Their private moment was suddenly crowded. And Tess wondered why she wasn't more grateful for the interruption.

Carter pivoted and picked up the pecan bag, instead of Tess's hand. He shook the bag and arched an eyebrow at her. His tone light and easy. "You know what these pecans are missing?"

Tess accepted the conversation shift and pushed the past back where it belonged. "What's that?"

"Ice cream." Carter set the pecan bag on the table and glanced at the others. "Anyone else want ice cream? Tess and I are headed to The Shivering Spoon."

While the others debated whether they wanted ice cream or gourmet donuts, Tess and Carter walked over to The Shivering Spoon. Tess ordered two scoops of the honey cherry pistachio and smiled at Carter. "I'm thinking you want butter pecan."

"You remembered." His gaze softened.

She could confess to remembering even more about him. If she wanted him to think he was important to her. But they were together until the wedding was complete. Tess placed their order and paid before Carter could pull out his wallet. "You bought dinner. Ice cream is on me."

"I have a good idea. You should open a chocolate food truck." Carter handed Tess her ice cream dish and picked up his bowl of two scoops of butter pecan. "Call it Silver Penny's Sweet Side."

Tess walked beside Carter to an empty picnic table. "You're serious?"

"Silver Penny's Sweet Side has a good ring to it." Carter chuckled. "You have to admit that."

"But a food truck," Tess said.

"Hear me out." Carter sat on the tabletop. "You could hand out chocolate samples to the crowd, so you'd still be giving some candy away."

"But I'd have to fill a food truck." She sat next to him and dug a frozen cherry out of her ice cream. "With chocolate and then drive it."

"I sense it's the food truck catching you up, so let's scratch that." Carter waved his spoon in the air. "You could have a tent-style booth like Nolan does for his barbecue sauces."

"And then sell my chocolate." Tess pressed her tongue to the roof of her mouth to stop the cold headache.

"Here's the best part." Carter nudged her knee with his hand. "You sell your chocolate and use the profits to buy books for your book nook at the general store."

Tess lowered her spoon and studied Carter.

"What?" he asked. "You love to be surrounded by books. I know it's not a library like where you used to work. But it could be a piece of one inside the general store."

Now she was caught off guard. That Carter remembered her love of books. She'd mentioned it once in passing. Even more, Carter had created a path for her to have something truly special. Something she wanted. But she'd have to sell her chocolate. And it felt like one of those rainbows Eric always told her not to reach for. What if it was nothing more than a doomed business idea like Eric had chased? Better to play it safe.

Carter covered her hand with his. "Don't make a decision now. Just think about it, okay?"

Tess nodded and resisted shifting her hand to link her fingers with his. As if they were a couple sharing plans for their future. She concentrated on her ice cream.

Beside her, Carter polished off his butter pecan and touched his stomach. "Okay, you have to hurry up and finish that."

"Why?" Tess glanced at him.

Amusement flashed in his gaze. "Because I ate way too much. And the only place to work it off that's convenient is the dance floor. You up for more?"

"Only if you think you can keep up." Tess worked on the last bites of her ice cream.

Carter jumped off the table and held his hand out. "I'm ready when you are."

Tess wiped a napkin across her mouth but couldn't stop the burst of happy inside her. Yeah, it was all going to end, but not tonight. And tonight was what she still had.

They weren't the last ones off the dance floor, but it was close. Harris walked Jodie to her car. Ryan helped Violet take down Nolan's barbecue tent.

"I have something for you," Carter said. "It's in my truck."

Tess walked beside Carter. Her head swirling with the country songs, her feet light and her heart quiet.

Carter opened his truck door, reached inside and handed Tess a bouquet of three oversize sunflowers. "Thanks for the help tonight with Roy and Sam."

Thanks for the dance. When can we have another? "I know it wasn't the conversation you wanted."

"It was a start." Carter tossed his cowboy hat in his truck and ran his hand through his hair. "And that has to count for something."

"Is that hope I hear in your voice?" she asked.

"Guess you're wearing off on me." He grinned.

And her cowboy was getting to her. "You don't have to sound like it's a bad thing."

He stepped closer to her and tucked her hair behind her ear. "You, Tess Palmer, could never be a bad thing."

But could I be your best thing? Because you could be... Tess stepped back and hugged the cellophane-wrapped sunflowers close and her heart even closer. Carter and she were only together until her cousin's I-dos. She was attaching too much meaning to one night and a few country dances. And that would only lead to trouble. She had to keep her feet on the ground and her eyes wide open. Falling in love with her cowboy would be a fall too far. She asked, "Do you have time for the last of the wedding checklist tomorrow before we make dinner?"

"I can make that work." He leaned an arm

against his open door. "Do you want me to come and get you?"

How about we meet in the middle? Two hearts. Same page. "I'll borrow Paige's car and come out to the farmhouse."

"Tomorrow it is," he said.

"'Night, Carter." Tess turned and walked toward Evan's truck.

"Tess," Carter called.

She turned around like her sunflowers toward the sun, then ordered her heart to stand down.

"Don't think tonight counts as the dance you promised me." His words were both a challenge and a promise.

And suddenly, Tess feared she had a heart-size cowboy problem on her hands.

CHAPTER SEVENTEEN

THE NEXT AFTERNOON Carter adjusted a stirrup on Catnip and watched Tess pull her sister's car to a stop in his driveway. He patted the bay's neck and said, "Here goes nothing."

Tess climbed out of the car and shielded her eyes with her hand. "Are you coming or going with those horses?"

"Hopefully going." He held the reins for both Whiskey Wind and Catnip and took Tess in as if he hadn't just seen her last night at the food truck rally. The night had been better than he'd imagined. Because of her. He'd woken up before sunrise, eager to see what unfolded this evening. Now it was here. Tess had arrived. And he was equal parts excited and nervous.

Tess glanced around the circular driveway. "Where is everyone?"

"They're all gone for the evening," Carter said.

Tess arched an eyebrow. "But we were supposed to have your family dinner night."

"They all requested rain checks." Convenient, certainly. Suspicious, definitely. But for once Carter wasn't in the mood to censure any matchmaking schemes. He said, "Jodie is taking Harris to the drive-in movie theater. Harris mentioned he'd never been. Sam and Boone are with Nolan, selling more barbecue sauce at a festival outside the city."

Tess's eyebrows drew together as if she was connecting the same matchmaking dots. "What about your brothers and uncle?"

"Ryan got called out to consult on a movie. He's also a stunt rider, and his director friend is filming outside of Albuquerque." That was real and unplanned. Carter added, "Uncle Roy announced visiting a real movie set was on his bucket list and refused to let Ryan leave without him. Caleb is still at the fire station."

"Then it's just us." Her teeth bit into her bottom lip.

And he wasn't the least bit disappointed about the situation. Carter nodded.

"What about that conversation between Sam and Roy?" Tess moved closer to Carter and the horses.

"I'm still working that out." And for reasons he didn't want to examine too closely tonight, he found himself not that worried. Which should concern him. Yet, all that concerned him was right now. With Tess. "I was thinking we could eat inside or outside on the porch. Then I thought we could try something entirely different."

"What's that?" Her gaze searched his face.

"It's best if I show you and that means us taking a ride on Catnip and Whiskey Wind." Carter walked the horses to her. "If it's not your cup of tea, we can come back. Cook in the kitchen and eat on the porch."

"Wouldn't you rather work?" she asked.

"Funny thing happened. I got all caught up today." He left out the part about how he'd spent the entire day clearing his plate so to speak to make time for her.

"And you're not anxious to get ahead." There was a hesitation to her words.

Carter wasn't certain if it was him or the horses. He gave her time to think things through. "It's quiet right now at the distillery. Maintenance and inspections are going on. Next week the harvest will take up most of my time. Then next month we get back to the distilling."

"Which is your favorite part?" She stroked her fingers along Catnip's neck.

Right now. With you. He kept his fingers curled around the reins. "There's something satisfying about plowing the wheat fields and knowing I had a hand in it. But there's magic in the distilling. I can't describe it."

"You don't have to. It's your passion." She

smiled. Her shoulders and expression relaxed. "I can see it on your face when you talk about it."

"That brings us back around to now," he said. "For some reason I had this notion to take a moment. And I figured we should take one together."

"I can't recall the last time I took a moment for myself." Her mouth dipped down.

"Neither can I." He laughed. "We can try it out together and see what we think."

"I like that plan," she said.

And I like you. Carter waited beside Catnip and guided Tess up into the saddle. He handed her the reins, then mounted Whiskey Wind. "There's no rush. So we'll keep it to an easy pace. Give you time to adjust to the saddle."

And give himself time to adjust to it being about himself and this special woman. Not duty, obligation or anything else. Even if it wasn't practical. Or viable for the long run. But for right now he planned to go with it. And if he was being selfish, he'd deal with all that later.

"It's quite beautiful out here." Tess's focus remained on the wheat fields stretching on either side of them for well over a mile. "I've never been past your farmhouse. Or seen it from this view."

"Thanks for agreeing to take a ride." Carter kept Whiskey Wind beside Catnip and the pace slow. "I've been trying to get Harris on a horse, but he keeps claiming he can't film and ride."

"How is all that going?"

"Not as awkward as I assumed," Carter admitted. "But I'm glad my interviews are over."

"I can't imagine you ever being awkward." She was still in the saddle, calm, if not completely confident. She added, "You're too…"

"Uptight," he filled in.

"I was going to say *put together*." Tess's gaze skipped to his and held for a beat. "Decisive and driven too."

"Some might call that closed off." *If I fell for you and your enchanting green eyes, would you shut me out too?*

She never blinked, kept her expressive gaze fixed on his. "Are you closed off?"

"Definitely." And that meant falling for her was impossible. She believed in romance and love. The kind that led to vows and lifelong commitments. She'd no doubt want his heart and its messy secrets as if love was somehow the great healer. But in the end, love hurt. He said, "There's a lot that people don't need to know about me."

"Like what?" Her interest was sincere. As if she was ready to listen if he was ready to share.

Carter settled his gaze on the trail ahead. He had a direction, a vision and goals. He kept his own counsel. Always. His knee brushed against her leg as if reminding him he wasn't alone. "Like I never wanted to be a wheat farmer like my grandfather, Tess. Never."

She nodded, easy and casual, as if they always rode horses side by side. Always shared truths with each other. As if they were some sort of safe place for each other. "What did you want to be?"

"A bull rider," Carter said. "On the national circuit."

"What happened?" She tipped her head toward him.

"I was the oldest grandson and living on a working farm." It wasn't complicated. It was assumed. And the debt he owed his grandparents for the home they'd given him growing up could never be fully repaid. Still, he tried his best and did what he had to for his family. "I had to drive the tractor, not ride the bull."

"What about your brothers?" Tess brushed a strand of hair off her cheek.

"Grant and the twins were too little. Ryan had a talent for riding as a kid and he only got better every season. He needed to go on to the rodeo circuit." And Carter needed to take care of things on the farm. That was the only way to make sure his brothers could have the choice to follow their dreams. And it was all working out.

Grant was on his way to becoming an orthopedic doctor. Josh was building his reputation as a leading horse trainer. His brothers were following their own paths.

"So you became Sam's right hand." Tess smiled. "And from Sam's praise you exceeded his expectations."

Carter motioned out toward the fields. "Farming was all I knew, and a farmer was all anyone expected me to become."

"Did you ever tell Sam you wanted to do something different?" Her gaze searched his face.

"No." Carter shook his head. "Leaving was never an option. Grandpa couldn't work the land alone. What if I left and he lost the farm? It's the only home my grandparents and my brothers and I have ever known."

"Where are your parents?" Her voice barely carried over the breeze. Again, no pressure to answer. More of an invitation to share.

"They divorced when I was seven." Carter sounded detached. He supposed he was after all the years since that summer. "My dad remarried, started a new life and never looked back. My mom brought us here to the farm and went on to become a world-class surgeon. She traded her kids for an operating room and a distinguished career."

"But you talk to her." Tess flexed her fingers on the reins and shifted in the saddle as if she found his confessions uncomfortable. "She's your mother after all."

"Those first years we did," Carter admitted. "Mostly phone calls. I give her credit, though. She never made any false promises about coming home or anything like that. So we weren't disappointed when she didn't show."

"But you were let down and hurt." The anger in her voice vibrated around her words. "You were kids. How could you not be?"

Tess would choose her family first. That realization comforted him. And like so many things about Tess it drew him to her even more. Carter said, "Our grandparents stepped in. Filled the void. Healed the hurt. They became our world. And this place became our home."

He slanted his gaze toward her. She'd gone quiet, not the soaking-in-nature kind of quiet, but rather the pensive kind. And so he waited.

Finally, she cleared her throat. "I came here because I had no place else to go. I had to sell our townhouse and belongings to pay off my husband's debt."

Carter absorbed that, turned it over and decided he didn't much care for her former husband. Tess should've been taken care of, protected, not taken advantage of.

"I planned on selling my grandparents' antiques inside the general store to get enough money to start over someplace else," she admitted, then met his gaze. "Three Springs was never my first choice either."

His knee brushed hers again as if he wanted her to feel the connection. "But it's your home now."

"Every day it's starting to feel a little bit more and more like it." She shifted in the saddle again, adjusted her grip on the reins and shifted topics. "What's next now that you have the success you've been working so hard for?"

"Now I need to keep it. Be certain it lasts." Then he'd know his family would always have a place to call home.

"Don't you want to enjoy it too?" A tease wrapped around her words.

There was no time for fun. Proving himself required a steadfast commitment and meticulous attention to every aspect of the farm and the distillery. He kept his focus on the horizon. "Who says I'm not?"

A warm breeze gusted around them, swirling dust and pollen and a pause into the air. He should want to take back his words, brush aside so many confessions.

"When did you stop having fun?" Her voice dipped into serious and heartfelt.

He met her gaze. "When did you?"

"After my father died." Sadness skirted across her downturned mouth. "I was nine and things got a lot more serious in our house."

"I'm sorry." He hurt for her loss. Understood the pain.

"It was a long time ago." Tess rolled her shoulders as if shifting away from the hard memories. "My grandparents moved across the street from us, and they made sure my sister and I had fun moments again. They took us to the state fair every summer and did so many other wonderful things for us."

"Sounds like we were both lucky to have our grandparents." The pond came into view and Carter slowed the horses beneath a group of trees. "We're here."

Tess glanced around and her grin grew wider and wider. "This is much better than eating inside."

"Glad you think so." Carter swung off Whiskey Wind and walked over to Catnip, then guided Tess off the horse.

She held on to him for balance. Then leaned in and brushed her fingertips across his forehead. "Thanks for this moment. I think it's just what I needed."

Her touch was feather soft. There and gone like a firefly's flash. Yet, it curved through Carter and settled inside him. Tempting him to reconsider every plan he'd ever made that hadn't included her. "It's only just beginning."

CHAPTER EIGHTEEN

TESS LEFT CATNIP under the trees with Whiskey Wind and walked over to the large pond. The late-afternoon sun reflected off the clear water. She turned back toward Carter. "Where are we?"

Carter unhooked a basket and blanket from Catnip's saddle and strolled toward her. "One of my favorite places on our property."

She could see why. Trees surrounded the clear water. Some with branches that swirled their leaves on the water's surface. Others that towered and protected. She took the basket from Carter and let her gaze drift over the scenery. "It's beautiful and peaceful." And private. And someplace she would want to return to again and again. With Carter. If it was hers. And he was hers. "I think I would be out here every day."

Carter laughed. "It gets a bit cold in the winter."

"But I bet it's still serene and inviting." There was something about the whole area that welcomed and encouraged her to sit and just be exactly who she was. And wasn't that what home was supposed to feel like? Except this belonged to Carter's family. She was only a visitor here and in his life. She hugged the basket tight against her stomach.

"It's fed by an underground stream. My grandparents brought us here to swim when we were kids." Carter shook out the blanket on the grass, then pointed across the water. "We used to have a tree swing and a small dock in the middle of the pond."

Tess set the basket on the blanket. "What happened to the swing?"

"It was more of a rope than a swing." Carter laughed. "We wore it and the tree branch out eventually. There was always someone trying to outdo the other one."

Tess could picture the young Sloan boys swinging out over the water and daring each other to go farther and higher. She smiled. "I'm surprised you didn't hang another rope."

"My brothers tried a few more tree branches over the years." Carter walked to the water's edge and picked up a rock. "Then we stopped coming out here."

That was a shame. Tess stood beside him. "This place is meant for fun. For family memory making. Time with your brothers. What were you doing instead?"

He turned a stone around in his fingers. Then he bent slightly and pitched it toward the pond with a snap of his wrist. The stone bounced a handful of times across the water's surface. A perfect skip. He said, "I was working. Farmwork never really ends."

His short reply was flat and had her heart sinking for the boy who'd believed he had to trade responsibility for happiness. "So you gave up time with your brothers for work."

"I didn't say that." One corner of his mouth tipped up and he reached for another rock. "It was more that my brothers and I found more excitement in the rodeo chute than out here. It's quite an adrenaline rush sitting on a bull in the chute for the first time, especially for a teenager."

"I don't know." Tess set her hands on her hips, considered the blanket, the setting sun and the privacy. Just him. Just her. That hint of romance and anticipation weaving through the air and circling around her. She faced Carter and kept her words light and playful. "This looks like a really good place for a teenage boy to bring a date." And share a first kiss.

Carter skimmed his stone across the water. "We never did."

And Tess and Carter had already shared their first and last kiss. And that was for the best.

Kissing Carter here might be unforgettable. One of those small things that mattered. And Carter already mattered too much to her. Tess searched for a flat rock. "Seriously? You never brought a date out here?"

"This was my grandparents' spot." Carter selected a rock and handed it to her.

His warm touch brushed against her palm. Tess curled her fingers around the stone and held on. Like she wanted to with Carter. They should go. Back to the farmhouse. Back to their lives. Back to where she knew where she stood and that her heart was safe. She tossed her stone, watched it sink, not skip. "I think I'm doing it wrong."

"It's about being fast. A quick snap like this." Carter released another stone. "Don't throw it so hard."

She could say the same about falling. Because if she fell for a cowboy like Carter, she feared it was going to be hard. And the recovery, not so quick. "Roy mentioned your grandparents got married out here."

"Yeah, but it was their spot before and after they exchanged vows." Carter took off his cowboy hat and messed up his hair. "Ryan and I came out one night to swim when we were in middle school. We caught Gran Claire and

Grandpa Sam sitting with their feet in the water, holding hands and laughing together."

"That's sweet." *Would you sit with me? Hold my hand?* Tess tossed her stone. "Did they see you?"

Carter shook his head. "We snuck away. But I never forgot how they were looking at each other. Like they were each other's world and the only place they wanted to be was right here. Together."

She knew that look. "My grandparents had a front porch swing." Tess closed her eyes, remembered the white wooden swing and hugged the memory of her grandparents' love close. "They'd sit out there and hold hands and talk for hours. Grandpa Harlan always said it was where they reconnected."

"I think my grandparents did the same sort of thing." Carter chuckled. "They'd always tell us they were going out for a walk to find something important. When they returned they always announced that they'd found it. I'm pretty sure they came here."

"It's a perfect place to escape for a reprieve." And for a shared secret moment together.

"Especially from five rambunctious boys. We went from sunup until sundown. Never stopped. I'm not sure how they did it." Carter shook his head and tucked his hands into the back pockets of his jeans. "In high school I figured they needed this place more than my brothers and I needed to swim."

He considered himself a reluctant farmer and lucky whiskey distiller. Tess was starting to consider him deeply layered. And she feared he was going to be hard to walk away from. But it was never supposed to be about their hearts. She wanted her own happiness, not heartbreak. And falling for a cowboy who'd vowed never to fall in love guaranteed heartbreak. "Does your grandfather ever visit now?"

"Not very often," Carter said. "But there've been a few times he's mentioned missing his Claire and I've found him out here."

"Grandpa Harlan sat on his porch swing and told me that was where he felt the closest to Grandma Opal after she passed. I would sit with him, and we'd talk about Grandma." Perhaps if she didn't talk about her time with Carter, her feelings would fade faster. Tess looked across the pond, watched several birds fly into the sky. "I always wanted a porch swing like that."

"Why didn't you get one?" Carter asked.

"I wanted the swing to be something Eric and I wanted together." She wrapped her arms loosely in front of her. Maybe it was the setting. Or maybe it was Carter. But the painful bits of her past no longer jammed her throat, making her breath catch. The retelling somehow became easier. "Not just something I sat in alone every night."

"Surely, your husband would have joined you," Carter said.

"No. I don't think he would have." Tess watched Carter's face darken and rushed to explain, "Not because he was mean or insensitive. He was just focused on his next big business opportunity. Or new investment that promised an even bigger payout than the last. Then his dreams would come true."

"What about your dreams?" Carter faced her.

"I thought what we wanted as a couple should come first." Tess curved her fingers around her arms. "My grandparents were always a team, and I always expected my marriage would be the same."

"So you gave up what you wanted." Carter stood beside her, his gaze on the water.

"Isn't that what you do when you are in love?" Tess countered. "Support what your partner wants, especially if it'll make things better for you both?"

"Not if you lost yourself in the process," he said.

"Well, I'm finding myself again. Here in Three Springs." On her own terms. It hadn't been fast or quick, but it was working. She would be completely happy soon with her family permanently settled and the general store just as it had always been. It was all she needed now.

"It's a good place to heal too," Carter said.

Tess grabbed a stone, tossed it and watched it hop two times then disappear. "I've done a lot of that as well."

Carter turned toward her. "What do you want now?"

To have you look at me like I'm everything you'll ever need. She met his gaze. "My family to be happy."

"I already know that. I want that for my own family." He stepped closer to her, took her hand and linked their fingers together. Then he reached up and trailed his fingers across her cheek. "What do you want for yourself?"

"I don't want to ever feel lonely again." Even more, she wanted to feel safe. Like she could be exactly who she was. No hiding. No pretending. Tess pressed her palm against his until she felt that really right place, then tightened her hold. "What do you want?"

"What I've wanted since I saw you. To kiss you. Right here. In this place where it's only you. Only me." His gaze, intense and warm, skimmed over her face as if memorizing everything about her. "But I should let you go."

"You're right." Tess closed the gap, moving

fully into him. His fingers drifted to her neck, rested over her pulse. Her heart slowed as if time had no meaning between them. She leaned into his palm, into him. "I should let go too."

Carter sucked in a breath. His eyes shuttered then locked back on to her. His gaze warmer yet more piercing. "Why don't you?"

"I'm not ready." Her words had no weight and dissolved inside her whispery voice. "What about you?"

"I'm thinking about it." His fingers sank into her hair, sent the warmest shiver along her spine. His gaze searched hers. The rasp in his voice let his words roll out unhurried. "Some decisions can't be rushed."

And some were meant to be taken slow. Better to absorb every detail of the moment. Better to imprint on the heart. And best if kept a secret. "And some things are a given."

"Then we agree we should let go." His voice was gentle.

His touch soft yet steady. Affectionate and reassuring. All the things her heart could want. If she wanted…

"We should definitely let go." And she did. She released him. Framed his face in her hands. And leaned in.

He met her halfway. For a kiss that felt like

pure joy. Belonging. And unspoken promises. For a kiss that was everything she'd been waiting for. Everything she never knew she needed.

CHAPTER NINETEEN

TESS WATCHED THE sky brighten outside her bedroom window at the Owl apartment and quickly braided her hair. She'd given Sam the master bedroom on the first floor. She was dressed, ready to get cooking before the general store opened, and smiling big. Today was the third morning in a row she'd woken up grinning, with thoughts of Carter and their kiss at the pond front and center.

Carter and she had traded texts to finalize wedding details, then shared late-night phone calls to keep sharing parts of themselves the past two days. Carter had inspectors at the distillery and unexpected tractor repairs in preparation for his upcoming harvest that had kept him home. Tess had been occupied with her own to-do list, including her contest chocolate sampler.

The weekend was approaching. She planned to start crafting her chocolates on Friday, break for the wedding festivities Saturday and finish on Sunday. Then it was off to Dallas and the festival.

Only to return ten thousand dollars richer. Time to get on with her day.

Tess's phone rang on the nightstand. She picked it up and answered the video call from her cousin. "Hey, Abs. How's the beach life?"

"What? Oh, it's good." Abby's face wobbled on the screen as if she was walking around. "I know it's early. But I also knew I'd catch you awake. What are you off to bake this morning?"

"Grandma Opal's triple chocolate pecan fudge for the Baker sisters' family reunion on Sunday." Tess had to finish the pecan dessert display to give herself time on Friday to work on her competition chocolate. Her phone propped against the bedside lamp, she reached for her sandals.

"Pecans and chocolate," Abby sighed. "Is there any better combination?"

Tess hoped not. At least not for the panel of judges in the Chocolate Corral Festival competition. She'd finally settled on the six chocolate candy recipes from Grandma Opal's personal cookbook for her competition sampler. She'd mixed and blended the cocoa powders from Abby's house to her satisfaction. The rest of the ingredients waited on the kitchen countertop. All except for that secret something missing in her grandma's contest-winning spiced ganache truffles. But she still had time to figure it out.

And ever since that kiss with Carter, she'd been feeling like she could conquer anything.

"Okay. You need to get baking and Faith is going to be awake soon and want to eat." Abby straightened and leaned closer to the camera. Her voice and expression suddenly serious. "So I'll get right to it. Wes and I know about the wedding planner."

"Oh, Abby." Tess dropped her sandals on the floor, pinched her eyes closed, then looked at the camera. Regret thickened her words. "I'm sorry I didn't tell you. We didn't want you to worry. We wanted to make it right first."

"And we love you for that." Abby blew a kiss from her hand toward the camera, then sobered. "Imagine my surprise and horror when I emailed our revised song list to the DJ, and he filled us in on our wedding planner's escape to the Bahamas."

"I'm really sorry, Abs." Tess pressed her hands against her cheeks, hoping she'd sound positive at least. "But listen, Carter and I have figured almost everything out to re-create your day here in Three Springs. I know it won't be exactly the same."

"Hold that thought." Abby held up her hand. Uncertainty crossed over her face. "Because I have news about the wedding too."

Tess stilled. They'd almost brought it all together with assistance from the locals. Delaney O'Neil as the photographer. Food from the local restaurants and their own mayor presiding. Even Boone and Sam were working on getting the backyards ready. Tess had planned to finalize the last of the checklist today with the party supply rental company.

"I know you've been organizing a wedding day for Wes and me. And I'm so very grateful." Abby paused and inhaled a deep breath, then announced, "But Wes and I decided to get married at the courthouse in Amarillo this coming Friday."

Courthouse? Tess reeled.

"There was a cancellation, and we got the last appointment on Friday." Abby's words rushed out and toppled over the other. From disappointment or excitement, it was too hard to tell. Abby added, "It's like it was meant to be."

Tess stared at her phone screen and searched Abby's face. Her cousin's smile wobbled. Tess's chest hurt for her and her cousin's crushed dream. "But it's not what you wanted."

"I never even considered my wedding planner would steal our deposits and leave us hanging. She seemed so professional and put together." Abby shook her arms as if she was warming up for an exercise class. Then wiped at her eyes, puffed out her cheeks and exhaled into a sincere smile. "But it's okay. It really is okay."

How could it be okay? This was her cousin's wedding day, not some canceled lunch reservation. Tess wasn't good with it. A courthouse wasn't a strong enough foundation. She knew that much. Tess grabbed both sides of her phone as if she was gripping her cousin's shoulders. "Tell me that you are really good with going to the courthouse?" *With giving up the wedding day you always wanted.*

"I wasn't," Abby admitted. She twisted her long hair up into a messy bun as if it was that easy to put everything to rights again. "Then Wes and I took Faith for a long walk on the boardwalk, and we talked. I realized it all comes down to one thing."

Not starting a marriage disappointed. Not starting off on the wrong foot and always struggling to find balance again. Tess inhaled around the tension building inside her chest. "What's that?"

"I want to marry Wes." Abby covered her engagement ring with her other fingers and pressed her clutched hands over her heart. Her voice was soft, her words honest. "It's not about the where or all the other stuff. It's about Wes and me and our commitment to each other."

But Tess had been part of a *we* too. Had spoken her own vows, heard her ex speak his. And still, that hadn't been enough. Tess cleared her throat. "What about your dream wedding day?"

"Sure, it's going to look different. But Friday night I'll be married to my best friend and the man I love." Abby's entire face brightened like the sun coming out from behind a cloud. "How can I not be excited about that?"

Tess wanted to be excited for her cousin and for Wes. "If you're absolutely sure about this. Because we can still…"

"Tess," Abby stopped her. She leaned close to the screen, her voice earnest. "Please be happy for us. And for yourself. You can stop all that wedding planning you took on and enjoy this upcoming weekend with us. That's all I ever wanted. The people I love around me while I marry the man I love."

"I am happy for you guys," Tess stressed. And she'd been more than happy wedding planning with Carter. Now it was over. Carter and Tess hadn't talked about what happened after the wedding. Would they end too? Whatever it was they had.

Abby's gaze narrowed. "Tell me that you will be there for the civil ceremony."

"Of course I'll be there." She had to be there. Had to be certain her cousin wasn't disappointed. She had to be certain Abby wasn't making one big mistake. Tess had gone it alone. But her cousin didn't have to.

Abby cheered and held up both hands. "Now our rehearsal dinner at The Champagne Rooftop Restaurant will be our reception dinner. I booked hotel rooms for everyone already at the Lavender Rain Hotel in Amarillo." Abby wrapped her arms around herself and swayed. "Wes and I reserved the honeymoon suite for the whole weekend. I'll text you the details for the times and locations."

Tess nodded. "What can I do for you?" *I promise I won't let you down.*

"Bring my dress." Abby's hands waved and her laughter spilled free. "I know it's a courthouse. But I want the dress."

"You got it." Tess grinned. "Anything else?"

"If we're throwing out wedding wishes, then Grandma Opal's Black Forest cake with her soaked dark cherries." Abby had a whimsical look on her face. "Like Grandma Opal had on her wedding day."

Tess knew the wedding cake well. It was one of her favorite pictures in her grandparents' wedding album. Their hands joined on the cake knife poised over the tiered confection, her grandparents had gazed at each other. Not at the camera. Not at the cake. And the tender devotion in their gazes captured their love story in one perfect picture. Tess's smile was wistful. "How many tiers?"

"Tess." Abby blinked into the screen. Her voice was stern. "I'm not asking you to make my wedding cake. I'm asking you to come to the ceremony. That's all."

"I already told you I was coming. I'll be there with your wedding dress and shoes." And maybe something more. Tess kept her tone offhand. "Grandma Opal had a wedding pull cake with the charms. Do you remember that?"

"I know." Abby rocked back and forth. "I already made the charms for mine. I was going to bring them to the bakery when we got back. Just like Grandma Opal hand made her charms. That's silly, isn't it?"

Not silly. Important. She saw that first hint of sadness in Abby. There at the edges of her cousin's eyes. Tess had wanted to honor and celebrate her grandparents at her own wedding too. But it hadn't worked out. Those connections to their grandparents, inconsequential to an outsider, but they meant so much to Tess and Abby and Paige. Tess asked, "Where are the charms?"

"You are not making a wedding pull cake for me, Tess. Are you listening to me?" Abby tipped her head and pursed her lips. "I arranged a dessert board with the restaurant. It's fine."

And it would be better when her cousin had

the wedding cake she'd envisioned. The pierce of a baby's cry streamed over the speaker. Tess thanked little Faith for her impeccable timing. "Sounds like Faith is awake."

"I've got to run." Abby blew kisses across the screen. "Love you, cousin! Remember, no cake. Just you and my bridal trousseau. See you for my wedding."

The video call ended. Tess slipped on a pair of flip-flops, grabbed her keys and headed for the front door of the Owl apartment. Then walked straight into Carter.

Carter's hands fell onto her shoulders and held her in place. "Where's the fire?"

"I have to get to the store and Abby's house." Tess inhaled and lifted her gaze to Carter's.

"Let's try this again." Carter leaned down, brushed a whisper-soft, but nerve-firing kiss across her mouth and said, "Good morning, Tess."

Tess pressed her palm over his heart and steadied herself. "It's good now."

One corner of his mouth tipped up. "Mine is better than good now too."

"Have you talked to Wes?" Tess shut the front door behind her, then headed toward the general store.

"Just got off the phone." Carter fell in step beside her. "A civil ceremony on Friday and dinner to follow."

"You sound excited about it." And that irritated her. But she shouldn't be the least bit surprised. Carter had been advocating for them to elope from the start.

"I am excited." Carter rubbed his palms together. "Now we can get back to work and the things that really matter."

"My cousin's wedding is important too." Frustration ping-ponged inside her. At him. At herself. He'd never pretended to be anyone but a wedding-averse cowboy.

"Abby and Wes are getting married how they want to." Carter slowed and touched her shoulder. Sounding confused, he asked, "Why aren't you happier about this?"

"Because it's not perfect. It's not the day Abby always imagined." Tess stopped in the middle of the street and rounded on him. "And no bride should start her life disappointed."

Carter scratched his cheek as if deciding which of her statements to debate first. "I talked to Wes, and he didn't sound the least bit disappointed."

"How can Abby not be disappointed?" Tess was exasperated down to her toes.

Carter tapped his cowboy hat higher on his forehead and studied her. "You're upset."

"Yes. I am." She was annoyed that even her voice trembled. She turned away from him. "Never mind. You don't get it."

"Help me understand." Carter's fingers touched her shoulder, stopping her. The concern in his voice turned her back to face him.

Tess searched his eyes. Found only concern and a hint of bewilderment. Still, he was there and seemed to want to understand. "Starting a marriage disappointed is bad luck for the rest of their lives. I don't want that for my cousin. She deserves better."

Carter rubbed his chin. His all-too-perceptive gaze narrowed on her. "Is that how your marriage started?"

Tess glanced over his shoulder and bit into her cheek to stop the quiver. How silly she was. Standing in the street, confessing old secrets when she should be concentrating on her cousin's wedding.

"Tess." Carter stretched out her name.

The tenderness in his voice tugged her gaze back to his. "We got married at the courthouse too. Four weeks after Eric proposed. It was fast, but not impossible that it couldn't work out. We were supposedly in love. I wanted to wait and get married on my grandparents' wedding anniversary for good luck. Eric promised we'd use the money we saved to buy a house to start our life together."

Carter's mouth thinned.

"You know the rest. He made promises and put things off. I thought we were investing in our future." She waved her hand as if that wiped it all away. "I was wrong about so much. I don't want Abby to get it wrong at the start too."

"But Abby and Wes are different people." His voice was mild, his point clear.

"They are in love with each other." And Tess's love had never been enough. Her smile was weak. "Eric loved me in his way. For a time. And in that time I would've done anything for him. For us."

"There isn't an expiration date on love." There was more force around his claim as if he fought for her.

"But sometimes there is." Tess searched his gaze. "It's why I want all the traditions for Abby and Wes. And anything that will bring them luck as they begin their lives together."

"Okay." Carter leaned in as if making sure he had her full attention. "What wedding traditions can we give them at the courthouse?"

Tess pulled back, but something like joy bubbled inside her. "You're serious?"

"I'm still standing here in the middle of Fortune Street with you." Carter opened his arms. "What do you think?"

Her joy burst free. Tess launched herself at Carter. He wrapped his arms around her, lifted her off her feet and held her close. And for the first time since Abby's revelation, Tess had hope.

CHAPTER TWENTY

TWENTY-FOUR HOURS LATER and Carter wasn't exactly certain the wedding traditions were worth all the trouble. But spending more time with Tess, well, that was more than worthwhile. And seeing Tess's face light up when they'd located her grandmother's wedding cake topper in a box in the general store basement yesterday, that triggered his own joy.

Carter parked outside the Owl apartment, grabbed the groceries he'd picked up from Five Star Grocery on his way into town, the takeout from White Olive Pizza Shop, and headed inside. Tomorrow afternoon was Abby and Wes's ceremony. They had a two-hour drive tomorrow to get to the courthouse and no time to waste tonight.

Carter nudged the door shut with his foot. "I've got the extra butter, powdered sugar and dinner."

"Tell me you got the handtied garlic knots and house marinara sauce?" Tess was a blur of constant motion in the kitchen. Her hair was pulled up into a bun that swayed to the side. She wore a hot-pink apron with Baker Queen and a crown imprinted on the front.

"That and red wine." Carter considered the kitchen counters that were completely covered with baking utensils, an industrial-looking stand mixer and bowls of every possible size. He set his packages on the dinner table instead. "What can I do?"

Tess chopped chocolate quickly like a wood-carver whittling wood. She grinned at him. "You can get out the plates for dinner. Open the wine."

"That I can do." Carter set the table, then opened the bottle of red wine. He filled two glasses and leaned against the counter to watch her work.

She was in her element. Chocolate melting in a pan on the stove. The mixer turned on low. She looked happy and content and alive. He knew that feeling. He felt the same inside the distillery, refining the mash blend and creating whiskey as he searched for a better sip. A better product. The joy had been difficult to find recently. And every day his grandfather and Uncle Roy continued their feud, Carter wondered if he'd ever find it again.

Then he stepped into Tess's space, felt a different sort of joy inside him and he wanted to focus on her. Not the duty. Not the responsibilities. That should be enough to send him walking out the door right now. Instead, he sipped his wine and tracked her progress around the kitchen.

She looked up and caught him watching her. She brushed the back of her hand across her cheek. "What? Do I have batter all over my face?"

"You'd look cute if you did." He picked up her wineglass and walked into the kitchen. Because if he was going to focus on her, he wanted to be closer to her. "But no, you don't."

"Then what's wrong?" she asked.

"Nothing." His interests were spreadsheets, barrel char levels and propagating his yeast. His interest shouldn't be a romantic like Tess. Her interest should definitely not be him. He was too rough around the edges and far from soft. Yet, that lightness in his chest expanded as if calling his bluff. He handed her a wineglass. "I think this is the happiest I've ever seen you."

"Grandma used to tell me that cooking is a way to put your love on a plate. And if I cooked with love, it was guaranteed to be there in every bite." She clinked her glass against his and took a sip. "She taught me how to love cooking."

"Watching you, I believe she excelled in her lessons." Carter leaned against the island. "What exactly are we making tonight?"

"The tiers for Abby's wedding cake." Tess

picked up a stainless-steel measuring cup. "It's going to be a long night. The cakes have to cook. Cool. Get iced. Cool again. Then get decorated."

"And that's all happening tonight?" Carter arched an eyebrow at her.

"Yes." Tess scooped flour into a measuring cup. "There won't be time tomorrow between the drive and the last-minute hair and nail appointments that Abby made for us at the hotel spa."

"Is that another wedding tradition?" he teased.

"I don't know about a tradition." Tess sipped her wine and smiled over the rim. "But it's certainly fun. And with Abby and Paige, even better."

"Then we better get baking." Carter set his wine on the dinner table, then moved beside her. He rubbed his palms together. "What can I do?"

"Hand me that bowl of cocoa powder." Tess set her wineglass to the side, stopped the stand mixer and lifted the beater from the large mixing bowl.

Carter picked up the cocoa powder bowl. His gaze caught on the opened cocoa powder containers on the far counter. The ones labeled *competition* on bright yellow sticky notes. He held the cocoa powder bowl out of her reach. "Wait, you can't use this now."

"I have to." Tess thrust out her arm. Her voice

was unyielding. "It's for the Black Forest cake. Abby requested the same cake my grandparents had. I have the photograph and my grandmother's recipe. My grandmother always used the best ingredients. I can't use anything less either."

"But this is for your contest sampler." Carter moved toward the other counter and peeked into the empty containers they'd taken from Abby's house the other day. Then he looked at the empty organic chocolate wrappers that had arrived in Tess's special order from the west coast. "I'm right, aren't I?"

"I didn't have time to drive to Belleridge for supplies. Five Star doesn't have the right ingredients. Abby's cake needs to be perfect." She switched out the beaters on the mixer. Scattered flour into cake pans. Scraped more chopped chocolate into a bowl. But never looked at him. "This is really important to my cousin. And it's important I do this for her. I'll figure something else out for the competition."

"Your goals are important too, Tess." Carter watched her.

"I have to do this for Abby." She paused and finally walked to him. "She's family. You'd do it for your family. I know you would."

He wouldn't be hanging his hopes on a contest in the first place. He ran his hand over his mouth and rearranged his approach. They'd shared one amazing kiss at the pond and several long conversations. That was hardly enough for him to presume to know what was right for her. He handed her the cocoa powder.

She leaned up, pressed the gentlest of kisses on his mouth. Then turned and focused on her cake mix, but not before he saw the tears pooled in her eyes.

Tess poured the last of the cocoa powder into the bowl and kept talking as if any pause would give her time to reconsider. Or second-guess herself. "Grandma Opal had a Black Forest wedding cake. Can't have that without chocolate. It'll have buttercream frosting and soaked tart cherries. Rosebuds and garland piped on the layers. And Abby will have a piece of our grandparents' cake on her own wedding day."

"Wasn't that why we searched for the wedding cake topper?" Carter waited and watched to make sure no tears escaped down Tess's cheeks.

"Yes. It's going to be an exact replica." She switched the mixer up to high speed as if signaling an end to the conversation and walked back over to him. She framed his face with her hands. "I appreciate your concern. I really do. But tonight is about Abby and making sure her wedding day is the best it can be."

"And that's admirable." Carter curved his

arms around her waist. "And I'm sure Abby will appreciate it."

Her fingers toyed with his hair. She said, "I sense a *but* coming."

He pulled her in closer. "But what you want matters too. And putting yourself first sometimes isn't a bad thing."

"I have time for all that later," she said.

If she kept on putting everyone else before herself, she'd run out of time. As it was, he wouldn't be surprised if she won the contest and gave the money away to help someone else. He admired her compassion, but he wanted her to succeed too. "If we focus on all things wedding tonight, promise me you'll let me help you get ready for the contest this weekend."

"I need a taste tester." She grinned at him.

"Accepted," he said. "I suppose it's time to get back to all things wedding."

"We have time for something else first."

"What's that?" he asked, but he was already moving toward her. Already meeting her halfway for one of those kisses that settled every restless bit inside him. But even as he lost himself in their kiss, he couldn't quite forget her tears.

CHAPTER TWENTY-ONE

"IT'S NOT THE rose-petal-strewn aisle we talked about, is it?" Abby whispered and fiddled with her bouquet of roses and lilies inside the lobby of the courthouse.

A chill whispered over Tess, the same as it had on her wedding day in that stark Chicago courthouse several years ago. Tess should've put more pennies for prosperity in the lavender ribbon she'd wrapped around Abby's bouquet that Paige had put together. Tess wiggled her toes in her strappy high heels and straightened her shoulders. It was all going to be fine. She'd infused as many wedding traditions as she could into the day. They had to work. Still, that chill remained.

Paige pressed her fingertips to the edges of her watery eyes and tried to catch her tears. "You're a stunning bride, Abs."

"Beautiful and stunning." Tess smiled at her cousin. Abby hadn't needed any luck to become a gorgeous bride.

"You know what, I feel stunning and so much

more." Abby threw her arms wide and spun in a slow circle. Joy washed over her face, chasing away any lingering doubt or disappointment. "It's my wedding day."

Tess channeled Abby's enthusiasm and tried to push aside her own apprehension. Carter wasn't wrong; Abby and Wes were two different people. But Tess worried. She wanted her cousin to begin her life with Wes the right way. Not the easy way.

Abby linked one arm around Tess's and the other around Paige's. "Ladies, it's time for me to get married."

The women pulled together for a quick embrace. How Tess would've welcomed their support at her wedding, but it wasn't time for Tess to look back. She had to be there for her cousin, as Abby and Wes looked forward.

The trio made their way up the marble staircase to the second floor. Delaney O'Neil had her professional camera raised to her eyes, capturing the bride's arrival.

Boone, Evan and Carter, each wearing dark suits and ties, waited on the second-floor veranda. Tess's gaze landed on Carter and stuck as if he was her forward. His gaze was fixed on her. And the warm admiration in his silver eyes banished that chill.

At their approach, Boone opened a door behind him, and Wes stepped into the foyer.

Abby gasped and squeezed Tess's arm. Her voice was raw with emotion. "That's my family."

Wes's smile wobbled, then spread across his face. The former Navy SEAL wore his full dress white naval uniform and held Abby's three-month-old daughter, Faith. Wes was focused on Abby as if she was his everything. The only one he'd ever need.

It was the look Tess's grandparents had shared. Likely the same one Carter had witnessed all those years ago at the pond between his own grandparents. Her gaze skipped to Carter for a beat and held. He gave her a small smile and soft nod as if he saw it too. And Tess's worry slowly began to drop away.

Wes kissed Faith's forehead and handed the three-month-old baby to Evan. Then he brushed the back of his fingers under his eye and stepped toward Abby. "I don't have the words. You're breathtaking."

Tess slipped her arm from Abby's and eased to the side, out of Delaney's camera lens. Paige joined Evan and scooped Faith into her arms.

"And you're more handsome than you were yesterday." Abby set her fingers over Wes's medals, then flattened her palm over his heart.

"And I love you more than yesterday. I never knew this kind of love was real."

"I know how you feel." Wes curved his fingers around Abby's as if he wanted to hold her against his heart always. "Ready for the I-dos?"

"I'm always ready since I have you." Abby's tears trailed down her cheeks.

Tess dabbed at her eye, catching a tear beneath her fingertip. Someone pressed a tissue in her other hand. Tess shifted and her gaze collided with Carter's. "Well, we made it to the wedding vows. I don't think they need us, but let's go cheer them on anyway." He offered her his arm.

It was only ever about the I-dos. After tonight Carter and Tess truly went back to their regularly scheduled lives. Yet, Tess wasn't certain she wanted to go back without Carter. They'd been too busy for that conversation. To dissect their futures and what it was between them. But she still had tonight. The wedding celebration wasn't over yet. And there would be time enough for those talks in the morning. Tess curved her arm around Carter's. "Lead the way."

Carter pulled her in close to his side and whispered, "I like your purple dress. It takes your eyes from striking to completely captivating."

Completely captivating. That was how she felt about Carter. Tess swept her hand over the flowy lavender chiffon skirt and steadied her racing heart. "Abby picked it out and it coordinates with your tie."

"A perfect match." Carter smoothed his hand over his light lavender-and-silver tie and escorted her into the judge's chambers. "So have you decided what song you want to dance to tonight?"

Tess's knee joints loosened. "Have you?"

"I've given it some serious thought." There was a hint of laughter and mystery in his voice.

The combination sent her pulse into overdrive. She watched Abby settle Faith in the stroller, then shake hands with the Honorable Judge Marlene Cain. "What do you have in mind?"

"Something slow. Although your dress was made for spinning across a dance floor." He paused and considered her. His voice thoughtful as he said, "But then you won't be where I want you."

Her next words were raspy as if snared by the enticing pull in what he'd just said. Or perhaps that was her own pull, that one drawing her ever closer to him. Unavoidable. Unstoppable. "Where is that?"

"In my arms." His voice was softer than a caress.

That captured her full attention. And she was caught by the heat in his gaze.

His chuckle rolled in his throat, barely more

than a whisper. "You should know not to ask a question if you're not ready for the answer."

Tess touched her neck, trailed her fingers over the sterling silver amethyst pendant Abby had given Tess for calm and clarity. But the stone was no match against playful Carter. And that kick start in her heart chased away her calm.

Carter gave her a small, secretive smile, then turned to greet the Honorable Judge Cain. Tess accepted Abby's bouquet and moved closer to the couple. Abby and Wes joined hands and the Honorable Judge Cain began the ceremony. Yet, the more Tess tried to concentrate on the vow exchange, the more aware she became of Carter beside her. From the brush of his jacket sleeve against her bare arm to his quiet breaths that came in time with hers. As if they were connected. The more she tried to shift her awareness, the more she sensed him. As if next to him had always been her place.

But she was on her own now and that was a good place. A few stolen kisses couldn't change that. And the promise of a dance wouldn't tempt her to give up her heart completely. Still, she had to be careful and so very cautious because being in Carter's arms, well, that could make her forget.

The Honorable Judge Cain pronounced Wes and Abby husband and wife. And the newlywed couple added an exclamation with a searing kiss. Cheers filled the judge's chambers.

Within minutes the wedding party was seated in the private dining room of The Champagne Rooftop Restaurant at the Lavender Rain Hotel. Wineglasses filled, toasts to the newlyweds rang across the table. Dinner conversation flowed steady and carefree from one course to the next. Finally, dessert arrived, and Tess clinked a butter knife against her wineglass. "I have a gift for Abby and Wes. Something that will add our grandparents to your wedding day. To honor the past and send you into your happy future together."

The waitstaff pushed a cart with Abby and Wes's three-tiered wedding cake into the room. The Black Forest cakes were covered in rich white buttercream frosting. A porcelain bride and groom stood on the top tier, surrounded by bouquets of buttercream roses. More buttercream rosebuds, garland swagging and leaves decorated the lower two tiers.

"Tess, I'm supposed to be all cried out." Tears trailed across Abby's cheeks. She hugged Tess, then took in her wedding cake. Her fingers and voice tremored. "It's perfect. It's just like Grandma's. Exactly what I wanted. We can't eat it. I want to keep it like this to always remember how I feel right now."

There. Tess closed her eyes against her own tears. There on Abby's face. The pure joy was all Tess had ever wanted. All she needed to know that she'd made the right choice. Knew then that she'd do it all over again for her cousin, despite the long hours and loss of her competition chocolate. Family was always worth her best effort.

Wes joined Abby and pressed a kiss on the back of his bride's hand. "Is that Opal and Harlan's cake topper too?"

Tess nodded and smiled. One more piece of luck to bring to their wedding day. "Carter helped me find it. We replaced the bride's tulle veil, but the rest is like it was on their cake."

Abby wiped away more tears, then gaped at the bottom tier. Her finger shook as she touched one of the pale purple silk ribbons hanging over the bottom cake plate. Wonder filled her words. "Tess, are those the charms I made too?"

"You wanted Grandma Opal's wedding cake." Tess touched her fingertip to one of the silk ribbons. "This is it."

"Come on, everyone." Abby motioned to the others, gathering them around the sweet treat. "It's a wedding cake pull. A tradition. You all take part in this."

"I thought we were here for the cake eating," Boone joked. "But I remember this from Opal and Harlan's wedding day, except it was for her bridesmaids."

"I changed the rules because I'm the bride and it's my day." Abby wrapped her arm around Boone's waist and squeezed the older cowboy. "This cake pull is for my family. And you are all my family."

"I love you too." Boone swiped at his own eye. His voice was slightly watery. "Now, do I get cake after this?"

Wes laughed. "I certainly hope so."

"Okay, everyone grab a ribbon." Abby pointed to the silk ribbons draped around the cake plate, extending from underneath the bottom layer. "There's one for each of you. Whatever charm you pull from the cake will be in your future."

Boone grinned and chuckled. "Here's hoping I pull a cake charm out."

Carter glanced at Abby. "Aren't you pulling?"

"No." Abby set her head on Wes's shoulder. "My wishes have come true, and I know what's in my future. It's your turn now."

Carter moved beside Tess and picked up a ribbon. Then he slanted his gaze at her, lifted his eyebrows and whispered, "What are you wishing for?"

You. Tess pressed her lips together, swept her wishes back into her heart. She was only getting swept away in wedding euphoria.

"Okay." Abby lifted her hand and counted on her fingers. "On three, everyone pull on their ribbon. One. Two. Three."

Tess tugged her ribbon from the cake. A silver heart hung on the end of the ribbon. *Love will come.* Her own heart thumped in her ears.

Wes passed around napkins to clean the cake from the charms and the ribbons. Abby smiled and clapped her hands. "This is the best part. Show me what you have, and I'll tell you what it means."

Tess concentrated on wiping buttercream from her charm. All too aware of Carter beside her. Love couldn't be her fortune. The polished charm sparkled in her palm.

Boone squinted at his charm in his palm. "Looks like a watering can of some sort."

"It means you're a blessing to others." Abby hugged the older cowboy tight. "I know you've been one to me and my family."

Boone patted Abby's back, then tucked the charm inside his suit jacket. He pressed his palm over his pocket and cleared his throat. "Well, that's a fine one to get, isn't it?"

She should ask for a trade. A heart for a watering can. Fair exchange.

Evan held his charm up into the light. "It's a wishbone, I think."

"It means your greatest wish will come true."

Abby's delighted gaze bounced from Evan to Paige and back.

"Do you have one of those?" Wes grinned at his friend and touched the polished white gold ring on his finger.

Evan took Paige's hand, pulled her firmly into his side, then wrapped his arm around her waist. "I think it's already come true."

"Maybe it's time to upgrade that wish," Wes suggested, then smiled at Paige. "Paige, what did you pull?"

"A castle." Paige dangled her charm in front of her. "I always wanted to live in one when I was a little girl."

Tess too. Another good swap. Paige deserved a fortune of love for her future. Tess was happy without it. She peered at Carter. Wasn't she?

"Now you have a cattle ranch." Wes's voice was dry and amused. He shrugged one shoulder. "Close enough, I guess. Castle. Cattle."

"It's not about living in a castle." Abby laughed and gave Wes a playful shove. "It means Paige will have her happily-ever-after."

Tess was on her way to making her own happily-ever-after.

"That's even better." Paige kissed Evan on the cheek. "I kind of like where I'm living a lot."

"Okay, Carter." Wes tilted his head and considered his best man. "I don't think they make spreadsheet charms, but if they did, you probably got it."

Evan and Wes shared a fist bump. Abby covered her laugh in her palms. "These are romantic charms. There's more to life than work."

"I know that." Wes grinned. "Tell that to Carter. He's all work and no romance."

Except her cowboy kissed like he knew more than he let on about romance. Tess felt her cheeks heat and tried to keep her gaze off her cowboy. And failed.

Carter's eyebrows drew together. "It's an owl."

"Guess that means you're going to be up all night for the harvest soon." Evan laughed and fist-bumped Wes again. "Get it. Night owl."

Abby frowned at Evan, then offered Carter an apologetic smile. "Ignore them, Carter. It means you are going to gain wisdom."

"In the wheat fields," Evan added.

Paige jabbed her elbow in Evan's side and said, "Tess, show us your charm."

"It's a heart." Tess lifted the polished charm up and avoided looking at Carter.

"That's my favorite." Abby pressed her palms together and set her steepled fingertips against her mouth. "You're going to be blessed with a life full of love."

"I already have that." Tess sighed and gathered

her sister and cousin close for a group embrace. "With you guys."

"I think it means the *in love* kind of love," Paige whispered. She touched the heart in Tess's palm. "The kind you have to open your whole heart for."

That wasn't possible. That was a risk she'd vowed never to take again. She would be beyond foolish to open her heart again. Tess's gaze slanted toward Carter as if her heart already knew and she just hadn't caught up yet.

"Who wants cake?" Abby called out. "We're eating, then hitting the dance floor."

Boone raised his hand. "I'll take the cake and skip the dancing if that's all right with everyone."

"One dance with me, please, Boone." Abby smiled.

Boone pretended to consider her request. "I could do that for a second slice of cake."

"I promised I'd send cake up to Riley and Ilene for taking care of Faith for us tonight." Abby unwrapped the ribbon from around the engraved cake knife and cake server Paige and Evan had gifted the newlyweds.

Tess opened her mouth to offer, but Carter grabbed her hand and squeezed her fingers. He shook his head at her. "You're not disappearing that easily. We still need to have that dance."

Tess linked her fingers around his and moved into his side. "Let me know when they're playing our song."

"Don't you worry about the cake. I'll deliver it and peek in on the baby too. Can't get enough time with little Faith." Boone's grin was sweet and affectionate. "You just enjoy your party with your husband."

"I like the sound of that." Abby turned toward Wes and handed him the cake knife. "Time to cut this cake together."

The entire cake-cutting ceremony was polite and restrained. Without any cake smashed on either the bride's or groom's face. It was unanimously agreed Tess's Black Forest cake rivaled the best bakeries in town. Abby and Boone headed to the dance floor and Wes prepared the to-go slices for Riley and Ilene.

Tess leaned back in her chair and sighed.

"Is that a sigh of success?" Carter finished the last of his cake.

"I think it is." Tess toyed with the ribbon on her charm and searched for any discontent. Any worry. Any concern for the newlyweds. She came up blank.

"Then it was a perfect wedding after all." Carter grinned at her.

"It was perfect for Abby and Wes." She had

only to look at them to know it in her core. And that was enough for her.

Wes traded places with Boone on the dance floor. Boone tipped his cowboy hat to Tess and Carter, picked up the to-go cake plates and slipped out the entrance.

"It's time for that dance." Carter held out his hand.

Tess set her hand in his. Carter twirled her onto the dance floor, then guided her smoothly into his arms. And Tess moved in as close as she could, let the slow music and Carter sweep her away for what was fast becoming the perfect end to a perfect day.

CHAPTER TWENTY-TWO

TESS EXITED THE dance floor on Carter's arm. She reached for her wineglass and swayed to the music.

"Sorry. I have my phone on silent, but it keeps vibrating with incoming calls." Carter pulled his phone from his pocket. A frown burrowed between his eyebrows. He picked up his hat from the chair at their table and stared at his phone screen. "I need to make a call. I'll be right back."

Tess watched him walk out of the restaurant. Apprehension swirled around her. She asked a passing waiter for the time and sat down to wait. Four songs later, Tess stood and signaled to Paige on the dance floor. She told her sister where she was going and headed out to find Carter.

She found him in the lobby, pacing in front of the ceiling-to-floor waterfall feature. The soft evening lights added a glow to the pooling water and an enchantment to the atmosphere.

There was nothing delightful about Carter's

expression. Or the tense grip he had on his phone pressed to his ear.

She walked over to him and waited for him to end his call.

His gaze settled on her, and his arm lowered.

"Everything okay?" She searched his face. Wondering when it'd all gone wrong. Because she knew without words something was wrong. Very wrong.

"That was Ryan." He dropped his phone into his pocket. "He's at the hospital in Belleridge with Uncle Roy and our grandpa. They were in an accident tonight."

"Are they okay?" Tess pressed her hand against her throat. "What happened?"

"An accident at the pond." Carter grimaced. "They were searching for that recipe. The one time they decide to work together, and they end up in the hospital."

"How serious are their injuries?" Concern washed over her like the water down the wall.

"Ryan said they're waiting on the doctor now." Carter looked left and right as if lost. "And they're keeping them both overnight for observation."

"That's good." Tess fought the tension knotting between her shoulders. "They're in the best place for the best care."

Carter paused and considered her. "I have to go."

"Of course you do." Tess pointed toward the hotel elevators. "You can get a good night's sleep and head out early in the morning."

He blinked at her. "I'm leaving now."

"It's late. And Ryan is already at the hospital with your grandfather and uncle," Tess said. "Is that really a good idea?"

"I have to be better than good when it comes to my family, Tess. I'm the one responsible for everyone, plus our home and the business. All of it." Worry and distress crowded around his words.

"But you're not alone. You have your brothers." *You have me.*

"You don't understand." He looked away. "I remember the lean times when my brothers and I moved to the farm. I watched my grandparents work tirelessly before the sun rose to after sunset. Day after day. They never complained, but I saw the toll it took. My brothers were too young to know."

And she saw now the toll it'd taken on him. She ached for the boy who'd assumed he'd have to shoulder it all himself. She ached for the man who still did.

"Grandpa would skip dinner to make sure our plates were full. He'd tell Grandma he wasn't hungry and slide his food onto my plate or Ryan's." Carter's eyes widened as if to stress his point. "It wasn't just a onetime thing, Tess. It was every week in the beginning, and it continued until I was ten."

Sam and Claire Sloan had five growing boys to feed. On a farm that according to Sam had seen good years and quite a few bad ones. "Your grandparents took proper care of you and your brothers. Did the best they could."

"Yes. And now it's my turn." Carter tapped his finger against his chest. "I vowed my grandparents wouldn't worry about missing a meal or losing their only home because they took me and my brothers in."

"And you've done that." Tess reached for him.

"But when I stop, look what happens." Carter flung his arms wide, avoiding her touch. "I can't risk distractions. Look at what happened tonight."

"Tonight was an accident." Tess clutched her hands together and tried to anchor herself. "It could've happened if you'd been at home."

Carter shook his head. "I would've stopped them from going out there."

"But what about the next time?" Tess asked. "You can't be there all the time."

"Yes, I can. I have to be. Don't you see?" Carter scrubbed his palms over his face, then settled his gaze on her. He seemed almost detached from her, from the moment. Almost indifferent except for the thread of grim resolve. "I'm doing what my parents failed to do. I'll always be there to look after my family. Always."

"But it's coming at a cost to you." Tess squeezed her hands together. Nothing soothed the squeeze in her heart.

"It doesn't matter so long as my family is taken care of," Carter argued.

"Of course you matter, Carter." *You matter to me. You really matter.* Her chest hurt now. A sharp slice of pain.

"What matters is that I was here and not with my family where I should've been all along." Regret and remorse hardened across his face.

"I want to go with you." She stepped toward him.

"You need to stay here. With your family." He retreated and held out his arm as if to stop her. "This is where you belong."

I belong beside you. Tess wanted to say the words out loud. "And where exactly do you belong?"

"On a farm, taking care of my brothers and grandfather, and my business." So matter-of-fact. So self-righteous. As if he'd always known his fate.

Without you. He didn't have to say those two

words. She saw the truth in the harsh creases around his eyes. In the steel depth of his frozen smoke-colored gaze. She lifted her chin and challenged. "And then what?"

"There is no more than that." He shook his head as if she was the one who lacked clarity or failed to understand. He added, "It's always been only ever that for me."

"You could have more." *You could have me too. You could have us.* That throb spread inside her chest. It was those first cracks of a heart breaking. Tess pressed her arms against her stomach, better to catch those shattered pieces.

"I have enough." His voice was flat.

"Do you?" She hadn't had enough. But she hadn't said enough. She railed on, "You spend so much time providing for your family. So much time leading the family, you're missing out on what it means to be a part of one."

"Don't talk to me about missing out." He flung his arms wide and his accusations wider. "Your life is all about taking care of other people. Everyone comes before you and what you want."

"I care about people." *I care about you.* Tess worked her voice around her closed throat. "There's nothing wrong with that."

"But you give and give as if there was no end and never ask for anything in return." He rammed his hands into his suit pant pockets and regarded her. "That way no one can let you down."

He was letting her down right now. "And you live as if the world already let you down."

"You can't be everything to everyone, Tess." He rocked back on his dress shoe heels.

"So that's it. You don't even try. You just walk away." Tess searched his face. Searched for the man she thought she knew. Saw only a shell. "You run away and get out before you get hurt."

"It's not about me." A storm flared in his silver gaze, then disappeared as if he'd contained it. As if he'd locked himself away again. "It's about what's best for my family."

"You're a fraud, Carter Sloan." Tess launched her conclusion like a curse.

Carter reared back. That storm swirled again in his gaze.

Tess didn't care. She was hurting and she was mad. At him. At herself. He wasn't supposed to hurt her. Not her heart. She was supposed to have been immune to this kind of breath-stealing heartbreak. "You use your family as an excuse. A shield. And everyone buys into it."

"But not you," he bit out.

"You're hiding behind all that self-inflicted duty and responsibility." Tess narrowed her gaze on him. "And we both know it."

"Is that right?" he said.

"Such a proud cowboy," Tess said. "You've locked everyone out, including your family. Diverted their attention with a distillery and profit lines and income streams. As if the value you bring to your family can only be measured on a spreadsheet and a big bank account balance."

"And you bring value by what? Not being able to say no to anyone. No matter what the request." He tipped his head and watched her. "No matter the cost to you."

"At least I let people in," Tess charged. "Do you know why I stayed in Three Springs? Because I felt like myself for the first time in years. Then my cousin and my sister needed help. And then I found a whole town that needed me too."

"And if someone needs you, then they won't leave you." His words hit true with quiet accuracy.

He was leaving her right now. "What's so wrong with not wanting to be alone? To want to be a part of something."

"What's wrong with letting someone love you?" His voice sounded raw. "Really love you. Not because of what you can do for them, but for who you are. Just as you are."

"Do you love me, Carter?" Tess's heart cracked completely. "Is that what you're saying?"

"You won't let me." He crossed his arms over his chest.

"That's ironic." Her mouth dipped into a deep frown. "I can claim the very same about you."

"I told you I vowed never to fall in love." He held her stare and didn't blink, but there was regret in his eyes. "I warned you."

"It doesn't matter. You're too afraid to love." Tess flung her arms to the sides as if daring him to take another shot at her heart. "You're too afraid your kind of love isn't worth sticking around for."

"I'm not the man you need."

"And this is the part where you walk away, right?" Tess shoved her shoulders back and leveled her gaze on his and walked to him. She grabbed his hand, jammed her charm against his palm and curled his fingers over the silver heart. "You can keep your kind of love. Now, I'll save you the trouble and leave first. Bye, Carter."

Tess dropped his hand and turned away.

"Tess."

His voice was a hurt-wrapped plea. Tess squeezed her eyes closed. One second. Then two. And then she finally faced him.

He lifted his arm, reached for his hat on his head, not her.

Tess let those pieces of her heart splinter.

There were no more words. Nothing left to

be said. Because if she ever risked her heart again, she had to know it was for a lifetime, not a moment.

I'm not the man you need. And it was past time for Tess to leave. Her chin quivered. Her voice trembled. "Please tell Sam and Roy I'll check on them tomorrow."

Tess spun away and began walking, steadying herself in her heels.

She wasn't falling apart. Not here. Not over Carter, as if she'd gone and fallen in love with the cowboy. Because that meant she'd fallen alone.

And she'd vowed that would never happen again.

CHAPTER TWENTY-THREE

CARTER WAITED FOR the valet to bring his truck around and looked back inside the glass doors of the lavish hotel lobby. The dinner crowd had departed several hours ago. A few late-night check-in guests stood at the reception desk. He was alone for the most part. Nothing he hadn't been countless times before.

Only now an emptiness gripped him. A numbness hollowed him out. He blamed Tess. But he blamed himself more.

He could go back inside. Apologize and tell her what? He wanted to want her, but he couldn't. Maybe in another lifetime. In another place. That emptiness crawled through him. If he was someone else. Someone meant to have it all. Not a cowboy bent on proving he could take care of his family better than his absentee parents. Better than anyone.

Headlights blurred his vision. He blinked and turned, watched his truck pull to a stop under the awning. *This is where you walk away.* Carter fisted his hand around Tess's heart charm. That numbness consumed him. As it should be. He had to walk away.

Family had always come first. He wouldn't make excuses for that. For hurting Tess, he hated himself for that. Carter shoved the charm into his pocket and took out his wallet. He tipped the valet and climbed into his truck. It was past time to go home.

He pulled out of the parking lot and watched the hotel fade in his rearview mirror. And wondered why it felt like home got farther and farther out of his reach. Like every mile away from Tess he became more lost. Two taps on the console screen pulled up his contact list; he hit his brother's name and pressed Dial.

Ryan picked up on the first ring. "Nothing new to report. Uncle Roy wants more chocolate pudding. And Grandpa wants to know if you have extra wedding cake."

"No cake." And no Tess. He pressed his fist against his chest. Against the cloying tightness. But he was numb. Shouldn't be able to feel anything. He never wanted to feel. He willed that cold detachment back. "I'm in my truck. On my way. I should be pulling into the hospital parking lot a little after midnight."

"You don't have to come here." There was a shuffling over the phone. Ryan's voice was hard. "I got this."

But for how long? He loved his brother, but this was his duty. Carter kept his focus on the road ahead of him. "I'm coming to the hospital. Tonight."

"Grandpa wants you to turn around and get some Black Forest wedding cake."

If Carter turned around, he was getting Tess, not cake. And if he turned around, he was choosing himself over his family. Like his parents had chosen their own selfish goals over their kids. And he'd promised he'd never be like them. *Family first.* It was equal parts curse and blessing. "There is no cake. Tell Grandpa to get more chocolate pudding like Uncle Roy."

Ryan sighed into the speaker, long and resigned. "They both want you to stay in Amarillo at that fancy hotel with Tess."

There was no staying with Tess as long as Carter had family to take care of. Why didn't anyone understand that? He rolled his frustration and worry over that hurt. Rammed that heartbreak deep. "I wanted Grandpa and Uncle Roy not to search for a moonshine recipe at night. Look how well that turned out."

"Nothing more than a stumble," Grandpa Sam grumbled over the speakerphone. "Everyone needs to stop making such a fuss about it."

Carter hadn't even begun. He clenched his fingers around the steering wheel. His voice was cold. The same as he was everywhere. "Everyone needs to start listening."

"Now they decided that they're tired. They've both closed their eyes." Ryan's voice carried a tolerance and acceptance across the speaker, as if none of it surprised him. "And they want you to know they'll start listening to you when you listen to them."

Carter ground his teeth together and worked the tension from his shoulders. "Let them know this conversation isn't over. I'll be there soon."

"Carter, hold on." A shuffling sounded across the phone line, then Ryan said, "I stepped outside their room. Look, I'm sorry about tonight. Sorry I ruined your evening with Tess."

Carter had ruined things with Tess all on his own. In a spectacular display. "It's not your fault, Ryan. Who would've thought they'd have snuck out while you were icing your leg? As of yesterday, they hadn't even been talking to each other."

"I should've been watching them closer." Regret was clear in his brother's voice.

No, Carter should've been doing that. That was his responsibility so his brothers could live their lives. "How is your injury, by the way?"

"Pain is almost gone." Ryan's voice was quietly hopeful. "Grant thinks I should be good to ride in Tulsa in two weeks, but I have to go see him in Dallas first. He wants you to come down too."

"Yeah, we'll see." Carter tossed his hat on the seat beside him. "The harvest is coming up. Gotta be here for that."

"Another rain check, then." Ryan's disappointment dropped across the phone line thick and unavoidable. "I'm going back in. We're on the fourth floor."

Ryan ended the call, leaving Carter with only the oppressive silence in his truck cab and his obligations.

Two hours later, inside Belleridge Regional Hospital, Carter won the argument with his brother in the hallway outside Sam and Roy's room. His brother tapped the elevator call button. Ryan was headed home to sleep in an actual bed. He needed the rest more than Carter. Ryan had an injury to heal. No amount of sleep was going to fix Carter.

Carter pulled open the door to the shared hospital room and stared at the two old-timers both snoring deep and in rhythm in their beds. Monitors beeped. Neither one twitched. And that worry inside Carter settled into a simmer. He pulled the covers up around Uncle Roy's chin, then tucked his grandfather's arm under the blanket. With a deep sigh, he dropped into the recliner, stacked his feet on the windowsill and tipped his cowboy hat over his face.

Carter watched a new day awaken outside the window and listened to his grandfather's sheets rustling beside him.

"I hope breakfast includes biscuits." His grandfather released a loud yawn, then grumbled, "Carter, you're not supposed to be here."

Carter settled his hat on his head, dropped his feet on the floor and braced his arms on his knees. Then he looked at his grandfather, took in his black eye and the butterfly bandage on his cheek. "I could say the same about you and Uncle Roy."

His grandfather flicked his wrist, but his wince ruined the brush-off. "Ain't nothing but a few scrapes and bruises."

"Uncle Roy's three broken fingers are more than a bruise." Carter steepled his hands under his chin.

Uncle Roy cleared his throat, rubbed his good hand over his head, waking up the silver curls before wiggling his fingers at Carter. "Still got these. And they're working just fine."

Carter inhaled, checked his frustration and his exasperation. He'd wanted his uncle and grandfather together, but not like this. "Anyone care to tell me exactly what happened last night?"

"Well, see…" Grandpa Sam started but pressed his lips together and peered at Roy.

Roy patted his head as if putting his words together. "It's a bit of a blur after the slip."

Carter had to be patient. He needed the details. Needed to know what they were thinking so he could prevent them from thinking it ever again. He said, "*Slip* as in a fall."

"No." Grandpa Sam frowned. His words came in a sort of hard bark. "Like a slip."

Roy nodded, curt and quick. "Like that. My boot on the rocks."

"In the pond," Carter added. He had a vague idea of what had happened from his brother. But he still wanted their version.

"Of course. Where else do you slip like that?" Uncle Roy shot back. "It's the water's fault."

"It's deeper on the east side than it used to be," Grandpa Sam mused.

And the east side was also the steepest. It's where the boys had their rope swing for the highest branches and tallest trees. Carter's mood darkened. "What were you doing over there?"

"Getting the moonshine recipe," Grandpa Sam announced. Pride curved across his face.

"That's right." Uncle Roy grinned. "We finally figured out where I'd buried it."

"Good place too," Grandpa Sam added, then

eyed Carter. "You and your brothers weren't the first to hang a rope swing there."

"And you never had a tree fort like we did. That was a perfect spot for it," Uncle Roy said. "We could have ridden out a monsoon in that thing."

Grandpa Sam chuckled.

Carter gaped at the pair. "Can we get back on point please?"

"You should be happy we're talking again," Grandpa Sam challenged. "That's what you wanted, isn't it?"

Carter pressed his palms against his eyes and stood. "I'm glad you've worked out your differences. And that you weren't seriously injured. I'm just wanting to understand."

"What's so complicated for you?" Uncle Roy watched him. "We went to the pond last night. Left Ryan a note where we were going. And dug around on the east side of the shore."

Grandpa Sam nodded. "Then Roy slipped on those rocks. Unfortunate for him. But I was quick and grabbed him. Unfortunate for me I was too quick. And we both tumbled into the water."

Uncle Roy studied his splintered fingers. "Slid clean into the water headfirst. Never done that before."

Maybe Carter didn't want the exact details. He

pictured all the ways their little outing could've gone entirely wrong. He shoved the what-ifs aside and tried to calm himself down.

"But we found the moonshine recipe," Uncle Roy declared. "So it was all for the best."

Carter stilled and glanced between the two men. "You actually found the recipe?"

"Of course," Grandpa Sam huffed. "We just told you that. But don't you be thinking we solved any of our differences."

"It's still my recipe." Uncle Roy jabbed his chest. "I have rights."

"But it's on my property," Grandpa Sam countered. "And I found it."

"Stop." Carter lifted his hands. "Where is the recipe?"

"Don't look at me." Uncle Roy frowned and patted his chest. "I got nothing but wires under this gown."

"It's in my jacket pocket." Grandpa Sam motioned toward the closet. "I zipped it up good and safe right before the rocks tripped up Roy."

Carter opened the small closet and stared at his grandfather's outdoor jacket. Part of him wanted to rip up the recipe and throw it out the window. Unread and forgotten. The other part had to know. Had to know if he'd built his success on a lie. That family first had never really been true for the Sloans after all. And his parents were the rule not the exception.

"I got a pocket on the inside for the good stuff," Grandpa Sam called out. "It's in there."

A tremor skated over Carter's hand. He reached for the jacket and opened the inner pocket. Sure enough, a clear plastic bag was crumpled inside. He opened the seal and pulled out a leather pouch no larger than his hand. He untied it and found a small black-and-white photograph of two young couples in swimming suits at the pond and a folded piece of worn notebook paper.

"Is it in there?" Roy asked, his voice hesitant.

Grandpa Sam pressed the button on his handheld remote and raised the bed so that he could sit up. "Come on, then. Show it to us."

Carter turned the picture around toward the pair. "Remember these people?"

"I don't have my glasses." Roy squinted. "Can't see a thing."

"Me either." Grandpa Sam rubbed his own eyes, then held his hand out. "Give me my glasses, Carter."

"It seems you both lost your glasses in the pond last night." Carter stepped between the two beds. "Let me tell you what I see when I look at this picture. Two brothers, the women they loved more than themselves and a happy family. So I ask you again, do you remember those brothers?"

Grandpa Sam fidgeted with the blankets.

Uncle Roy scratched his cheek. "I thought for sure I'd buried the recipe with that photograph."

Carter tossed the photograph on his grandfather's bed and unfolded the piece of notebook paper. "It's right here."

The room stilled as if it held its breath too. Carter read the recipe scrawled across the paper. Blinked. And read it again. The knot of tension uncoiled between his shoulders. And his world slowly tipped back into balance.

He dropped the piece of paper on his uncle's bed. "It's for dandelion moonshine." *Dandelion moonshine.* "Not whiskey." No corn. No barley. No mash bill. No ownership claims or lengthy legal battles. Carter pointed at the door and shifted his gaze between the two cantankerous cowboys. "Now, I'm walking out that door. I need food and a shower. As for you two, you can sit here and decide if it was all worth it. And maybe even remember who you once were. Sloan brothers. Used to be that bond meant something."

Carter tipped his hat at the pair and walked into the hallway.

He pulled the door closed. A grin spread across his face. At the elevators, his laughter erupted. The nurses at their station frowned at him. Carter sobered, gave them an apologetic grin and stepped on the elevator. He reached for his phone to call Tess. She had to hear this. Then he paused. There was nothing Tess wanted to hear from him.

And just like that, his laughter evaporated.

CHAPTER TWENTY-FOUR

THE NEXT MORNING Tess stood near the valet stand, pressed her hand against her stomach and reconsidered ordering homemade granola and honey vanilla yogurt for breakfast. She'd lost her appetite after her showdown with Carter the evening before and hadn't recovered it yet. But she hadn't wanted unnecessary questions from her sister during breakfast. At least she'd made it through the meal without crying. And now she'd have Evan's truck all to herself for her drive home. And if she cried across county lines there'd be no one to stop her.

"Step aside, Tess." Paige tipped the valet and accepted the keys to Evan's truck before Tess could pull out her wallet. "I'm driving us home."

"Paige, what are you doing?" Tess adjusted the strap of her overnight bag on her shoulder and frowned at her sister. "You're supposed to be spending the day with Evan."

"Evan is riding home with Boone after they go check out one of the new stockyards in town."

Paige opened the back passenger door of the truck and dropped her suitcase inside.

"But that wasn't the plan over breakfast." Tess crossed her arms and waited in the loading zone.

"Things changed." Paige grinned at her, but it was closemouthed and determined. Her sister opened the front passenger door and motioned Tess inside with the flourish of a carnival ride attendant.

"Why do I think you changed things?" Tess dug around inside her purse.

"Because I did. And stop frowning at me," Paige ordered. "You've been crying. And don't even try to deny it."

Tess shoved on her sunglasses. "I just didn't sleep well."

"I'm driving, which means I'm in charge." Paige waved the truck keys at Tess.

"That's not what that means." Tess gave in and climbed into the truck. Her sister had the keys and an unshakable resolve. And if she was honest, she kind of didn't want to be alone.

"Well, we have two hours together. Buckle up, sister, and get spilling." Paige started Evan's truck and pointed at Tess. "And don't even try to wait me out. Or it will get very uncomfortable in here."

"You're scary when you get bossy." Tess reached for her seat belt.

"I get bossy when my sister is upset and keeping things from me." Paige pulled out of the hotel parking lot. "How can I fix things if my sister refuses to tell me what's going on?"

There was nothing to fix. Nothing to resolve but her broken heart. And time, she hoped, would do its magic healing that. She leaned back against the headrest, stared out the window and confessed, "I kissed Carter. But it's not going anywhere. I was silly. I don't want to talk about it."

Paige was quiet for several minutes as if processing Tess's admissions. Finally, she said, "We kind of have to talk about this."

"No. No, we really don't." Talking would make her upset. When she got upset, she cried. Then her sister would get upset too. And none of it changed anything. Carter was gone. And Tess was sad. "We can play one of those car games instead, like we used to with Grandma and Grandpa when we went on our summer road trips. I spy something blue."

"The sky. Game over." Paige's voice softened. She reached over and squeezed Tess's arm. "What happened?"

"I got things wrong." When she'd known the right thing to do was keep her heart locked up tight. She set her elbow on the door and propped her head in her hand. "I got swept up in all the wedding excitement and bliss. It was my fault."

"You are telling me you kissed Carter. And the fallout was your fault and you made yourself cry," Paige said. "Does that sound right?"

"Sounds exactly right." Tess refused to look at her sister. There would have been no crying if she hadn't cracked open her heart.

Paige tsked. "I'm calling Evan to give Carter the third degree."

"No. Don't do that." Tess grabbed her sister's phone from the drink holder in the center console. "Carter and I are fine. We are on the same page."

Paige's fingers drummed against the steering wheel. "But you're hurting, Tess."

"It'll pass." Eventually. She hoped.

Paige gave her a doubtful look.

"It's for the best. We're too different. We have too much going on. We wouldn't have time for each other anyway." Although she'd wanted to make time for him. Not important. Tess rushed on, "What kind of relationship is that? It's for the best, really."

"If you're sure." Paige stretched out her words, clearly unconvinced.

Tess hoped if she only repeated it enough times, she'd believe it too. Her sister's phone rang in Tess's lap. Tess picked it up and jumped on the distraction. "Look, it's an after-hours call for your clinic."

"Let it go to voice mail," Paige said.

"That's not good business," Tess countered.

"You come first, Tess," Paige said. "Send it to voice mail."

"Can't do it." Tess shook her head. "Your patients are relying on you."

Paige's eyebrows drew down toward her sunglasses. "I'm warning you. This conversation isn't over."

Maybe not for Paige. But Tess was over talking about it. How else was she supposed to move on? She ignored the dull ache in her chest and the tears pooling in her eyes. *It was for the best.* Then she forced her mouth into a stiff grin she aimed at her sister before pressing Answer on the phone screen. She said, "Three Springs Pet Clinic, how can we make your pet's day?"

Thankfully, it proved to be an active morning for the Three Springs Pet Clinic's after-hours line and the emergency phone call took up most of the drive back home. Between patient calls, they'd had to phone Doc Conrad, Paige's partner and mentor, to fill prescription orders and add patients to the following week's schedule. And when they walked up the staircase to Tess's second-floor apartment two hours later, Paige still hadn't been able to return to the original conversation.

Tess dug in her purse for her apartment key.

"What's with all the boxes on your front step?" Paige bent over and picked up the stack.

"They're most likely for the store, but some of the delivery people leave everything up here." Finally, Tess located her keys in the bottom of her purse and opened her front door. "Just set them inside. I'll deal with them later."

Paige set the stack of four boxes on the kitchen counter and faced Tess. "Are you sure I can't stay here with you?"

"You have to get to Country Time to pick up that medicine for the Picketts." Tess took a water bottle out of her refrigerator and handed it to her sister. "Be sure to get to the Pickett farm this afternoon before any more goats get sick."

"I just don't want to leave you by yourself." Paige hugged Tess. "Not when you're sad."

"Come by later." Tess grabbed a water bottle for herself. "We'll eat brownies and ice cream and watch movies."

"I'll be here." Paige's phone rang again.

Tess shooed her sister toward the door and carried her overnight duffel bag into her bedroom. Exhaustion pressed against her shoulders. It was the weight of a broken heart. She heard a shuffling in the front room and shook her head. She walked down the hall. "Really, Paige. I'm fine."

But it wasn't Paige standing in her front entryway. It was Carter, holding a large box and looking uncertain. Tess tilted her chin up.

His gaze searched her face as if to be sure she was telling the truth about being okay. "Paige told me to come on in."

Of course she had. Tess reached for a smile, then gave up. She was fine, but she wasn't in the mood to smile about it. "Hey, Carter. Why are you here?"

"I'm dropping off supplies." He adjusted his hold on the box. "Where do you want them?"

"On the counter." Tess stepped to the side to let him pass. "What are they for?"

"For the chocolate competition." He set the box on the counter and turned toward her. "I raided practically every pantry in the county so you can enter the competition."

Tess was floored. She peeked into the box, everything from cocoa powder to brown sugar to assorted candy bars was inside. And so much more. "I don't know what to say."

"You deserve to have your dreams come true, Tess." His voice was sincere, but his gaze was guarded as if those doors were still locked against her. He added, "The whole town thinks so too. We're all rooting for you."

Even you? She left the box and ignored her heart and asked, "How are Roy and Sam?"

"They're getting discharged this afternoon." Carter took a step backward. "I'm heading to the hospital now to bring them home."

"That's good news." Was it good to see her? She wanted to hate that he was here now. Standing in her apartment. Invading her space. But she couldn't feel anything but despair.

"Grandpa Sam won't be staying at the Owl apartment anymore." An apology was there in the wince around his eyes.

"Sam will be home where he belongs." And Tess would be alone like she wanted. Not alone, she corrected. On her own. With her family around her.

"They found the original moonshine recipe." Carter tucked his hands into his pockets as if unsure what to do next.

"Wow. Then it was all worth it to them." *Was it worth it to you? To kiss me like I was all you ever wanted?* And then to walk away. As if it was nothing. That sadness came in a wave. Tess kept her head up. She wouldn't sink yet.

"Depends on your perspective," Carter said, his voice neutral. "It turned out to be a recipe for dandelion moonshine, not whiskey."

"That's unexpected." She'd never expected to be standing this close to Carter. This soon. It wasn't the unexpected part. It was the hard part getting to her.

"I thought so." He adjusted his hat. "Look. I have to get going. Sam and Roy are waiting at the hospital."

And Tess was waiting for her heart to stop breaking. She nodded. "Thanks for all this."

"See you around, Tess." He disappeared outside.

The soft click of her front door was the opening she'd been needing all morning. And her tears finally spilled free and unchecked. She left the supply box untouched on the counter.

What was the use if she couldn't have what she wanted? And what she wanted was Carter. Tess wrapped herself in one of her grandmother's handmade quilts and curled up on the couch.

TESS WOKE UP in the early morning hours, still tucked on the couch in Grandma Opal's quilt. Restless and certain her mind wouldn't let her go back to sleep, she picked up the boxes Paige had carried into the apartment. Work fulfilled her. She'd lean into that distraction now.

She opened the first two boxes, checked the special-order items for any damage and set them aside. It was too early to call her customers to tell them that their special orders had arrived. She reached for the next box and stilled.

This one didn't have an address or shipping label. But it had a name. *Her* name was written in bold black marker across the top. She knew that handwriting well. It was the same cursive in Grandma Opal's cookbooks. And she recognized instantly what the box was.

It was the third of its kind. Paige and Tess had both received boxes from their grandparents in the past year. Each box had arrived at a particularly meaningful time. None of them had quite figured out where the boxes came from, but they had their suspicions.

Tess twisted her hair into a bun, picked up a pair of scissors from the end table and set the box on her lap. Then she simply sat and stared at it. She wanted the letter and whatever her grandparents had deemed important enough to leave for her. But more, she wanted to share one more thing with her grandparents. One more hug. One more day spent in the kitchen. One more evening spent around the dining room table. One more time to feel loved and be loved.

Those tears gained traction again. Tess swiped at her cheeks, then opened the box. An envelope with the same handwriting on it sat on top of the wrapping paper. Tess trembled and opened the letter.

Dearest Tessie,
I'm starting this letter off. It seems Grandma
and I both have something to leave to you.
And I got to the pen and paper first.

Grandpa Harlan. Tess pressed her hand against
her mouth. How she missed his laugh. His hugs.

Your grandma is telling me to get on with
it. We're wasting the day already. Don't
waste your days, Tessie. Or your nights.
Embrace each one because it's the one you
got. But that's not what you need to hear.

Tess smiled through her tears.

So, listen well. You don't need something
big to have a solid foundation. Sometimes
even the smallest thing, like say a silver
coin, can give you the courage and strength
to reach for your dreams. Even the smallest
thing can give you the strength to believe
in yourself and your vision.
All you need is to hold on to that and
trust in yourself, Tessie. And if you're re-
ally lucky, you'll realize, all you ever truly
needed was inside you all along. But keep
that lucky charm close, Tessie. Just to re-
mind yourself of where you've been and

where you're going. I promise it'll be worth more than any silver coin.

Now I'm handing the pen over to your grandma. And don't go telling Paige and Abby that you got two things and we loved you more. It's just how things work out sometimes. And sometimes things have to go to the ones that need them the most.

Oh, Tess! How proud I am of you. I'm proud of all my granddaughters. But you and I had our adventures in the kitchen, didn't we? You must promise to have those same adventures with your own one day. Pass down what you learned from me and teach them what your life and your kitchen have taught you.

And to get you started, you're going to need your own cookbook. I've included my own favorite quotes and tips to inspire you. Not that you need them.

But the pages, well, Tess, those are blank. They're waiting for the recipes you create. The ones with your spin. Your own flare. Never be afraid to add a dash of cayenne or a sprinkle of cardamom. After all, it's the unexpected that adds spice to our food and life.

And remember. Soufflés will collapse no matter how softly you walk. Caramel will burn, no matter how closely you tend to it. Cookies will crumble. Just brush off your hands, pick up a new bowl and start again. But always start again, Tess. I promise you won't regret it.

And lastly my dear, just as lasagna and pots of chili are meant to be shared, so are big hearts like yours. Share your heart, Tess. Allow yourself to be loved and love with all you have. It's a journey more valuable than any treasure.

With love from our dinner table to yours, Grandma Opal and Grandpa Harlan.

Tess dropped the letter on the couch beside her. She lifted off the wrapping paper and reached inside for the vintage leather-bound cookbook. Tess hugged the cookbook to her chest, then set it aside. She removed more paper and gasped at the object in the bottom.

The silver coin in its original frame waited inside the box. So much searching. So much conjecture. And it'd been here all this time in a box labeled with Tess's name. She lifted it out of the box and set her hand against the glass. One silver coin that had started the Silver Penny and helped build the community of Three Springs.

Tess's gaze skipped to the box Carter had left. An entire community had contributed to her chocolate sampler. She had the support of the people of Three Springs. Because she'd supported them.

Tess carefully wrapped the silver coin frame and set it back in the box. Then she stood and sorted through the ingredients inside Carter's box. Dried blueberries, blackberries and strawberries were in a glass jar labeled Kinney's Garden. Honey from Whitney Carson's farmers' market. Pecans from the Baker sisters. Hazelnuts from Mayor Molina. Chocolate bars from Violet Myers. Smoked sea salt from Margot McKee and a note of thanks for the snapdragons. And a bottle of Misty Grove private select single barrel bourbon whiskey and a note: *For Luck.* Tess lined the items up across the counter and opened her new cookbook. Several hours later she had a sampler created on paper and an urgency to get baking.

She picked up her phone and called Paige. Her sister answered on the first ring. "Are you up for a road trip? I have a chocolate competition to win."

CHAPTER TWENTY-FIVE

TWENTY-FOUR HOURS, a dozen chocolate molds and one five-hour drive later, Tess stood inside the entrants' circle for the results of the Best Up and Coming Chocolatier at the Chocolate Corral Festival in Dallas. Excitement and nerves blended together like the sweet honey and tart blackberry inside her dark chocolate ganache truffle. "I can't believe I'm here."

"I can't believe I never knew this place existed." Paige sipped her peppermint pattie cocktail, cradling the sample-size glass like a rare jewel. "I mean chocolate vodka is a real thing. I'm drinking it and it's divine. I think it's the best thing I've ever tasted."

Tess laughed and grinned at Abby. "Didn't she just say that about the chocolate-covered peanut butter and banana frozen bite?"

"I think it was the chocolate-covered potato chip." Abby chuckled and rocked baby Faith's stroller back and forth.

"I'm really nervous." Paige set the cocktail glass on the round bar table between them and picked a chocolate-covered raspberry from the tray of a passing waiter. She popped the raspberry into her mouth and grinned around the bite. "I can't help it. I eat when I'm nervous. And it's chocolate."

"How are you holding up?" Abby grabbed Tess's hand and squeezed. "I can get you a Death by Chocolate cocktail to settle the nerves."

"You guys being here is keeping me calm." Tess reached for Paige's hand. "Thanks for coming with me."

"Thanks for asking." Paige toasted Tess with her cocktail. "And know that we would've been here beside you if it was a beet and kale festival. I mean this is way tastier than that, but you get it."

And she did. Her family was there for her too. Waiting and willing to give back to her as much as she gave to them. There was a joy in that knowledge that anchored her.

Movement up on the stage caught their attention.

Abby bounced and whispered, "I think it's time."

Valerie Joyce, the contest organizer who'd greeted Tess and accepted her competition sampler several hours ago, tapped her fingers against the microphone and smiled. "Is everybody ready to crown our next rising chocolatier?

I'll tell you. This was one of the best collections of entries we've ever tasted. And I've been judging for the past ten years so I know a little something about this. Talk about a chocolate rush."

Tess swallowed around her own rush of nerves and kept her hands inside Abby's and Paige's. She sent a silent surge of gratitude to Grandma Opal for getting her there. Whatever happened, Tess knew she had her family's support. And with that support, she knew she could follow her dreams again. If she fell, they'd be there to soften the impact. "Well, here goes."

"We're breaking from tradition this year. The other judges and I had such a hard time deciding on our favorites from the over three dozen contestants." Valerie chuckled and set her fingertips against the hinges on her coral-red eyeglasses and adjusted the frames on her face. "We decided to hand out an honorable mention to a chocolate craftsman that has a bright future."

Anticipation swelled around the crowd.

"I'm more than delighted to announce this year's honorable mention goes to Tess Palmer." Valerie accepted a bouquet of white- and dark-chocolate roses from an assistant, then said, "And I'm hopeful Ms. Palmer might tell me her secret to her salted chocolate-covered bourbon vanilla caramels."

Tess smiled. *Honorable mention.* It was a

start. Especially for a chocolate sampler that was all her own from the flavors to the decorations. She'd used Grandma Opal's recipes only as a foundation and had jumped off from there.

Abby and Paige hugged her, offering congratulations and that anchor. Around her, the crowd applauded and cheered. Tess made her way to the stage.

"Your bourbon caramels were hands down my favorite bite of the competition." Valerie handed Tess the chocolate bouquet and wrapped Tess in a warm embrace. "Can you tell me your secret?"

Tess's gaze landed on Paige, Abby and baby Faith cradled in her mother's arms. Tess glanced at Valerie and nodded. "It's simple. Love."

Understanding flashed up into Valerie's bright eyes. "I use that too. Can't ever add too much love." Valerie clapped for Tess and turned to the microphone. "Congratulations, Ms. Palmer. I know I'll be waiting to see what delightful confections Ms. Palmer brings to us from Three Springs. And I speak for all the judges when I say we hope to see Ms. Palmer here next year."

Tess returned to her family. She cheered on the third-place winner and the first runner-up. Both contestants she'd met on her arrival, and connections had been made over a mutual affection for chocolate. But Tess also sensed the beginnings of a long friendship with both chocolatiers. Then she congratulated the best up-and-coming chocolatier and recipient of the ten-thousand-dollar award.

Back at Evan's truck, Tess folded baby Faith's stroller and lifted it into the bed. She sagged into the front passenger seat, felt the adrenaline that had carried for the past day and a half finally dissolve. "I don't know about you guys, but I'm exhausted."

Abby secured baby Faith's car seat in the back, climbed onto the bench seat and shut her door. "I don't care what you say, Tess. Those judges were plain wrong."

"Their taste buds were clearly off." Paige started the truck and said cheerily, "Honorable mention is wonderful. I'm so proud of you, Tess."

Abby leaned between the seats. Her words were affection-laced and protective. "But you were seriously robbed. You should've won. I ate those vanilla bourbon caramels all the way down here. They are the best. The. Best. Ever."

Tess soaked in their frustration and aggravation on her behalf. She was running seriously low on energy. She chuckled and dropped back against the headrest. "It's okay. There's always next year." And she knew there would be a next year. At the competition. And more importantly, for her, in Three Springs. Felt it deep in her bones. She was building her future there with her family.

Abby huffed. "Well, I'll promise you this much. We're all going to be there to make sure you win."

Tess glanced back at her cousin. "What are you going to do?"

"I don't know." Abby crossed her arms over her chest and grinned. "But I have a year to figure it out."

Laughter spilled through Tess. How she loved these two women who would always have her back just as she would always have theirs.

"And I'm going to be right beside Abby," Paige promised, then tipped her head toward the rose bouquet resting on the center console. "Don't you think we should eat those roses before they melt?"

"Paige Palmer," Abby scolded. "Haven't you had enough chocolate today?"

"Said no one ever." Paige extended her arm and wiggled her fingers. "Come on, Tess. Give me a rose. There's no way it's as good as yours anyway. Might as well let me eat it."

"Have as many as you want." Tess touched the pink cellophane. "I already have an idea for how to make my own chocolate bouquets."

"That's our girl. Best them at their own game." Abby's voice was encouraging. She slid the rose bouquet off the console and into the backseat.

"Abby, what are you doing?" Paige frowned into the rearview mirror.

"Taking the first pick of the roses." Abby snapped a white chocolate morsel from its wire stem, clasped the rest of the bouquet like a winner in a pageant and grinned at Paige. "Oh, these are pretty good. You should try one."

"Don't make me stop this truck, Abs," Paige warned.

Tess smiled and turned her face to the sun streaming through the window, enjoying their easy banter.

Abby laughed, snapped another chocolate off the bouquet and passed it to Paige. "Better now?"

Paige bit into the chocolate and sighed. "Not quite."

Abby groaned. "You're not eating this whole thing. If you can't set chocolate boundaries, I'm going to have to."

"This has nothing to do with chocolate." Paige finished her truffle and tapped her fingers on the steering wheel. Curiosity with the smallest dash of sympathy circled her words. "This has to do with a certain unfinished conversation."

Tess stiffened in the plush leather seat. That contentment soured like burned caramel. She knew it'd been too much to hope her sister had forgotten. She'd been doing an outstanding job of forgetting herself. Perhaps not completely. Truthfully, not at all, but that was her secret. And besides, it was her broken heart, not theirs.

"What conversation is this? It sounds important." Abby sounded interested and a little hurt. "And why wasn't I included?"

"Because you got married and were spending the night with your new husband." Paige's voice was casual and matter-of-fact.

"Well, okay." Abby giggled, then sobered. "But I'm here now. Faith is asleep and I'm all ears."

Paige glanced at Tess. One eyebrow arched over her sunglasses. "Do you want to tell her, or do you want me to?"

"I don't know what you're talking about." Tess stared straight ahead and willed her sister to let it go.

"Have it your way." Paige shook her head. "Tess kissed Carter. Carter broke her heart. And now we're mad at him."

Abby squealed and slammed her hands over her mouth, casting an eye toward her sleeping daughter. "You and Carter kissed. When?" she whispered.

"That's not the important part." Tess twisted

in her seat to glance over at her cousin. "The point is that it's never happening again."

"Why not?" Abby studied Tess.

"Did you not hear the part about the broken heart?" Tess asked softly.

"That can be fixed." Abby waved her hand as if it was as easy as sweeping up spilled sugar.

Tess dropped her cheek on the headrest. "He doesn't want a relationship."

"That's nothing unusual," Paige offered and shrugged one shoulder. "I wasn't looking for one either. And then I met Evan, and nothing was the same after that."

"But I like the same." It was comfortable. She knew what to expect. "And I don't want a relationship either." *Liar.*

"We're going about this all wrong." Abby leaned forward and touched Tess's arm. "Tess, do you love Carter?"

Love Carter. Tess tightened her lips. Shook her head. *Love Carter.* As if she was that foolish.

"Tess." Her sister stretched her name into several syllables. Hope and wonder wove through Paige's voice. "Are you in love with Carter?"

"I'm a widow," Tess blurted. "I'm immune to falling in love."

Paige's eyebrows boomeranged together as if she wasn't sure where to begin with that.

"Love isn't a disease," Abby stated. A hint of humor framed her words.

"And it's not something you can always avoid," Paige added. "Most times it just happens."

"And there's no rule that states a widow can't fall in love again." Abby's voice was gentle.

Tess slipped her fingers under her sunglasses and covered her eyes. As if that would keep her from seeing the truth. As if that would keep her from feeling the absolute rightness. *Her heart. Carter. Love for a lifetime.* And the impossibility of it all. "I cannot be in love with Carter. I can not."

"Why not?" Abby pressed.

"Don't you see?" Tess dropped her hands to her lap. "It makes it all much worse if I'm in love with him." Harder. Lonelier. She worked the truth around the ache in her throat. The one she had to accept and deal with. "Because he's not in love with me."

"But he might be and just can't admit it," Paige suggested.

"Stop looking for the silver lining," Tess countered. "There isn't one."

Abby's fingers drummed on the center console. "Paige has a point. Wes told me he would never have believed in a million years that Carter planned a wedding for us."

Because Tess had made him. Tess tried to forget that conversation.

Paige nodded. "And Evan told me that he'd never seen Carter dance. Not at the Owl. Not anywhere until the other night. With you, Tess."

Tess pushed the memory away. Still, something like hope started to tingle close to her heart. "That's not love."

"And he took an afternoon off work." Paige dropped that revelation like a hot potato between them. "To take you to his family's pond."

"Wait." Abby folded her arms in front of her. "Back up. When was this?"

"Last weekend. We had wedding things to do. And we were supposed to cook dinner together." Tess's argument trailed off at the disbelief on Abby's face. "It was nothing." Except it was everything.

"Carter is in love with you, Tess." Wonder filled Abby's smile and voice. "I have to admit I never thought I'd see the day. It's work first and last with Carter all the time."

"Except with Tess." Paige's voice was frank and straightforward. "When it comes to Tess, Carter puts her first."

Was it true? Dare she believe it? A slideshow of all the things Carter had done skipped through her mind. From the sunflowers to letting her put up a vision board in his man cave to bringing her the chocolate supplies to so much more. The first of her tears escaped. "I'm in love with a cowboy."

Abby raised her arms in a quiet cheer.

Paige beamed. "And now you need to show him that he's in love with you too."

"Cowboys like them can be a stubborn bunch." Abby flopped back onto the bench. Her tone pensive. "We have to have a good plan for Tess to convince her cowboy."

How to convince a cowboy like Carter? Tess knew. "I know the perfect place. But we're calling in help." Tess was already reaching for her phone. "To pull this off, it's going to require all hands on deck."

"I'm in," Abby said. "Whatever you need."

"Count me in too," Paige said.

And for the first time ever, Tess was counting on love to win.

CHAPTER TWENTY-SIX

ONE WEEK LATER the wheat harvest almost complete and Harris back in the city overseeing Misty Grove's national launch, Carter still hadn't laughed. Or found his focus. It was as if without Tess beside him, he had suddenly lost all sense of direction. And worse, he wasn't in the mood to find it. He reined Whiskey Wind in at the pond, dismounted and took in the solitary figure standing near the water. *Grandpa Sam.*

It was minutes past sunrise. He should've been alone. No sense turning around. His grandfather would've heard Whiskey Wind's approach long before now. Carter walked over to the water's edge. Noted his grandfather's black eye had changed colors again to a deep purple. His boots were planted steady on the shore and his clothes weren't wet. Carter released his worry. "Morning, Grandpa."

Sam tapped his hat farther up on his forehead and eyed Carter. "I couldn't sleep. Got tired of staring at the ceiling fan."

Carter could relate. He'd spent most of the

night listening to the whisper whirl of the ceiling fan blades and staring into the darkness. As if in those late-night hours he'd find some sort of clarity. The only thing he'd learned was that he missed Tess more with every hour. And he still hurt. Deep and unrelenting and as unavoidable as a boulder in the road. "I know that feeling."

"Always meant to put a bench out here for your grandmother and me." Sam motioned toward the trees where Whiskey Wind grazed. "Right over there. Nice spot of shade and a good view."

"Why didn't you?" Carter shoved his hands into the back pockets of his jeans and let his gaze wander over the pond.

"Suppose I just got too busy with life to get around to it." Sam stroked his fingers through his beard. "Always seemed there was something else that I should be doing first."

Putting off those small things to concentrate on something bigger. Something better. Carter lived his life like that. And he'd been good at it. Until Tess. Until one wisp of a woman showed him those little things he skipped over. Riding double. Holding hands. Kissing at the pond. They all meant something. Were important to him, to everyone.

He reached inside his pocket, curled his fingers around the silver heart he'd put there that morning. He'd carried the silver charm with him since Tess had crammed it against his palm. "But you and Gran Claire still found time to come out here."

Affection smoothed across Sam's wistful smile. "I always made space for my Claire, just as she made space for me."

Tess had done the same. Opened her heart to him. But when she'd reached for his, he'd blocked her. *Access denied.* That was for the best, wasn't it? Carter squeezed the silver charm. "You and Gran Claire didn't need that bench after all." Just as Tess didn't need a cowboy like him. But him. He still needed her. *Selfish.*

"I can't deny a bench would be quite nice right about now." Sam adjusted his stand. "Wouldn't mind sitting for a spell."

Carter focused on his grandfather, scanned the older cowboy for signs of distress or pain. The doctors had warned them that the bruised ribs would be slow to heal.

"I'm perfectly fine. Stop looking at me like that," Sam grumbled and jammed his cowboy hat lower on his head as if blocking out Carter's assessment. "I'm only wanting to sit with my memories. And out here seems like the proper place to do it."

Carter wasn't interested in sitting with his memories or his regret. He pointed across the pond. "I just came out to fill the holes on the other side." And repair any damage his grandfather and uncle might've unintentionally caused and return it to rights.

"You could probably use that bench more than me." One corner of his grandfather's mouth twitched, lifting his white beard.

"I'll leave memory lane to you if it's all the same," Carter said.

"Sometimes looking back can give you what you need to move forward." Sam's voice was wisdom-filled and his expression thoughtful.

"What if there's nothing in my past I want to learn from?" Carter crossed his arms over his chest.

"I got more years under this belt buckle than I care to confess to," Sam admitted. "And yet I'm still learning how to get this life thing right. Just look at me and your uncle."

Carter was sure he could get back to living his life right once he got past his hurt. But looking into his past only hurt more. And he was certain the answers weren't waiting there. "You know what my past taught me? It taught me how not to be like my parents. How not to abandon my own family." Like a pile of junk.

Sam never flinched at the harsh bite in Carter's tone. Carter heaved a sigh and reached for his apology. His grandfather deserved better. Carter was supposed to be better. He blamed that incessant hurt consuming him. He really needed to keep to himself until it passed.

Sam's gaze remained fixed on the water. "Your mom never gave up on you boys. And I'm to blame if you believe that."

His grandfather deserved all the credit. And his Gran Claire. They'd given Carter a home. "Mom never came back." Not once. Despite his prayers. His silent pleas as a kid.

"She came." Sam rolled his shoulders as if coming to some internal decision, and finally shifted his gaze to Carter. "You just didn't know it."

"When?" Bewildered, Carter stared at his grandfather, looking for the catch.

"After Lillian had finished medical school." Sam stroked his fingers through his long beard. "You were probably around fourteen. Lillian had a tiny studio apartment, a whopping school debt and was barely supporting herself. You and your brothers were settled here by then. Friends and school and sports. We all agreed we didn't want to uproot you."

"Fine. Mom could have moved here." Where her family was. He heard the anger and bitterness in his voice. He recognized it, but he wasn't just letting it go. His mom had come home. Once. Not good enough.

"Your mother was determined. She wasn't coming home." Sam's voice was resigned as if he, too, recognized forgiveness wouldn't come in one pond-side chat. He continued, "Lillian swore on the day she left that she'd never move back. She kept her promise too."

Carter stepped closer to his grandpa. "But we were here."

"True, and I suppose for some people that's all it would've taken." Sam's gaze was all too patient. All too knowing. "But your mom wanted things beyond what Three Springs could give her."

"She wanted her career more than her family." There was no way to argue that simple, family-fracturing fact.

"But she provided for you boys when she could," Sam admitted.

Carter was reeling. His grandfather was certainly full of surprise admissions this morning. But memory lane wasn't giving him clarity, only more frustration and aggravation. "When was that?"

"Where did you think the new tractors came from?" Sam asked. "Or the forklift? The plow."

Carter sputtered.

Sam continued, "She sent money when she'd made a name for herself in the medical world."

"You never told me," Carter said.

"You wouldn't have taken it," Sam countered. "You would've told me to send it back."

His grandfather was right. She hadn't wanted them. They had learned not to need her. Not to depend on her. Carter said, "I'm still mad at her."

"I reckon that's your right." Sam hooked his thumbs in his belt loops and considered Carter. "And it's something you'll need to deal with one day like Roy and I had things to figure out."

"I'm not figuring it out today." Carter turned toward the pond.

Sam chuckled. "You're not so different from your mother, you know."

Carter gaped at his grandfather as if the man had just cannonballed into the pond and drenched Carter from head to boots.

"You wanted to get out of Three Springs too," his grandpa accused. "Leave the farm as far behind as you possibly could."

Carter stilled. "How did you know that?"

"I raised you boys." Sam chuckled again and shook his head. "And if I missed something when it came to you and your brothers, your grandmother was quick to point it out."

"Why didn't you say anything?" Carter searched his grandfather's weathered face. A proud man with a stronger love for his family. Always protecting his own.

"Same could be asked of you." Sam lifted one shoulder and scratched his cheek. "You stayed. So I figured it was something you would work out for yourself eventually. Have you worked things out, then?"

Carter bent down, grabbed a stone and pitched it across the pond. The pebble never bounced and simply sank. Sort of like Carter since he'd walked away from Tess. "It feels like I have nothing figured out."

"You know one of the things I'm most proud of?" Sam's voice was casual.

Carter shook his head.

"For a time, I had it all." Sam touched his pinky finger where he still wore Gran Claire's wedding band. "I was married to the love of my life and teaching my grandsons everything I knew about life. I was surrounded by family and good friends. Oh, so happy. So full."

"What about the farm?" Carter asked.

"I loved it." Sam's chin dipped down, but his gaze remained on Carter. "Not the same way I loved your grandmother or you and your brothers. But I'm grateful to the land for everything it's given me. Because of the farm I had the space for five young boys. Because of this place, we were part of a community." His grandfather tapped a loose fist over his heart. "It meant something in here. And that's when you know your life has been worthwhile and well lived."

Carter rubbed his chest. He'd been living. Rushing toward a future he couldn't quite see. But could he claim he'd been living well? For a brief time. With Tess. He'd felt alive. Then he'd run.

"I know you never loved the farming, but I always hoped through the farming you'd find your way. Your own path." Pride filled Sam's smile. "And you have with the distillery. It's a part of you the same way the wheat and all is a part of me. Now, it'll be up to your kids, Carter, to build on what we've done. To make it even better."

Kids. Something inside Carter slid into place. As if he'd just surfaced from the bottom of the pond and caught his breath. He wanted kids. *His own.* Carter's heart thumped in his chest. He wanted to teach his kids the same as his grandfather had taught him. He wanted a family on this land. "Grandpa, have I ever thanked you?"

Surprise shifted across Sam's face. "For what?"

"Never giving up on me," Carter said.

"We don't give up on each other." His grandpa's voice had gone gruff and tight. He cleared his throat. "You boys needed us, but I also know I needed you all too. When you boys moved in, your grandmother and I had a reason to do what we loved. A real purpose to keep the farm up and running."

His heart picked up speed. The future unfolded in front of him.

"You've got your own reason now to keep things running." His grandpa set his hand on Carter's shoulder and squeezed. "But you probably need to go tell her that."

"Tess." She made it all worthwhile.

"Knew you'd get it all worked out eventually." Sam patted Carter's shoulder.

"I don't think it's quite worked out." Carter had walked away. Essentially given up on them. Now he had to work out how to repair the damage he'd caused.

"When your gran and I were dating, we hit a bit of a bumpy patch." Sam arched an eyebrow at Carter; one corner of his mouth tipped up. "Well, your gran stormed onto my parents' front porch one evening, set her hands on her hips and said *Samuel Corbin Sloan, you about done taking up that entire swing all by yourself?*"

Carter eyed his grandfather. "What did you do?"

"What every man who loves a woman does." Grandpa Sam grinned. "Scooted over and made space. Best decision I ever made. Your gran sat down. I took her hand and vowed never to let go ever again." Grandpa Sam adjusted his hat on his head and glanced at the trees. He mused, "Still, should've built that bench. I need some breakfast."

Grandpa Sam walked back to the UTV and headed to the farmhouse. And Carter headed for Whiskey Wind. He knew exactly what he had to do.

CHAPTER TWENTY-SEVEN

TESS SAT IN the back of Evan's truck and struggled not to fidget. And rethink every part of her outfit. As if her choice of a billowy top and jean shorts would affect the outcome somehow. She wiggled her toes inside her new cowboy boots. The light denim blue boots could possibly trip her up. Literally. She should've worn the sandals. Kept to her comfort zone. If she had her car she could've turned around, run home quickly and changed. "I really have to get a new car."

"You told me you don't really need one," Paige said from the front seat. "With the general store and everything all within walking distance."

She hadn't needed a car until tonight. When she wanted to turn around and take a moment. And telling Evan to slow down and pull over would cause a scene. She aimed the back row air-conditioning vent at her face. "It's nice to have."

"Well, in the meantime you have us." Paige smiled, then reached across the console for

Evan's hand. "And we're nice to have around too."

"Yes, you both are." Tess tapped her fingers on her knees. "What if Carter isn't home?"

"He's home." Evan seemed to press on the gas pedal as if he heard Tess's nerves spike. "Ryan has been texting me updates on his whereabouts all day."

"What if he has plans?" What if she was making a big mistake? Maybe the other day she'd just been riding that chocolate rush wave and gotten it all wrong in her head. And her heart.

"We've worked out the details with everyone." Paige's voice was calm and soothing. "Carter thinks they're having a family dinner tonight."

Tess knew he would show for a family dinner. But would he walk when he saw her in his kitchen? She thought she'd covered all contingencies. The food was cooked and sitting beside her on the bench seat. Sam and Roy were setting the Sloan dining room table. They'd all be seated around the table when Carter walked in for dinner. And Tess would stand and convince him to love her. Oh no! What had she been thinking? It was a ridiculous plan. Tess rocked back and forth on the seat and rubbed at the chill skating over her arms. "Why did you guys go along with this? It's no good." *Abort! Abort!*

"It's going to work out," Paige reassured her. "Really. It's going to be fine."

"You have to say that. You're my sister," Tess charged. "Evan's not talking. He agrees with me. We must cancel tonight. Call it a scratch and reset."

"Hey. I'm just the driver." Evan coughed and held up his hand. "And I think it's a fine plan."

"What do you know?" Tess frowned at him. "You let my sister get on a plane and fly back to Chicago without telling her that you loved her."

Paige reached over and patted Evan's leg. "But then he came and got me on his horse, and it was very romantic."

Evan smiled at Paige. "It was, wasn't it?"

"I have no romance." Tess popped her head between the two front seats. "Evan, you have to pull over. I can't do this without something romantic."

"Tess, you're flushed." Paige touched Tess's cheeks. "Sit back and breathe. I don't think I've ever seen you this nervous before."

"It's no big deal." Tess inhaled and exhaled. "Just my heart on the line. My future."

Paige's shoulders shook as her laughter tumbled through the cab.

"Stop it." Tess pointed at her sister. "I'm having a panic attack. You're not supposed to laugh at me."

"I can't help it." More of Paige's laughter slipped free.

Tess dropped her head back and stared at the ceiling. Her smile came first followed by a slow roll of laughter. "What is wrong with me?"

"You're in love," Evan chimed in as if all too happy about her condition. "It's the most grounding and terrifying feeling ever. You're at once on top of the world and free-falling."

Exactly. Tess met Evan's gaze in the rearview mirror. "Does it get any better?"

Evan took Paige's hand in his. "No, but you're both in it together and you realize that's all that really matters."

Paige shifted and studied Tess. Her lips pulled to the side in a partial frown. "Evan, you don't think this is a preview of what she's going to be like at her wedding, do you?"

Evan's laughter burst free.

"Paige." Tess tried to sound disapproving, but she knew what her sister was doing. Distracting her. And she loved her all the more for it.

Evan slowed the truck in the Sloans' circular driveway, set his truck in Park and left the engine running. "We're here. Operation Convince a Cowboy is a go."

"Tess, you get out and leave the food to Evan and me." Paige opened her car door. "I'm sure you want to check Roy and Sam's handiwork in the dining room first anyway. Maybe light some candles for that romance you want."

Tess climbed out, rocked in her new boots and tucked her nerves away. She'd be surrounded by her family. How bad could it be?

Sam and Roy waved from the back porch and headed toward the truck.

Roy reached Tess first and gave her a bear hug. "Tess. Welcome to the family."

"I haven't talked to Carter yet," Tess said.

"Don't you worry about all those details." Sam hugged her next. "As far as I'm concerned it's a done deal."

Tess appreciated the older duo's confidence. "Thanks. Should I just head on inside?"

"Yes. Yes. Family only ever uses the back door." Sam waved her on. "We'll just see what needs bringing in from the truck."

Tess headed toward the stairs leading to the back porch but stopped halfway there. Behind her two car doors slammed shut, although Tess kept her focus front and center. On her cowboy.

Carter came down the stairs and paused. He tucked his phone into his back pocket and stared at her. "Tess."

He wasn't supposed to be there yet. She was supposed to have more time. To rehearse what she'd wanted to tell him. All that was in her heart and more. But all she managed to say was a weak, "Hey, Carter."

"What are you doing here?" He stepped closer but stopped way out of her reach.

I was coming to convince a cowboy. Do you know any? She chewed on the corner of her lip. "What are you doing?"

"I was going to go see you, but you're here." A small smile worked around the edges of his mouth.

"That's convenient because I was coming to…" Her voice trailed off as Ryan appeared, leading Whiskey Wind and Catnip and wearing a big, cheek-to-cheek grin. Tess asked, "What's going on?"

Carter turned and stared at his brother. Confusion covered his words. "I have no idea."

Ryan touched his finger to the brim of his hat and greeted Tess. Then he glanced at his older brother. "Thought you two might want to take a ride. Looks like it's going to be quite a nice evening."

Ryan handed the reins of both horses to Carter, tipped his hat once more at Tess and walked away whistling.

"I thought there was a family dinner tonight," Carter called out.

Ryan turned around, spread his arms out and walked backward toward Evan's truck. "Yeah.

I'm gonna have to take a rain check on that dinner. Grandpa and Uncle Roy too."

Tess peered at Evan's truck. Roy and Sam were already in the backseat, wearing matching grins. Paige rolled down her window. "Get a move on, Ryan. The food's getting cold in here."

Carter moved beside Tess. "I think they're leaving us."

"With our dinner too," Tess said.

Ryan climbed into the backseat of Evan's truck and shut the door.

Paige leaned out her window and called to them, "Sorry, Tess. Your plan was fine. But our plan was better."

And with that, Tess's support pulled out of the driveway, leaving only dust and dirt behind. Tess turned toward Carter. "What do we do now?"

Carter rubbed his forehead. "I think we take that ride."

"Carter, I…"

He took her hand and stopped her. "Tess, there's so much I need to say. So much I want to tell you. But not here. Will you please take that ride with me?"

Tess searched his face. But the shadow cast from his cowboy hat and the late-afternoon sun guarded his gaze.

"Please, Tess." He shifted his grip and turned

her hand over in his. He reached into his pocket and set something in her palm.

She stared at the silver heart charm from Abby and Wes's wedding. Her heart charm. "You kept it?"

"You can't have it back." One corner of his mouth tipped up. "I've become a bit attached to it. But you can hold it for now. Until I've said what I need to say."

Tess curled her fingers around the charm. "I'll take that ride with you."

Carter guided her up into Catnip's saddle, mounted Whiskey Wind and led them off toward the wheat fields. The wheat was gone now, but the view was no less appealing. Carter kept the pace quick as if he didn't want to risk Tess changing her mind. Tess used the time to work out her own confessions. To find the right words for all that was in her heart.

At the pond, Carter slowed the horses to a stop. And Tess lost all those words again. She asked, "Is that a swing?"

Carter dismounted and walked over to Tess, but he didn't reach for her. "I know it's not a front porch swing like you always wanted."

It was better. A white wooden swing hung from a sturdy wooden frame. A blanket had been draped across the back and a long pillow sat on the bench seat.

"I like the view here more than from the porch at the farmhouse," Carter added. "I was hoping you would too."

"You built that swing for me?" Tess searched his face. And that free fall she'd been feeling in the truck slowed.

"I built it for us." Carter reached for her and helped her dismount. Then he pushed his hat higher on his forehead, revealing his intensely warm gaze. "If you'll forgive me, Tess. I'm sorry for walking away."

Tess gripped his arms, steadying her balance. Nothing steadied her heart.

"I stand by what I told you. I'm not the man you need." His voice was serious.

She opened her mouth.

He continued before she could speak, "But I'm a man who loves you more than I could possibly ever show you. I intend to try to show you every single day. And the swing is the first start."

Tears pooled in her eyes. Her heart swelled. This was love and its inevitable free fall. But the landing would be soft together. "I love the swing. I love you, Carter."

He pulled her closer. "I don't think I heard you."

"I love you, Carter Sloan." She moved fully into his space.

"I don't think I'm ever going to get tired of hearing that." He pressed a soft, promise-laced kiss against her lips. "I love you too, Tess."

Tess kissed him with all the love inside her heart. And those words she discovered weren't really required. And she hadn't needed to rehearse. After all, her heart knew exactly what to say. She pulled back and tipped her head. "Can we try out that swing now?"

"Thought you'd never ask." Carter took her hand and guided her to the swing. When she sat down, he lifted her legs and set her boots on his lap. "Nice cowboy boots."

Tess shifted and leaned against the armrest. "Thanks. I bought them to convince a cowboy."

"How'd that work out for you?" His smile lifted into his eyes.

"Pretty good." She leaned forward and pressed her silver heart charm into his palm. "He has my heart and I have his."

"Always." And her cowboy sealed that promise with a kiss.

EPILOGUE

One week later...

CARTER'S HOUSE WAS FULL with family. His heart was full with love.

His gaze tracked Tess around the kitchen. She washed the dinner dishes and argued with Ryan, who dried the pans, and Caleb, who put them away. He'd tried to help earlier, and they'd all told him to go sit down. Carter turned his glass in his hands and took a sip of his whiskey.

"What seems to be the problem over there?" Sam dropped into the chair beside Carter and set his plate of Tess's homemade strawberry short-cake on the place mat.

"They're having a disagreement about the best way to make a s'more." Carter tapped his fingers against his glass. He knew his brothers' goal. Now he waited to see who would win. "Tess believes Caleb and Ryan need to expand their taste buds with candied bacon, roasted berries and spices on their s'mores."

Uncle Roy finished his strawberry shortcake

and leaned back in his chair. "Can't make a s'more without a proper fire."

"I'm already working on that." A fire pit at the pond. For s'mores and warmth on those cooler nights when Tess and Carter wanted to take that walk to find that something important. The same as Grandpa Sam and Gran Claire had taken their walks all those years ago.

"I knew Tess was gonna fit right in this family from the first time I met her." Uncle Roy dipped his spoon into the bowl of extra whipped cream.

"Me too." Sam nodded.

Carter grinned into his glass. These days his grandfather and uncle agreed on almost everything. And the pair could be found with Boone either at the general store or the Feisty Owl, offering advice to the locals and visitors alike. The back door opened, and the rest of Tess's family poured inside. Boone headed for the far end to sit beside Roy and Sam. Abby and Paige stepped into the kitchen for quick hugs with Tess.

"Please tell me there is strawberry shortcake left. I took Faith for an extra-long run today for a heaping helping of Tess's homemade ice cream." Wes carried baby Faith on one arm, a diaper bag on his shoulder, and looked more content than Carter had ever seen him. Wes's wedding band gleamed on his finger.

One more thing Carter was working on. A

ring. Proposal. And all the romance that came with it. But that wasn't for tonight. Tonight was about family.

"I'll take a single pour neat, if you're serving." Evan squeezed Carter's shoulder and lowered into the chair beside him.

"Count me in too." Paige sat in a chair across from Carter. "Riley and I went roller skating today in Belleridge. I don't remember it being so hard. My legs hurt."

"Where is Riley? I thought she'd be here for the strawberry shortcake." Evan's young daughter had declared herself and Carter as Tess's go-to taste testers for all things dessert-related. Carter set a tumbler of whiskey in front of Paige.

"At a sleepover," Paige replied, grinning. "But Riley told me to remind you that you promised to take her swimming in the pond on July Fourth. And that you would put up a rope swing."

Carter nudged his elbow into Evan's side. "Want to help me hang a rope swing tomorrow?"

"Only if I can try it out first. Riley is going to be thrilled." Evan cupped his hands around his mouth and called out to Tess, lifting his voice over the multiple conversations. "Hey, Tess. Where's all the chocolate? I don't want the fruit. Did Ryan and Caleb eat it all?"

"Only the test batches." Tess smiled, picked

up a glass dish from the side counter and walked over to the dinner table.

The antique oak table had seating for ten. Carter glanced around the room. One more thing he would have to look into. Seating for all his family.

"These are *the* Three Springs chocolates." Tess lifted the lid. "I've used as many ingredients from the locals as I could find. Nothing is final. So if you don't like something, I need to know." She reached over and set her hand in Carter's. "These are going to be for sale in Silver Penny's Sweet Side."

Carter squeezed her hand and pulled her onto his lap. One perk of not enough chairs. Tess had met with a contractor to inquire about renovating the second alcove in the general store into a small candy shop. He reached for one of the bourbon vanilla caramels. "Still my favorite."

She kissed him. "Mine too." She stood; a quick flash of concern dulled her gaze. Carter eyed her. "Tess?"

"I'm fine." Tess faced the table. "It's just I didn't bring everyone here to only sample chocolate." The conversations around the table stalled. Tess continued, "I found something, and I wanted us to be together when I shared it."

"Sounds serious." Sam's eyebrows dragged downward. Boone frowned beside his friend.

Tess picked up a Silver Penny paper bag she'd left in the corner and pulled a frame out. "I'm not going to drag this out." She turned the frame around and smiled wide. "It's the missing silver penny we've been searching for."

Carter blinked. It wasn't that he hadn't believed. He'd just never expected the silver penny to be found. It'd seemed like they'd all searched every corner of the town for the past year. His gaze landed on Tess. But then he knew sometimes things were found when a person wasn't even looking.

"It sure is." Amazement threaded through Boone's words.

Abby pressed her hands to her cheeks. "I knew it existed. I can't believe it's back and Tess is holding it."

"It's exactly like I remember." Sam's eyes were wide, his voice soaked in wonder. "Where'd you find it?"

Tess walked to Sam's chair and set the frame in front of the three old-timers. "I'm thinking you and Boone might know a little something about that."

"Don't reckon we do." Sam stroked his fingers through his beard.

But his grandfather knew something. Carter could see it on his face.

"Maybe you didn't know *what* was in those

three boxes." Tess pressed a kiss on Sam's cheek. "But you and Boone knew about the boxes that our grandparents had packed and left for us."

"Finally figured it out, did you?" Boone grinned with pride. "Of course we knew. Who do you think kept those boxes safe for you three all these years?"

Sam handed Abby the frame. Wes leaned closer to Abby to look over her shoulder. Abby asked, "So Grandpa Harlan and Grandma Opal never told you what was inside our boxes?"

"Never told us." Sam sipped his whiskey.

"And we never asked." Boone accepted the frame from Abby and passed it over to Evan and Paige. "They told us they'd let us know when the time was right."

"After they passed and you three returned here, Boone and I decided it was up to us to decide when the time was right." Affection filled Sam's gaze as he looked around the table. "I think we did a pretty good job."

"I think so too." Tess clasped her hands together and looked at the trio of old-timers. "But there's one more thing we need to do. Open it."

"Tess is right." Paige set the frame on the table. "Someone needs to open it to see if there's a treasure map inside. Who gets the honor?"

The three old-timers shared a look and nodded.

"It should be you, Tess." Boone smiled. "It

was given to you by your grandparents. It belongs in your general store."

Tess looked at Paige and Abby. They nodded. Abby rubbed her hands together. "I'm so ready for a treasure hunt."

Laughter and anticipation rumbled through the room. Even Carter's brothers had scooted their chairs closer to the table as if joining the treasure hunt crew.

"For the first time ever, my heart is full." Tess glanced around the table and her gaze landed on Carter. "Treasure map or not, I've already found what I was missing. And no gold is going to ever change that."

"Let's look anyway," Carter said. "We've come this far together."

Tess carefully removed the hinges of the frame and lifted off the thick backing. A browned envelope was inside. She held it up for everyone to see. Surprised murmurs were heard from around the table. Carter wasn't sure what he'd been expecting, but not an envelope.

Tess peeked into the envelope. More surprise splashed around her words. "It's pictures."

She shook the pictures, mostly black-and-white photos, onto the table. Carter picked up a pair. "Really old pictures from the looks of it."

"This one isn't so old. It's all of us." Boone tapped one photo and laughed. "Harlan, Opal,

Sam, Claire, Millie, Roy, my own Rose and me out front of the general store."

Sam slipped on his glasses and lifted up the picture. "Sure is." He turned over the picture and read. "The Three Springs Adventurers. Never lose hope."

Roy gazed at the backs of several photographs. "These others are all marked the Three Springs Adventurers too. But these folks I don't recognize."

"And their clothes look like last century. It's like these are different generations of Three Springs Adventurers." Abby picked up one, then another and glanced at her sister. "Can I take these, Tess? Do some research on who these people are?"

"Certainly." Tess put the frame back together. "They might work well on your City Hall display about Three Springs's history, Abby."

"This might help, Abby. This photo has more writing the back." Carter took Tess's hand in his and read out loud. "'To the future Three Springs Adventurers, use these photographs of generations past to remember the giving community that came before you. And that together you are stronger. You never need a treasure map if you have each other.'"

"Then, that's it." Evan stretched his hands out

and picked up another chocolate. "There's no treasure map. No treasure."

"Not one associated with the silver coin," Abby corrected, then sent an apologetic gaze toward the older cowboys.

"What do we do now?" Roy shrugged.

"We'll convene the historical committee tomorrow and decide." Boone nodded. "And Harris will be coming back this weekend to see Jodie. We can speak to him about next steps."

"Why are you all acting as if you lost?" Carter asked. Everyone at the table looked at him. "The missing treasure did what it was rumored to have done all those centuries ago. It brought this community together. Through your search for the map, you all found new friends. Good friends. And Boone and Sam, you're preserving those community stories for the future. That's the real treasure."

"You know. Carter is right." Tess moved to his side.

Carter stood and curved an arm around her shoulder and pulled her in tight.

Tess continued, "We've already won. We do have each other and we are stronger for it."

"Well, if we aren't going to be treasure hunting any longer, we need to pick up a new hobby," Sam mused.

Ryan leaned in to grab a chocolate from the

dessert tray and Sam nudged Boone and Roy. Sam said, "Hey, Ryan. You should come down to the Owl. There's someone we think you should meet."

Ryan popped the candy into his mouth and backed away from the table. "I'm sure I'm busy that day, Grandpa. Why don't you ask Caleb? He's single too."

"Don't you be worrying about your brother." Uncle Roy laughed and waggled a finger at Ryan. "We'll get to him in good time."

Boone rose and set a hand on Ryan's arm as if to slow his escape. "Seems we've got time on our hands. What with not having a treasure map to find. Did you ever hear the tale about how Sam and I saved a runaway bride and her cold-footed groom?"

Ryan cast a helpless look at Carter. Carter smiled and shook his head. "I think Ryan would love to hear that matchmaking story again. Caleb too."

Caleb sprinted into the family room. Uncle Roy and Grandpa Sam were hot on his boot heels. Clearly, the old-timers had landed on a new chapter for their matchmaking story.

Tess chuckled. "Ryan looks like he might be ill."

"That's payback for all the meddling he's done over the years." Carter laughed louder.

"And besides, falling in love could be the best thing for my brother."

Tess shifted and studied him. "You think so?"

"I know it was for me." Carter kissed her softly and then pulled away. "I love you, Tess. Today. Tomorrow. And always."

* * * * *

*If you missed the other enchanting romances
in the Three Springs miniseries
by Cari Lynn Webb,
visit www.Harlequin.com today!*

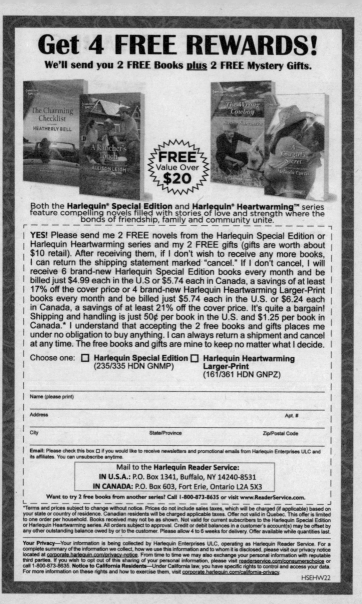

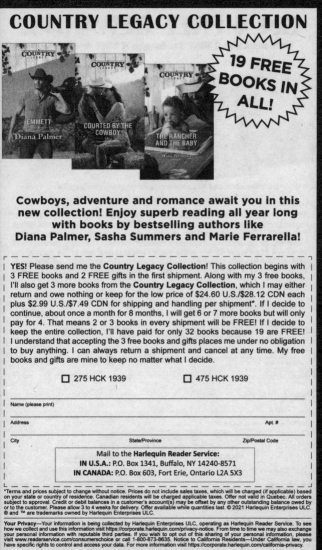

Get 4 FREE REWARDS!

We'll send you 2 FREE Books plus 2 FREE Mystery Gifts.

FREE
Value Over
$20

Both the **Romance** and **Suspense** collections feature compelling novels written by many of today's bestselling authors.

YES! Please send me 2 FREE novels from the Essential Romance or Essential Suspense Collection and my 2 FREE gifts (gifts are worth about $10 retail). After receiving them, if I don't wish to receive any more books, I can return the shipping statement marked "cancel." If I don't cancel, I will receive 4 brand-new novels every month and be billed just $7.24 each in the U.S. or $7.49 each in Canada. That's a savings of up to 28% off the cover price. It's quite a bargain! Shipping and handling is just 50¢ per book in the U.S. and $1.25 per book in Canada.* I understand that accepting the 2 free books and gifts places me under no obligation to buy anything. I can always return a shipment and cancel at any time. The free books and gifts are mine to keep no matter what I decide.

Choose one: ☐ **Essential Romance**   ☐ **Essential Suspense**
                    (194/394 MDN GQ6M)   (191/391 MDN GQ6M)

Name (please print)

Address   Apt. #

City   State/Province   Zip/Postal Code

Email: Please check this box ☐ if you would like to receive newsletters and promotional emails from Harlequin Enterprises ULC and its affiliates. You can unsubscribe anytime.

Mail to the Harlequin Reader Service:
IN U.S.A.: P.O. Box 1341, Buffalo, NY 14240-8531
IN CANADA: P.O. Box 603, Fort Erie, Ontario L2A 5X3

Want to try 2 free books from another series! Call 1-800-873-8635 or visit www.ReaderService.com.

STRS22

#431 WYOMING PROMISE
The Blackwells of Eagle Springs
by Anna J. Stewart

Horse trainer Corliss Blackwell needs a loan to save her grandmother's ranch. Firefighter Ryder Talbot can help. He's back in Wyoming with his young daughter and is shifting Corliss's focus from the Flying Spur to thoughts of a forever family—with him!

#432 A COWBOY IN AMISH COUNTRY
Amish Country Haven • by Patricia Johns

Wilder Westhouse needs a ranch hand—and Sue Schmidt is the best person for the job. The only problem? His ranch neighbors the farm of Sue's family—the Amish family she ran away from years ago.

#433 THE BULL RIDER'S SECRET SON
by Susan Breeden

When bull rider Cody Sayers attempts to surprise a young fan, the surprise is on him! The boy's mother is Cody's ex-wife. He still loves Becca Haring, but she has a secret that could tear them apart...or bring them together.

#434 WINNING THE VETERAN'S HEART
Veterans' Road • by Cheryl Harper

Peter Kim needs the best attorney in Florida for his nephew's case—that's Lauren Duncan, his college rival. But she's tired of the grind. He'll help show her work-life balance...and that old rivals can be so much more.

HWCNM0622

Visit
ReaderService.com
Today!

**As a valued member of the
Harlequin Reader Service,
you'll find these benefits and more at
ReaderService.com:**

- Try 2 free books from any series
- Access risk-free special offers
- View your account history & manage payments
- Browse the latest Bonus Bucks catalog